Copyrights

Content Warning

This story contains detailed descriptions of depression, anxiety, and panic attacks, as well as brief instances of physical violence that may be upsetting for some readers.

It's okay to step away when needed. Your well-being matters. ❤

Rocky Crescendo

Latasha Crystal

1

On Monday morning, fourteen-year-old Rocky Coleman woke up at 5:45 a.m., fifteen minutes before her alarm clock. She barely slept a wink the night before, as her anxiety kept her tossing and turning most of the night. Today was her first day of high school, and she was anything but excited. Growing up, Rocky had always been socially awkward. Talking to people made her feel uneasy, so it was difficult for her to make friends.

As she lay awake in bed, heart racing and hands clamming up, all the worst-case scenarios of her first day of high school kept running through her mind.

She wouldn't be wearing the latest trend, so the popular girls would tease her about it. Somebody would point out an insecurity of hers, such as her height. She was just under 5 feet tall. Would someone make fun of Rocky's looks? She was chubby, struggled with breakouts, and had acne scars. Her flat feet and pigeon toes make her gait a bit funny.

Rocky felt her eyes well up with tears when she realized there was no turning back. In less than two hours, she was going to be a high school freshman. The thought terrified her, so she took some deep breaths and focused on the ceiling fan above her to prevent an anxiety attack. When her alarm clock finally sounded, Rocky reached over to her nightstand to shut it off but didn't get out of bed. She felt exhausted and tried to get five extra minutes of sleep.

The sound of her mother barging into her room startled Rocky awake. "Rocky!" she exclaimed. "It's almost 6:30.

Why aren't you awake? You're going to be late for school if you don't start getting ready now."

Rocky turned to look at the time and immediately sat up when she saw the large red numbers read 6:25. How could all that time have passed? It felt like she was asleep for less than five minutes.

"Get up," Rocky's mom said. "You don't want to be late for your first day of high school."

Yes, I do, Rocky thought. "Okay," she mumbled as she got out of bed and shuffled to the bathroom.

Rocky's mom, Rochelle, was already dressed in her scrubs. She was a medical assistant and usually went straight to work after dropping Rocky off at school.

Rochelle was way more excited about her first day of school than Rocky. Mostly, this was because Rocky would be attending Rochelle's old school, Lennox High School of the Arts. She would always tell Rocky how exciting it was and that it was impossible to be bored there. Something was always going on at Lennox, from random flash mobs between classes to live entertainment by students during lunch once a week.

Rochelle went to Lennox for vocals, which is what Rocky is there for as well. After Rocky's mom graduated, she sang professionally for about five years until she met Rocky's dad. He was also a professional singer, and they met while touring. They dated for three months before getting engaged and got married six months later. Not long after they got married, Rochelle found out she was pregnant. After Rocky was born, Rochelle and Rocky's dad both stopped singing professionally. Rocky couldn't help but feel responsible for ending her parents' successful singing careers. Rochelle would always reassure her that they both chose to stop singing by choice.

Rocky's dad joined the U.S. Coast Guard, and Rochelle was a stay-at-home mom. When Rocky was eight, her dad died in a freak accident at work. Rochelle went into a deep depression for months after Rocky's dad died. Six years later, it still devastated Rocky that he was gone. It was difficult to see how sad her mom would be, especially on the anniversary of his death.

She wished that she could've had the opportunity to spend more time with him and always cherished the moments he was here.

After Rocky finished getting ready for school, she went to the kitchen for breakfast. She was pouring herself a bowl of cereal when she noticed her mother staring at her.

"What?" Rocky asked.

"You're going to school with your bonnet on?" she asked.

Rocky put her hand on her head and realized she had forgotten to do her hair. It was still twisted up, and she still had on her nighttime bonnet. "Oh, man," she said as she took it off. Rocky had coily hair that could be difficult to deal with at times. It usually took her about half an hour to get her hair to cooperate with her and get it styled how she wanted it. Rocky begged her mother to let her get a perm over the years, but Rochelle refused. She always told her perms would damage her hair and that she should embrace her natural hair. "I don't have time to do it without being late," Rocky said.

"Well, figure something out quickly."

Rocky ran back to the bathroom and started untwisting her hair. By the time she finished, it was tangled and unpresentable. With a sigh of frustration, she put some detangling cream in her hair and combed through the tangles, making it easier to manage. Rocky already knew she wasn't going to like how her hair turned out and didn't have the time nor the patience to perfect her hairstyle. It looks like today would be a high bun day. After looking at herself in the mirror for a while, she started to hate what she saw. Rocky always wore her hair down to hide most of her face. Her high bun made her feel exposed, and she couldn't stand the sight of her chubby, acne-scarred face. She started to restyle her hair but stopped when she heard her mother yelling from the kitchen.

"Rocky, you're going to be late!" Rochelle called out.

"I'm coming!" she called back. She sighed and tried her hardest not to worry too much about her hair. Once she returned to the kitchen, her mother already had her keys in her hand.

"Eat your cereal in the car," Rochelle said. "We can't waste any more time. You're going to be late."

"Mom, calm down," Rocky said. "I'll get there on time."

Rocky began to feel more uncomfortable about starting high school now that her mother was rushing her out of the house. Was high school stricter on tardiness than middle school? Would they suspend her on the first day of school for being late? What if she got lost trying to find her class? All those questions flowed through her head until Rochelle called her name again.

"Rocky, come on," she shouted at her.

Rocky shook her head and followed her mom outside to the car. They lived about five minutes from Lennox, but the drive seemed to take an eternity. She felt her eyes water, and her hands began to tremble once the car pulled up to the student drop-off. The school seemed much bigger than when she was there a couple of weeks ago for the freshman orientation. She couldn't bring herself to leave the comfort of the car.

"Man, this place hasn't changed since I graduated," Rochelle reminisced, unaware of Rocky's increasing anxiety. "I miss it."

Rocky's heart pounded inside her chest, and she felt like she was suffocating. *Please, not another panic attack*, Rocky thought. "Mom," Rocky managed to utter.

Rochelle noticed Rocky's intense anxiety and went into nurse mode. "Hey, you're okay. Deep breaths, Rocky." Rochelle guided Rocky with some deep breathing until Rocky's breath was back to normal. She loved her mother for being patient and helping her through these intense anxiety attacks.

"What's on your mind?" Rochelle asked once Rocky was calm.

"I'm just scared," Rocky said in between breaths. "I'm scared of what can go wrong."

"Oh, Rocky," Rochelle said, hugging her. "I know high school can seem scary, but it's not. Just be yourself and have fun. Everything will be fine."

"What if nobody likes me?"

"I find that hard to believe. You are such a beautiful, talented, and wonderful person. I have no doubt you'll make some great friends here. And you'll already have Hayley and Adam here."

Hayley Wolfe and Adam Marin are Rocky's best and only friends. She met them both in the seventh grade, and Rocky felt they were the only two people with whom she could be herself without feeling judged. The three of them were inseparable due to their love and passion for music.

"I have a bit of advice for you," Rochelle said. "Be yourself. Don't get caught up in all the drama, and you'll have such a great high school experience. You're a freshman now, and it seems like four years will take forever. But you'll be wondering where the time went once you're a senior. Trust me."

Rochelle took Rocky's hand in hers and gave it a gentle squeeze. "It'll be fine," she reassured her daughter. "Go on."

Rocky took a deep breath before leaving the car. Her mom waved at her once more before driving away. Rocky soon began to feel lonely and wanted to run after the car and go back home. She stared at the front entrance of Lennox for a moment before entering. The courtyard was full of students who looked so much older than her. She noticed the girls in high school were more developed than the middle school girls. The boys were way taller and had more facial hair than the boys in middle school. Everyone looked like young men and women.

Rocky noticed cliques of friends hanging out and talking about what they did over the summer. Everyone seemed happy and in their own worlds. They were completely oblivious to the awkward freshman standing by herself.

Her eyes searched desperately for Hayley or Adam. Then as though her prayers were answered, she heard a familiar voice.

"Hey, Rocky! Over here." It was Adam walking through the entrance waving at her. Rocky flung herself onto Adam, and they both almost went tumbling down.

Rocky and Adam were close but not as close as she was with Hayley, even though she and Adam had much more in common. He was also shy but not quite as socially awkward as Rocky. Adam could make friends with anybody and was always a pleasure to have around. He also avoids attention like Rocky and is a bit on the short side, although he doesn't seem to care as much as Rocky does. She met Adam through Hayley. When she first introduced her to him, her exact words were, "She's literally the female version of you. You guys will be great friends!" And she was right! The three started hanging out more, and that was when Rocky knew she had found her best friends.

"You act like you haven't seen me in years," Adam laughed, trying to regain his balance. "What's up?"

Rocky laughed, too. "Sorry," she said. "I'm just glad I found someone I know. High school seems like a whole different world."

"Oh, relax. It's going to be fun. I know people who graduated from Lennox, and they say it's a blast here."

"I know. I hear it from my mother, 24/7." Rocky rolled her eyes. She'd heard many stories of Rochelle's high school life at Lennox. At first, they were interesting, but it got annoying after hearing about them every day.

"Oh yeah. I forgot your mom went to school here," Adam said.

Adam got taller over the summer, Rocky noticed. He and Rocky were about the same height in the eighth grade, but he sprouted a few inches. Still, he looked tiny compared to the 6-foot boys at the school.

"Did you get your class schedule in the mail?" Adam asked.

Rocky gasped once she realized she'd left her schedule on her bedroom dresser. "Oh, no. I left it at home!"

"Wow," Adam said. "That's not good."

"Dang it!" Rocky sighed in frustration. "I knew my first day of high school was going to be a disaster. I don't even know where to go for my classes. What am I going to do?"

Adam gently placed his hands on Rocky's shoulders. "Rocky, breathe," he said. "It's not the end of the world. Just go to the main office and ask them to give you another schedule."

"I don't know where the main office is," Rocky said.

"Straight across the courtyard. It's that building with 'Main Office' written on the window in big, bold letters." Adam joked.

Rocky laughed and swatted Adam. "Don't get sarcastic with me, mister. Can you come with me?"

"Of course. Remember, you don't have to be scared," Adam assured her.

As Rocky and Adam walked across the courtyard, Rocky's eyes darted around at the campus. *This is so not middle school anymore*, she thought to herself. She let Adam take the lead inside the building as she followed close behind him.

"Good morning," Adam greeted the lady at the desk.

"How can I help you?" the lady asked.

Adam looked at Rocky, who was cowering behind him. "Come on, Rocky," he told her gently. "Just ask her."

Rocky repositioned herself next to Adam. "Um, hi," she stammered. "I um. I kind of need my schedule. Um, I accidentally left mine at home."

"Not a problem. Do you know your student I.D. number?" the lady asked.

Rocky shook her head.

"Okay. What's your name?"

"Raquel Coleman."

The lady started typing and clicking away on her computer. The sound of the printer firing up followed shortly after. "Okay, Miss Coleman. Your schedule is printing now."

Rocky's hands trembled as the lady took her class schedule from the printer and handed it to her.

"You're all set," she said with a smile.

"Thanks," Rocky said and sped out.

"See, Rocky. That wasn't so bad, was it?" Adam said once they got back to the courtyard.

"She looked mean," Rocky told him.

"But she wasn't. You need to loosen up a bit. You're in high school now."

Rocky rolled her eyes and looked at her schedule. "What classes are you taking?" she asked Adam.

Adam handed his schedule to Rocky. "My schedule seems okay," he said. "What do you think of yours?"

"I think we have no classes together except for P.E.," Rocky said.

"Bummer," Adam said. Their schedules were almost the same, except they had different teachers. They both were studying music, but Adam focused on band music, and Rocky focused on vocals. It made sense why their classes and some of their electives were different. The only class Rocky looked forward to was chorus with Ms. Rose, who was also Rochelle's teacher. Her mother adored that woman and would be thrilled to hear Ms. Rose was still teaching at Lennox.

"I wonder where Hayley is," Adam said, looking at his watch. "School is about to start."

Rocky started thinking about Hayley. Her anxiety increased as she wondered why her best friend wasn't at school yet. "I hope everything's okay with her."

Adam opened his mouth to respond but was interrupted by the school bell ringing. The crowd started scattering in different directions, and Rocky felt her heart racing. The class she and Adam shared wasn't until later in the day, but she didn't want to walk to her first-period class alone. She was also worrying herself, wondering why Hayley wasn't here yet.

"I'll see you later then," Adam said.

Rocky stood paralyzed in fear. Adam took her by the hand. "You can do this. There's nothing to be afraid of."

Rocky tried her best to stay calm but felt close to tears. She didn't think she would be able to do this.

"Do you want me to walk you to your class?" Adam asked her. "Will that make you feel better?"

Rocky started to nod but changed her mind and shook her head instead. She wanted to be brave. "Thanks, but you have to find your class. I think I should be okay."

"You sure?"

"Yeah. I appreciate the offer. I'll see you in P.E." Rocky hugged Adam before they parted. As soon as he left, she instantly regretted telling him no. She felt so alone, but she forced herself to find her class.

Rocky's first period was Algebra, and she found the classroom easily. It was the first door to her left when she walked into the building. When she entered, the teacher was standing at the front of the class, and two other students were sitting at desks.

"Last name?" the teacher asked.

"Coleman."

The teacher scanned a sheet of paper Rocky assumed was a seating chart, then she looked back at Rocky and smiled. "Nice to meet you, Miss Coleman. My name is Mrs. Hawthorne. Your seat will be the last desk in the first row."

Rocky smiled back at Mrs. Hawthorne and went to her assigned seat. Rocky never liked sitting in the back of the classroom because she had difficulty seeing the board from so far away. Rocky did have glasses but never wore them since she thought they made her look nerdy, and she didn't like having something sitting on her face. Also, all the tall people somehow always get the seat right in front of Rocky, making it even harder to see. This time was no different. Mrs. Hawthorne directed a guy who had to be at least 6'7 to the seat in front of Rocky. She sighed. *Every year,* she thought to herself.

When she looked at the door, she saw someone familiar walking in and smiled. It was Hayley! It felt so great to have her first class of the day with her best friend because they could walk to class together every morning. When Hayley noticed Rocky, she smiled back and waved. Mrs. Hawthorne directed Hayley to the last seat in the last row, so it was safe to assume the seating chart was in alphabetical order. Rocky hated that because whenever she had a class with Hayley, they would be on opposite sides of the room. Hayley put her things in her assigned seat, walked over to Rocky's desk, and squeezed her.

Rocky thought it was funny how she and Hayley were the best of friends even though they were complete opposites. Being outgoing, social, and loving attention, Hayley was the friendliest person anyone could ever meet, which is what initially drew Rocky to Hayley. In the seventh grade, they sat next to each other in math class. Hayley would chat with Rocky every day, which was awkward for Rocky at first since she never knew what to say. She felt more comfortable as she started getting to know Hayley a little more each day. Rocky assumed Hayley was such a social butterfly because of her large family. Hayley was the third of five siblings, while Rocky was an only child. Her outgoing personality made her a perfect candidate for the theater program at Lennox.

Hayley and Rocky even contrasted physically. Hayley was almost six feet tall, had waist-length jet black hair, almond-shaped brown eyes, and a delicate heart-shaped face with a cute little button nose. She was one of the most drop-dead gorgeous girls Rocky had ever met. She turned heads whenever she walked by; meanwhile, Rocky struggled to get a boy to notice her. Sometimes, Rocky was a little jealous of Hayley because of her good looks. She got her beauty from her mother, Miyoko, who used to be a professional model.

"I'm so glad to see a familiar face," Rocky told Hayley. "Where were you this morning?"

"My mom couldn't find her car keys. My stupid little brother hid them, and he wouldn't tell us where they were," Hayley explained.

"Why would he do that?"

"He thought if Mom couldn't find her keys, then we wouldn't have to go to school. And you know my mom has to make two other stops before coming here."

Hayley's mother dropped her little brother Henry off at his elementary school first, then her younger sister Hanna at her middle school, and Hayley and her older brother Hector at Lennox. Hector was a senior, and her oldest brother Harold was in college.

Rocky giggled. "Typical Henry," she said.

"I guess he wasn't ready for summer to end. It took us twenty minutes to get him to confess where he hid them. I got to school right when the bell rang." Hayley sighed. "Now that I'm here, let me see your schedule. Don't you love high school life now?"

Rocky handed Hayley her schedule. "Girl, when I got here, everything already went downhill. I forgot my class schedule at home, so I had to get a new one printed in the office. It was so embarrassing. I had to tell the lady I needed a new schedule because I was careless and left my original one at home."

"You're so overreacting," Hayley giggled. "You're human, and you forget sometimes. It's no biggie. Hey, we have four classes together!"

"Really? Which ones?"

"This one, obviously, third-period P.E., fourth-period English, and eighth-period home economics."

"Adam has P.E. with us, too."

"That's so awesome! It's the first time the three of us all have a class together."

The final bell rang, and it was time to begin class. Hayley returned to her assigned seat on the other side of the room. Rocky was disappointed her best friend wouldn't be sitting close to her. She hoped the other classes they had together didn't seat students alphabetically.

Throughout the class, Rocky kept thinking about what a long year it would be. Math was her worst subject, it was too early in the morning, and Mrs. Hawthorne had a soft and monotonous voice. She almost fell asleep during the first fifteen minutes of class. Luckily, the school's block scheduling meant Rocky had third-period P.E. next. She was even more excited about spending it with Hayley and Adam. Then they had lunch right after, so they all went together.

So far, high school has been going well for Rocky. Her next class after lunch was fifth-period chorus, and she was super stoked about it. The only sad part was Rocky didn't have any more classes with Hayley or Adam for the rest of the day.

As the three of them got to the cafeteria door, they heard a group of boys singing together, and they sounded fantastic. They stopped to listen.

"Finally, a spontaneous performance!" Hayley squealed. "Where is it coming from?"

They all turned around and saw four guys harmonizing "If I Ever Fall in Love." The lead singer had dark, round eyes, a strong jawline, and a phenomenal baritone voice. He immediately caught Rocky's attention.

"They're amazing," Hayley said in awe.

"I know," Rocky agreed, keeping her eyes on the lead singer.

Adam glared at the four boys without saying anything. It looked like he had his eyes on the same guy Rocky was admiring — only Adam looked at him with hatred.

The four boys got everyone's attention, and the crowd around them grew by the second. It wasn't long before Rocky couldn't see the singers anymore. Once they finished the song, everyone cheered loudly for them. As the crowd was dispersing, she stole another glance at the boy she had her eye on. For a moment, their eyes met, but she panicked and looked away.

"Wow, those boys can sing," Hayley said. "And the lead singer is too cute."

Rocky smiled shyly, still thinking about their brief eye contact.

"Yeah, yeah," Adam said impatiently. "Let's get to the lunch line before it gets too long."

"They sounded just like Shai," Hayley continued, completely ignoring Adam.

"Maybe a little better," Rocky agreed.

"Do you think they'll be famous? Or maybe they're already famous. We're probably going to school with celebrities!"

"Hayley, get real," Adam jumped in. "They're not famous. They're amateurs just like us."

"That was so not an amateur performance," Hayley shot back. "Those guys are crazy talented."

Adam rolled his eyes. "Whatever. While you keep gushing over those guys, I'm going to get something to eat before I starve to death." He went inside the cafeteria, leaving Rocky and Hayley outside.

"What's his deal?" Rocky asked.

Hayley shrugged and then giggled. "Probably jealous."

"I doubt it. Adam's talented too, and he's not the type to lose it if he thinks someone else is better than him."

"You know what would be cool? We should put on an impromptu performance. We'll start getting noticed."

Rocky looked down at her feet. "Oh, I don't know about that," she said quietly.

"But it'll be so much fun! We'll start building a reputation, and maybe by our senior year, we'll be as popular as those guys."

Rocky wanted to be popular and break out of her shyness, but she didn't want to start randomly singing in the middle of the courtyard. It was only the first day of school, and she wanted to feel comfortable before putting on an impromptu performance.

"Let's wait for Adam," Rocky said, switching the subject.

When they walked into the cafeteria, another crowd of people was cheering on the other side. Eager to know what was happening, Hayley and Rocky joined the group. They couldn't see much, but Rocky did get a glimpse of a guy and girl break dancing to "Pump it Up" by Joe Budden. The flips, handstands, and head spins they were doing seemed unreal. They looked like professionals!

"How do they *move* like that?" Rocky asked, astonished. Hayley was just as amazed and speechless for once.

The couple spun on their heads in unison, which got the crowd roaring. Then they got back on their feet and took a bow as the song finished; both were breathing hard and had beads of sweat on their foreheads. The boy kissed the girl on the cheek, and they walked away holding hands.

"This school really *is* filled with talented people," Hayley said. "It's like *High School Musical*."

"You better not bust out with 'We're All in this Together,'" Adam's voice came from behind Rocky and Hayley, then he laughed. "Let's go outside. I want to see more performances."

"I want to sing something, too," Hayley said as she and Rocky followed Adam outside.

"You guys should," Adam said. "Get yourselves noticed now."

Rocky felt her heartbeat get faster at the thought of singing in front of all these people. "What if we're not as good as everyone else?"

Hayley and Adam stopped in their tracks and looked at Rocky in shock.

"I know you did not just ask that question," Adam said.

"Rocky, we wouldn't be here if we weren't as good as everyone else," Hayley told her. We're exceptional. Do you know how many times we're told that?"

"Yeah, by family members. They're supposed to encourage us. And besides, we're just little freshmen. Nobody's going to want to listen to us trying to get noticed."

Hayley put her hand to her chest and gasped dramatically. "I think I'm going to faint. Adam, you might have to catch me." Hayley pretended to pass out, and Adam caught her.

Rocky rolled her eyes. "I'm serious. Nobody's going to care about us. Let's not even waste our time."

Rocky had always been a pessimist. She would rather expect the worst in every situation than hope for the best and end up disappointed. Rocky never even thought she would be good enough to get into Lennox. She wasn't even brave enough to audition in person at the school. She had a massive anxiety attack the morning of her audition. It was so bad that her mom took her to the hospital because she thought it was a heart condition. The school agreed to let Rocky record her audition and send it in rather than coming to the school.

Rocky found it hard to believe that, as a freshman, she would get noticed by the other students at Lennox, especially not on the first day of school. There were about three performances Rocky saw today, and they all were incredible. She was almost positive they were all upperclassmen. There was no way two little freshman girls were going to get noticed.

"Rocky Coleman," Adam said. "I'm so tired of your pessimistic ways. You're singing. Right now."

"What?" Rocky said.

"You heard me. You and Hayley are going to sing, you guys will get a standing ovation, and you're going to prove to yourself that you *are* just as talented as anyone else in this school."

"Adam..." Rocky pleaded.

"Come on, Rocky, please," Hayley begged.

Rocky had never felt more grateful for a school bell than when she heard it ring to go to fifth period. "Whoops, there's the bell," she said. "Better get to class." She rushed away before Hayley or Adam could say another word.

2

It didn't take long for Rocky to find the chorus room because it was close to the cafeteria. As a result, she was the first person in the classroom. She noticed an elderly woman standing in the storage room, and she assumed it was her teacher. From how her mom spoke so highly of Ms. Rose, Rocky almost felt like she was meeting a celebrity.

"Hi, Ms. Rose," she said quietly.

The lady turned around and looked confused. "Oh, I'm not Ms. Rose," she told her. "She's in here."

Rocky felt her face get hot and held her head down. Well, that was embarrassing.

"A student already?" asked a voice in the storage room. Then out came Ms. Rose, and Rocky almost didn't believe it. She was in awe at how youthful Ms. Rose looked. She looked great for someone who was probably in her late 50s. "Okay, I'll see you later then."

At first, Rocky thought Ms. Rose was talking to her but realized she was talking to the lady whom she thought was Ms. Rose. After the other lady left, Ms. Rose smiled at Rocky. "Hello," she said.

"Hi," Rocky said shyly. "You know my mother, Rochelle. She had your class when she went to school here."

Ms. Rose smiled widely. "Oh, yeah. I remember Rochelle, all right," she said. "I've been teaching at Lennox for over 20 years, and she was one of my best students."

Rocky knew her mother would greatly appreciate the compliment. "She loved having your class."

"She was such a joy to have. Rochelle was so sweet and humble and a remarkable singer." Ms. Rose grinned at Rocky again. "You look a lot like her, too. I have high hopes you'll be just as wonderful as your mother."

Rocky smiled and took a seat as more students started filling in. The number of unfamiliar faces made her anxious, but she took some deep breaths to calm herself. *Just think about how fun this class will be*, she reminded herself.

Rocky looked at the door and recognized one of the four boys from lunch who sang "If I Ever Fall in Love." She expected, and really hoped, to see the rest of the guys walk in, but it was only him. It wasn't even the one who caught Rocky's attention. When he sat next to her, Rocky felt her heart rate increase, and she looked down at her lap. Someone popular and very attractive sat down next to her! She wanted to compliment him and his boys on their fantastic singing but couldn't bring herself to talk to him. He probably wouldn't want to have a conversation with her anyway.

"Okay, my lovelies," Ms. Rose said as soon as everyone was seated. "Let's cut right to the chase and get a few things settled so we can have a great school year. I assume you all want to be singers. Otherwise, you wouldn't be at this school or taking my chorus class. Please know that I am a no-nonsense woman. I will push you to work hard, and sometimes you won't like me."

Rochelle mentioned to Rocky a few times that Ms. Rose was the sweetest person ever but also the strictest teacher ever. It's like she wasn't the same happy-go-lucky lady she saw right before class started. This worried Rocky a bit.

"You will participate and do work in my class, or you will fail my class," Ms. Rose continued. "If you have no intention of participating in my class, please do us both a favor and make your way to the office right now to have your schedules changed."

Rocky wondered if anybody else was intimidated by Ms. Rose.

"Secondly, my name is Ms. Rose. My name is *not* Ms. Lady, or Miss, or Ay. You will address me as Ms. Rose, or you won't address me at all."

Rocky heard somebody scoff in the back of the classroom.

"If you want to speak, you will raise your hand and wait patiently to be called on. You will be ignored if you call out." Ms. Rose paced back and forth as she spoke in front of the classroom. "And I don't do attitudes, disrespect, or fighting. Leave all negativity and beef outside of this classroom. Chewing gum is not allowed in this room. This is a chorus class, and we sing. We cannot sing when we are chewing gum. And lastly, there is absolutely, positively no profanity used in this room whatsoever. If I hear it, I'm kicking you out. No questions asked. Are we okay with the rules?"

The room was silent as everyone looked back and forth between each other and Ms. Rose.

"I did ask a question," Ms. Rose said.

A little less than half of the class answered yes. Rocky was sure everyone was intimidated by Ms. Rose.

"Okay, my children. First things first, we'll practice some vocal warmups together. After that, I'll call you up individually to the grand piano. From there, I'll determine your vocal range and voice type. Let's all stand, please."

Rocky had always felt silly doing vocal exercises, but knowing everyone else in the room was also doing these exercises made her feel less uneasy. Ms. Rose showed the class several types of vocal warmups. They practiced humming, lip buzzing, yawning and sighing, tongue trills (those were especially challenging for Rocky), and two-octave pitch glides. Everything took about five minutes. After everyone finished, Ms. Rose went to her desk and picked up her attendance book.

"Now that our voices are nice and warm, let's find your range and voice type," she said. "I'll call you up alphabetically. Absolutely no talking. The first person is Tracey Adams. Come on down."

A tall, lanky girl with short hair and thick glasses stood up and went to the grand piano. The class was quiet as Ms. Rose played some notes on the piano while Tracey sang what Ms. Rose was playing.

The thought of going to the front of the class and having everyone hear her sing made Rocky want to vomit. Why couldn't Ms. Rose find their vocal range in private? And she was going in alphabetical order, which meant Rocky would be going up soon.

The last thing Rocky wanted was to have a panic attack in the middle of class, so she tried to clear her mind and focus on her breathing. Her leg kept shaking, and she couldn't relax. What if she messed up and everyone laughed at her? Rocky didn't want that at all. She looked at the guy from the singing group next to her and noticed how relaxed he seemed as he casually sat back and watched. Something about his persona made her relax a little.

After about four more students went, it was Rocky's turn.

"Raquel Coleman," Ms. Rose called out.

Rocky's face turned warm the moment she heard her name. Maybe she could pretend she had a sore throat so she wouldn't have to sing in front of the class. But she remembered talking to Ms. Rose before class started, so she'd know Rocky was faking. It could probably be one of those out-of-the-blue sore throats.

"Miss Coleman, are you here today?" Ms. Rose asked. "Please make your way to the grand piano. There's a lot of you to get through, and I don't have all day."

Rocky got up and walked to the grand piano with trembling legs. Ms. Rose smiled at her. "Ah, my mini-Rochelle," she said. "Class, you know her mother was my student many, many years ago. She became a successful singer after graduating."

Nobody seemed to care. Either that or nobody wanted to say anything because they were scared Ms. Rose would scold them for talking.

"Okay, Raquel," Ms. Rose continued. "We'll start you on middle C, then go down the scale until you can't comfortably sing any lower. Then we're going to go up until you can't sing any higher. Shall we begin?"

Rocky cleared her throat and turned to face away from the rest of the class. Not looking at everybody else made her feel less nervous and was the closest she could get to hiding. As Ms. Rose played middle C, Rocky sang along, but for some reason, her voice cracked. She heard a snicker in the back of the room and felt near to tears. Rocky closed her eyes and put her hand over her mouth.

"Excuse me," Ms. Rose called out. "Why do I hear voices? I said I want it quiet in here, and I know I said to keep all negativity outside of this classroom."

Once again, the class went silent. "Okay," Ms. Rose said, looking back at Rocky. "Let's try that again, but this time I need you to relax and project your voice a bit more. Don't worry about everyone else."

Rocky cleared her throat and tried again, this time with her eyes closed. She imagined being the only person in the room. As Ms. Rose played the scale in descending order, Rocky could only comfortably go down a few steps until her voice started feeling way too breathy. She stopped singing after going down five notes. "Okay," Ms. Rose said, writing something next to her name on the roster. "This note is E3. Now let's see how high you can sing. Starting with middle C again, we're going up the scale."

Rocky already knew she sang soprano, but she never knew exactly what her vocal range was. She sang along as Ms. Rose went up the scale and felt her voice crack again as she was nearing her second octave.

"Okay," Ms. Rose stopped her. "This note is G5. You have a little over a two-octave vocal range, which is pretty good. With a range like that, I'll have you singing soprano. Just like your mom did," she said with a smile. Was Rocky going to be compared to her mom all year? She sure hoped that wouldn't be the case. "Thank you, sweetie. You can sit down now."

Rocky nodded and went back to her seat. Her mouth was dry, her neck felt hot, and her legs were still shaking from all the adrenaline. At least she finally got that over with.

"My next victim is Ethan Curry," Ms. Rose said. "Come on down."

About ten other students went after Ethan, and before Rocky knew it, class was almost over. After Ms. Rose finished with another female student, she got up from the grand piano and stood in front of everyone.

"Only about half of the class went, and we're almost out of time. Next time we meet, we'll continue and start with Marcus McKinsey. Until the bell rings, you all are free to talk."

There was a moment of silence before the other students began talking to their friends. Rocky stayed silent.

Rocky's last class of the day was science, which was also a bore, but at least she got to go home right after. Her first day of high school was finally over! Rocky had to admit her first day went a little better than expected. Her classes were mostly okay, and she saw a decent number of talented students put on an impromptu show.

Now that the school day was done, all she wanted to do was go home and relax. Since Rocky's mom would not be back from work until later in the evening, Rocky decided to stay at Hayley's house until her mom got off.

Rocky and Adam were always at Hayley's house because her dad turned their family's attic into a musical instrument gallery; they called it The Studio. It had a grand piano, several guitars, a drum set, some keyboards, and a few other smaller percussion instruments (maracas, tambourines, etc.).

It was clear where Hayley developed her passion for music from! Whenever Rocky, Hayley, and Adam would meet, they would make music for hours in The Studio. Sometimes until their fingers would hurt or their voices would go hoarse. Whenever Rocky had to sing in front of other people, she always closed her eyes and imagined being in The Studio since it was her happy place. Whenever she was in that room, she felt invincible.

Rocky and Hayley were hanging out in The Studio while Hayley's parents cooked dinner. Hayley was playing the guitar, and Rocky sat at the keyboard, watching.

"You're getting a lot better," Rocky told her. "Your chord transitioning has really improved."

"Thanks," Hayley smiled. "I've been practicing. One day, I'll master every instrument in this room. Then I'll master every instrument in the world."

Rocky laughed at her. "That's a lot of instruments to learn," she said. "I'll be fine mastering the piano and guitar. But I also want to learn how to play the steel drums. I wish your dad had those here."

"He might get some if we ask. Or beg." Hayley chuckled. "How did you enjoy the first day of school?"

"It was okay. Today turned out better than I expected. There are a lot of crazy talented people at Lennox."

"Seriously. Especially those hot guys who sang during lunch," Hayley giggled. "Out of all the spontaneous performances, I enjoyed theirs the most."

Rocky smiled as she thought about the lunchtime performance today. She enjoyed their singing the most as well. "You know, one of them is in my chorus class," she told Hayley. "He sat right next to me today."

"No way! Which one?"

"The one with the blue eyes and the brown curly hair. He's so cute."

"They *all* are cute!" Hayley giggled again. "But you know, I heard a lot about them in my last-period class today."

"Like what?"

"You remember the lead singing guy? His name is Aiden Benjamin, he's a sophomore, and his family is really powerful in the music industry."

"Really?"

"Yeah, he's practically famous. Did you know he met Usher?"

"No way! Like, *the* Usher?"

"Yes, girl! I couldn't believe it either. Aiden and his boys are, like, the best singing group in the entire school. Rumor has it that one singer tried to prove he was better than Aiden last year. The day after, Aiden supposedly pulled some strings and got him expelled from Lennox."

"Oh, my gosh."

"Then the guy tried to confront him about it in front of the whole school! Later that week, news spread that the guy had a throat injury and could never sing the same way again. His chances of becoming a professional singer were destroyed."

Rocky was tense. It must have been terrible for a singer to damage their voice box so badly that they'd never be able to sing the same way again. Thinking about it made her shudder. "That's scary," was all she could say. "How did he injure himself?"

"Nobody knows. There are so many different theories about what happened. Some people think Aiden hired somcone to hurt the guy for trying to embarrass him in front of the school, and others think it was just bad karma or something. All I do know is that nobody ever tried to outshine Aiden again. Everybody gets too scared they might end up getting expelled or never being able to sing again."

Hearing that story made Rocky even more anxious about singing in front of everyone at school. All she wanted was to be popular in school just once in her life. She was tired of being in her shell. She wanted to have more friends, get invited to parties, and be accepted as one of the cool kids.

"What do you think about that?" Rocky asked worriedly.

"Honestly, I think it's a bunch of baloney. I mean, Aiden is incredibly talented, but I don't think anybody can be capable of hurting someone so they can feel better about themselves. That's just cruel."

"What else can you tell me about them?" Rocky asked.

Hayley shrugged. "That's all I got," she said. After a brief silence, Hayley picked up her guitar again. "Hey, my dad taught me how to play 'Listcn to the Music,'" she mentioned as she began strumming some chords.

"That old song from the 70s?" Rocky laughed.

Hayley laughed along with Rocky. "Yes, and don't laugh. It's a catchy tune." She started playing the chords to the song. "Go ahead and sing it. You know you want to."

Rocky laughed again but began singing the first verse. Hayley joined in with Rocky, and by the time they finished singing the chorus, they couldn't stop laughing. Rocky loved moments like this.

After some time, it was beginning to get dark outside, which meant Rocky's mother would be home from work soon. She grabbed her things and prepared to leave.

"It felt like we've only been here for like twenty minutes," Rocky said.

"Time flies when you're having a great time," Hayley replied.

As the two girls were leaving The Studio, the savory smell of freshly made chicken filled the air. While Hayley's parents were in the kitchen finishing the food, Hayley's younger brother and sister were watching TV in the living room.

Hayley's mom, Miyoko, turned around and smiled at the girls. "Hey, I was just going to call you guys for dinner," she said.

It was amazing how beautiful Hayley's mom was. She looked youthful for her age and had a great figure for having five children.

"Why don't you stay for dinner?" Hayley asked.

"We'd love that," said Hayley's dad, Bruno.

"I probably should get home," Rocky said. "My mom might be expecting me."

"You can invite Rochelle over," Miyoko told her. "I'm sure she wouldn't mind having dinner with us after a long day at the hospital."

It was difficult to say no to Hayley's family because they were always welcoming and generous.

"I can call and ask her," Rocky replied. "I'm sure she'll want to stay, too."

"Oh, no problem," Bruno said. "Hector! Harold! Dinner!" He called Hayley's older brothers upstairs. "Hanna, Henry, turn off the TV and come help set the dinner table."

While Hayley's family started setting the dinner table, Rocky stepped away from all the noise to call her mother. When she picked up, it sounded like she was driving.

"Hey, Rocky," Rochelle said. "What's up?"

"Hey, Mom. Hayley's parents wanted to know if you'd come over for dinner."

"Oh, absolutely," Rochelle said immediately. "I was on my way home thinking I had to cook dinner and all, and now I don't have to. My prayers are answered!"

Rocky laughed. "I'll let them know you're coming then. Where are you now?"

"I'm about five minutes from Hayley's house."

"Great! See you in a little bit." Rocky said before hanging up the phone and returning to the dining room. Hayley and her siblings were nearly finished setting the table.

"My mom is on her way," Rocky told them.

"Fantastic!" Miyoko said. "Hayley, get another chair and placemat for me, please."

Rocky always loved how large Hayley's family was and how close they were. Things weren't as fun in a house of two as they would be in a house of seven. Sometimes, Rocky wondered if she would have still been shy if she had grown up in a big family like Hayley's.

Rocky also loved how Rochelle and Miyoko were great friends like Rocky and Hayley. They often had family dinners and outings, which were a lot of fun.

After dinner was over, Rocky and Rochelle went home.

"I never got to ask you how your first day of school was," Rochelle said once they got inside the house. "Tell me everything!"

"Oh, it was pretty good," Rocky told her. "Lennox is exactly like how you said it would be. Ms. Rose is still there, too, and she remembers who you are."

Rochelle's face brightened up. "She's still there? Oh, Rocky, you're going to love her."

"It seems like she really loves *you*," Rocky chuckled. "She always compares me to you. I've been dubbed her mini-Rochelle."

Rochelle laughed too. "I figured she would do something like that. She's such a character. I need to visit her one of these days."

"I'm sure she'd enjoy seeing you again."

"How are your other classes?"

"They're not too bad. My classes aren't what I'm worried about."

Rochelle understood how much Rocky wanted to break out of her shell. She put her arm around her daughter and hugged her gently. "It's only your first day," she told her. "I'm sure you'll grow out of your shyness eventually. Who knows? Maybe by graduation, you'll be nothing but a friendly chatterbox."

They both laughed, then Rochelle looked at Rocky.

"But don't let breaking out of your shyness be your top priority. Remember that what you're learning in school is way more important than being popular. Also, make sure you choose your friends wisely. Soft-spoken people like you can get taken advantage of easily."

Rocky nodded. "Okay," she said.

"Alright, girly, it's getting late. Go on and get ready for bed. Let's not have a repeat of what happened this morning."

Rocky rolled her eyes but laughed. "We weren't even late," she said.

"True, but maybe tomorrow, you'll have enough time to do your hair and eat breakfast in the house."

Rocky laughed again. "Goodnight, Mom."

"Night, sweetheart."

3

The first two weeks of school went well for Rocky, and she was starting to enjoy Lennox's spontaneity. Between the random flash mobs throughout the day and the lunchtime concerts every Friday in the cafeteria, there was always something new to experience. Aiden and his boys performed every week, and nobody ever got tired of hearing them — or at least Rocky never got tired of hearing them.

"I can't believe we've been here for two weeks, and we still haven't sung anything," Hayley complained on Thursday morning in the courtyard.

"I can't believe it either," Adam agreed. He and Hayley both looked at Rocky, waiting for her to say something.

"I just don't know if I'm ready yet," Rocky said meekly.

"If you wait until you're 'ready,' you'll be waiting for the rest of your life," Adam told her. "You have to push yourself to take that first step eventually."

"And I will. Eventually. When I feel comfortable enough to do so."

"Come on, Rocky," Hayley pleaded. "If you ever want to get noticed at this school or become a professional singer, you have to...well, sing. It's literally the only way people here will know who you are."

"Maybe I like being unknown," Rocky protested.

"That's not true, and you know it," Adam said. "I thought this was the year you wanted to break out of your shyness."

"I know I said that. It's easier said than done, though."

"I get it, but you'll have to make yourself uncomfortable at one point so you can stop letting your anxiety control your life."

Rocky looked away from Hayley and Adam. It was always a constant battle between wanting to be popular and wanting to hide in her comfort zone. She wanted to be a singer, but being on stage in front of a large audience terrified her. Rocky didn't even know what she wanted anymore.

"You know how the famous saying goes," Hayley said. "Great things happen outside your comfort zone — or however the quote goes." Hayley laughed at herself, and Adam shook his head.

"What are we supposed to do? Just randomly start singing?" Rocky asked.

"Yeah, pretty much," Adam laughed.

"Remember the step dance routine we made up over the summer to 'Titanium?'" Hayley pipped up.

"Yeah, but..."

"We should totally do that! That'll get us noticed for sure."

"But..."

Hayley didn't even wait for Rocky to finish her statement before she began the routine. They only showed it to Adam and their parents, and they all thought the routine was terrific. Although Rocky knew the steps and enjoyed doing it with Hayley, she couldn't help but be a little annoyed at Hayley for making her do this without warning.

When Hayley began singing the first verse of the song to the rhythm of the step dance, Rocky spun her head around to see if anyone noticed. No one had yet. Hayley projected her voice and caught some of the students' attention little by little. Before Hayley got to the chorus, she paused and nudged Rocky, her eyes begging her to join in.

Rocky took some deep breaths, closed her eyes, and imagined she was in The Studio with only Hayley and Adam. The Studio was her happy place, and she felt her nerves slowly ease as she joined Hayley with the step routine and song. It wasn't long before a crowd started forming around the two, which terrified Rocky. To keep herself calm, Rocky kept her eyes closed and focused on staying in harmony with Hayley rather than all the eyes on her. This was difficult for her because her legs were shaking, and her mouth started to feel dry. Basically, she felt like the opposite of titanium.

When they finally finished their routine, everyone cheered loudly. Rocky opened her eyes and immediately looked at the ground when she noticed how many people were watching her. She didn't know how to react, so she kept her head down and prayed everyone would leave already. For the past two weeks, she had been the one in the crowd, watching and cheering for whoever was performing. For Rocky, it felt odd to be the center of attention.

"Now, do you believe you're as talented as the others in this school?" Adam asked Rocky when the crowd began to disperse.

"I'll answer you as soon as I've calmed down," Rocky said while sitting on the floor and trying to control her breathing. The anxiety of that mini performance had her adrenaline pumping, and her heart was pounding in her chest. Her legs were still shaking, she felt lightheaded, and she desperately needed water for her dry mouth.

Adam knelt next to her and placed his hand on her shoulder. "Hey, you're okay," he said gently. "You guys were wonderful, and everyone loved your performance."

Hayley sat on the other side of Rocky and hugged her. "I'm so proud of you, girl," she said. "That was amazing."

Rocky felt her body becoming less tense while her friends sat next to her.

Two female students from the crowd approached the three of them. "Hey, you girls were fantastic," one of them said.

"Yeah," the other one agreed. "By far, the best performance since school started."

"You really think so?" Hayley asked in disbelief.

"Totally," the first one said. "Your voices blend so perfectly together. I'd watch out for Aiden if I were you."

"Don't scare them like that," the second one whispered harshly.

"What? I'm just being real. Did you guys hear about the time...?"

"Okay, thank you," Adam cut her off.

"I apologize for her," the second one said. "Anyway, great performance!" She grabbed the first one by the arm and pulled her away.

Trying to change the subject, Hayley looked at Rocky and smiled big. "Did you hear that? They thought we gave the best performance since school started!"

"They also said we should watch out for Aiden," Rocky warned.

"Forget Aiden," Adam said.

"But if Aiden sees us as a threat, our popularity won't last very long. *We* won't be here very long."

"Rocky, forget him," he repeated. "He and his boys got nothing on you."

Rocky looked to the floor and didn't respond. She was proud of herself for performing as well as everyone said she did, but how long would it be until Aiden found out about them? Not very long, Rocky thought. Would he think she and Hayley were trying to outshine him, even though she knew they weren't? Rocky enjoyed being at Lennox and didn't want to leave on her second week because of Aiden. She also didn't want her singing voice to get ruined.

The bell rang, interrupting Rocky's worries. Hayley, Rocky, and Adam all stood up, said their goodbyes, and parted ways to their classes. Rocky's legs were still shaking from the performance.

***

By the time Monday came around, everyone in the school knew who Hayley and Rocky were. It was more intimidating for Rocky than she'd imagined. After being unnoticed all her life, it was hard to get used to people speaking to her in the hallways or complimenting her singing. She never knew what to say, so she smiled, nodded, and kept walking.

Rocky also never realized how draining it was to be popular. Whenever she and Hayley were together, some people would often stop them and ask them to sing something. Although Rocky genuinely loved singing, it became tedious to start singing on command.

Rocky, Hayley, and Adam were all in the cafeteria eating lunch during the middle of the week when a girl came up to them, smiling as if they were celebrities. It felt so weird to Rocky.

"Hayley and Rocky," she said excitedly.

"Yeah, what's up?" Hayley said.

"So, today is my birthday, and it would completely make my day if you sang 'Happy Birthday' to me because your voices are so beautiful. Do you think you could do that for me, please?"

Rocky smiled at her, but she was screaming internally. *I just want to eat lunch with my friends!*

"Happy birthday," Adam told her. "How old are you?"

"I'm fifteen," she said. "If you guys wouldn't mind, could you please sing for me?"

Hayley and Rocky exchanged looks. "I mean, I don't mind," Hayley said. "What about you, Rocky?"

Even though she didn't feel like doing it, she would've felt awful telling this sweet and innocent girl no. Besides, this was the life she would have to get used to if she became a professional singer. "Um, sure, I guess," Rocky said.

The birthday girl excitedly jumped up and down and squealed.

Hayley stood up on the cafeteria table, grabbed Rocky by the hand, and pulled her up on the table with her. Rocky wasn't expecting that at all.

"Do we really have to stand on the table?" Rocky whispered to her. She noticed people staring at her and felt her heart begin to race. She positioned herself slightly behind Hayley.

"Hey, everyone!" Hayley called out. "Today is our friend's birthday, and we're going to sing to her." She looked down at her and whispered, "What's your name?"

"Crystal," she answered.

Hayley looked back at Rocky. "Ready?"

"Ready to get this over with," Rocky said softly.

Hayley cleared her throat and started off. Rocky joined in shortly after, staying in perfect harmony with Hayley. Rocky kept her head down as she sang, but when she glanced at Crystal and saw her smiling from ear to ear, she felt great about herself for once. She felt honored to make somebody that happy, even if it was something as simple as singing "Happy Birthday." When the girls finished singing, everyone cheered, and a few students who were close by hugged Crystal and told her happy birthday. Rocky and Hayley climbed down from the table, and Crystal hugged them tightly.

"Thanks so much, you guys!" she said happily. "You're the best. I'll never get tired of hearing you two sing."

"You're so welcome," Hayley said. "We hope you have a good rest of your day."

Crystal gave them both another hug before running to her friends.

Rocky was filled with pride. This nice girl they just met actually said she and Hayley were the best *and* that she'd never get tired of hearing them sing. What a wonderful compliment!

"Aww, look at you two doing good deeds for your peers," Adam laughed.

Hayley giggled, too. "It feels like we're celebrities. This is so surreal."

"I'm glad we made her day," Rocky said. "Seeing how happy she was made me feel so great."

"That's great," Adam said. "Slowly but surely, you're breaking out of that shell of yours. Soon you'll be standing on tables singing your heart out without Hayley begging or forcing you to do so."

Rocky laughed and shoved Adam. "It feels like Hayley and I are the celebrities while you're, like, just there. Why don't you sing with us?"

Adam shrugged. "I don't mind being your entourage. In fact, I enjoy it."

Hayley rolled her eyes. "I'll get you to sing with us someday," she told him. "It took some effort to get Rocky to sing, but you'll be a piece of cake, Adam."

Adam chuckled, and Rocky laughed, too. When they walked outside, there was a performance going on. It was Aiden and his boys singing "On Bended Knee" by Boyz II Men, and they sounded terrific.

"I'll be over there," Adam said, irritation filling his voice. He walked in the other direction, leaving Rocky and Hayley to watch the boys' performance until the end. They cheered along with the rest of the crowd after their song was finished. Rocky and Aiden locked eyes again, but he smiled at her this time! The butterflies in her stomach became intense, so she looked away. Rocky couldn't believe the cutest guy at school just smiled at her. Or maybe he smiled in her direction and not necessarily *at* her?

"Should we go find Adam?" Hayley asked.

Rocky glanced over to where Aiden and his boys were standing but couldn't see them anymore. "Um, yeah," Rocky said. "Let's find him."

"I wonder why he never wants to stay and hear the guys sing," Hayley said.

Rocky shrugged and wondered the same thing. She and Hayley went to the courtyard and found Adam sitting on a bench with his headphones on. He removed them when he saw Hayley and Rocky approach him.

"Dude, why'd you leave?" Hayley asked him.

"I get so tired of hearing that narcissist," he rolled his eyes.

"Oh, come on, Adam. Do you even know him like that to call him a narcissist?"

"Yes, I do know him like that, Hayley. He's a joke. I hope he pops his jaw out of place, so he won't be able to sing again."

"Adam," Rocky said, appalled at his rudeness. "Don't say stuff like that."

Rocky wondered if there really was something wrong with Aiden for Adam to have so much hatred towards him. Or maybe Adam was jealous of him? Rocky didn't think Adam was the jealous type or that he should have any reason to be jealous.

Later that evening, Rocky was in the living room watching TV when her mother came home from work. She's been waiting all day to tell Rochelle about what happened today at school.

"Hey, Mom!" Rocky called out as soon as Rochelle walked in.

"What!" Rochelle called back.

"You'll never guess what happened at school today."

Rochelle walked into the living room and sat next to Rocky. "What's up?"

"Hayley and I are getting noticed around school since we started singing."

"Oh, that's great to hear! I'm so happy for you guys."

Rocky smiled as her mother gave her a tight hug. "It's strange, and it can be a little overwhelming at times. But I think I kind of like it. This girl asked us to sing 'Happy Birthday' to her today, and she told us that she would never get tired of hearing us sing."

"Aww, that was nice. I'm glad you're starting to branch out and make new friends. I knew you could do it."

"But," Rocky continued. "There's this talented group of singers that are like the best in the entire school. There's this rumor that if anyone tries to be better than the lead singer, he'll pull some strings to get you expelled from Lennox. And when you try to confront him about it, he'll hire someone to ruin your singing voice."

Rochelle couldn't stop laughing. "You can't be serious."

"I am," Rocky said. "The last person who tried to outshine him got expelled, ended up with a throat injury, and could never sing the same again. A lot of people are paying more attention to Hayley and me. I'm scared he might think we're trying to show off, and he'll get us kicked out of Lennox. And I don't want to injure my throat."

"Rocky, would you relax? Nobody is better than anybody. Back when I was at Lennox, nobody ever competed for who was the best in the school. We all just had fun being creative. There's no way some teenagers will 'pull strings' to get you expelled. I promise."

"How can you be so sure if you don't even know them?"

"You don't know them, either. You heard all this nonsense from a rumor. How can *you* be so sure it's true?"

Rocky hesitated. "I don't know. It just feels right, I guess. Someone even warned us to watch out for them."

Rochelle rolled her eyes and laughed again.

"Mom, it's not funny," Rocky whined. "I'm really scared."

"Rocky. Honey. You will be fine. I can guarantee you no student has that much power. Just keep doing you, and you'll have a wonderful school year."

Rocky kept her head down as her thoughts raced all over the place. How could her mom be so nonchalant about the whole thing? The thought of getting expelled from such an exciting school terrified her. She didn't even want to think about what her life would be like if she could never sing the same way again. Rocky was a little upset that her mom didn't seem to take this as seriously as she wanted.

"I'm going to make something to eat," Rochelle said while standing up and stretching her arms. "You want anything special?"

Rocky shook her head, then Rochelle left for the kitchen. Rocky sat on the couch and tried to think happier thoughts, but she couldn't stop worrying about what Aiden could do if he thought she was better than him.

***

On Thursday, Rocky, Hayley, and Adam were all having lunch together when she saw a teacher walking up to them. Rocky recognized her as the lady who arranged for the singers, dancers, and musicians at school to perform during lunch. Rocky also noticed Aiden and his boys following her from a distance and stopped when she stopped at their table. Was Aiden watching them? Rocky's heart skipped a few beats as she tried not to look at the guys.

"Hayley and Rocky," the teacher said happily. "Just the girls I was looking for."

Hayley and Rocky both smiled at her.

"In case you didn't know, my name is Mrs. Miller, and I'm in charge of collecting the names of students who'd like to perform for Friday's lunch concerts. Someone had to drop out at the last minute, so there's an opening for tomorrow's concert if you girls are interested in performing."

Hayley squealed with delight, but Rocky felt her face get warm. Singing on stage was a lot different than putting on impromptu performances in the courtyard. Rocky wanted to be as excited as Hayley was, but her anxiety was getting the best of her.

"Rocky, do you want to do it?" Hayley asked. "It would be so great to perform up on stage."

Rocky hesitated. She knew how much it would mean to Hayley for them to sing on stage together, and she knew she would have to get over her stage fright one way or another. Rocky wanted to perform but didn't want to at the same time. She also knew having Hayley on stage with her would make her feel a little less anxious. "Uh, sure," she said meekly.

"Okay, perfect." Mrs. Miller said, writing their names down on her clipboard. "You ladies are now scheduled to sing tomorrow during lunch. After your third-period classes, come straight to my classroom. It's the one right next to the cafeteria. I'll see you guys then!"

As Mrs. Miller was about to leave, Aiden finally walked over to their table and stopped her. "Wait, Mrs. Miller. You didn't ask if me and the boys wanted to sing for tomorrow."

"Yes," Mrs. Miller said. "Tomorrow is completely full. Rocky and Hayley just filled the last spot."

"But we perform every Friday," Aiden protested. "Why did you skip over us?"

"I didn't skip over you, Aiden. Like you said, you boys perform *every* Friday. People want to see something new. Hayley and Rocky are, like, the next big thing."

"But that's not fair, Mrs. Miller. You know how much this means to us."

"Aiden, listen, I need to go." Mrs. Miller seemed almost impatient. "You and your boys can perform next week," she said as she rushed out of the cafeteria.

Aiden glared at Rocky, Adam, and Hayley for a moment and briefly locked eyes with Rocky before turning away to face his boys. This was the one time Aiden broke eye contact with Rocky first, and it ate her up inside.

"Unbelievable," he said with disappointment in his voice. "Let's get out of here." Aiden walked away, and his boys followed behind him.

"Aiden looked really upset," Rocky told Hayley and Adam after they left. "Should we drop out, so he and his boys can perform instead?"

"Of course not!" Adam exclaimed.

"No way!" Hayley cried at the same time.

"But what about Aiden?" Rocky asked.

"What about that fool?" Adam retorted. "Like he said, he performs all the time, and I'm sure some people get tired of hearing him."

"Rocky, this is our first real performance," Hayley said. "We can't just drop out because Aiden got upset."

"But remember what everyone said about the guy who got expelled and couldn't sing the same after he tried to show Aiden up?"

"We're technically not *trying* to show him up," Hayley laughed. "We're just having fun, doing us, and we happen to be better than him."

Adam cracked up and high-fived Hayley.

"Besides, Aiden is way too cocky," Adam added. "He needs his ego crushed, and I *really* want you guys to be the ones to do it."

"Don't get me wrong," Hayley said. "I adore Aiden and his boys, but I love singing with you more. And if Aiden has a problem with us, well, he'll just have to get over it."

Rocky looked around to see if Aiden or any of the boys were within earshot.

"Now quit worrying about Aiden and start figuring out what you and Hayley are going to sing tomorrow," Adam told her.

Rocky sighed. She thought that maybe she deserved to leave Lennox and not be a singer. What kind of singer had social anxiety anyway? She might as well enjoy her 15 minutes of fame since she would get kicked out of Lennox and lose her singing voice for good. It took everything in her to keep herself from crying. Rocky turned to face away from her friends, so they wouldn't see her angst.

"Why don't you come on stage with us, Adam?" Rocky heard Hayley ask. "We can sing, and you could play your guitar."

"You probably should've told Mrs. Miller about that then," Adam said. "She has you and Rocky down to perform, not me."

"Shoot! I just thought about it," Hayley sighed, looked at the cafeteria's exit, then back to Adam. "Maybe if we could find her and..."

"Nah, don't sweat it," Adam chuckled. "It's fine."

"Adam, you're not going to be our entourage!"

"I'll perform with you next time."

The bell rang for them to go to their next class. As they stood up, Hayley gave Rocky a gentle nudge.

"Hey girl, is everything okay?" she asked.

"I'll be fine," Rocky said quietly.

"Everyone at school already loves you," Adam assured her. "Don't get worked up because of a stupid rumor. Nothing bad is going to happen."

Rocky wasn't too convinced. She was ready for the day to be over, so she could go home and lock herself in her bedroom.

"Text me, so we can figure out what we're going to sing tomorrow," Hayley told Rocky.

"Okay," Rocky said.

"This is going to be so much fun, Rocky. I can't wait!"

"Yeah, me neither," Rocky responded, her voice sounding the opposite of thrilled.

Rocky couldn't get over the fact that tomorrow would be her first time singing on a stage with an entire audience watching. Between that and worrying about Aiden being threatened by her, she couldn't keep her mind at ease. Sure, the lunch performance would be the first step in breaking out of her shell, but what was the point if she could never perform again?

4

Rocky and Hayley were standing backstage while an all-girl group performed an a cappella version of "Stand by Me." They sounded magnificent, and the crowd loved them! However, Rocky had trouble enjoying the show because she and Hayley were going to perform after them, and she was trying not to panic.

"I think it's so cool how people can make music like that with just their voices," Hayley said in awe.

"I know. They're fantastic," Rocky agreed. Then her pessimism got the best of her. "How are we supposed to compete with that?"

"Rocky, please don't start with the negativity."

"I'm sorry. I'm just nervous. I've never sung up on a stage before." Even the brief thought of being on stage made Rocky's heart start beating faster and her mouth dry. "I'm so thirsty."

"There's absolutely nothing to be worried about," Hayley reassured Rocky as she handed her a water bottle. Rocky began gulping it down.

"I'm going to be up on stage with you, and Adam said he's going to be right there in the front row. Everyone at school has already heard us sing, and they say we sound great. *We* know we sound great. Everything will be fine, I promise."

Rocky finished the entire water bottle, yet she was still incredibly thirsty. She noticed Mrs. Miller walking up to her and Hayley. Rocky's nerves were so intense that she could barely move. *Please don't have an anxiety attack. Please don't have an anxiety attack.*

"Okay, girls," she said excitedly. "You're up next. How are we feeling?"

Hayley looked over at Rocky and gave her a gentle pat on the back when she saw how distraught she looked.

"She has performance anxiety," Hayley said.

Mrs. Miller smiled at Rocky. "Sweetie, you'll be wonderful. You know you have such a beautiful voice."

Rocky wanted to turn around and forget about the performance. She couldn't bring herself to do it – not with all those people out there watching. The a cappella girls were finishing their song, to her dismay, and the crowd was going nuts for them. The terror soon became too overwhelming for Rocky, and she started freaking out.

"Hayley, I can't do this!" she exclaimed. Tears started rolling down her face. The last thing Rocky wanted was to have an anxiety attack in public without her mom around. Thinking about that only worsened her anxiety, and she started hyperventilating.

Luckily, Hayley stayed calm. Although she didn't have much experience dealing with Rocky's panic attacks, she tried everything she could to calm her down. She pulled Rocky into a tight embrace. "Rocky, you're okay. Just breathe. You're okay." It sounded like she was holding back tears of her own.

Now Rocky felt like she was letting Hayley down, which only amplified her agitation. So many thoughts were racing through Rocky's mind at that moment: She was terrified about singing onstage, embarrassed about having a panic attack in public, and worried that her not performing would upset Mrs. Miller and Hayley. She desperately wanted her mother to be there to help stop this panic attack. What would happen if she and Hayley couldn't perform anymore? What if she had to go to the hospital?

I know this will fade away, Rocky thought to herself over and over again. She remembered her mother whispering that to her repeatedly during some of her worst panic attacks, which usually helped stop them. *I know this will fade away. I know this will fade away.*

Slowly, Rocky started controlling her breathing and was coming back to reality. She didn't even realize how many worried people were surrounding her. This was one of the reasons why she hated having panic attacks in public.

"How are you feeling?" Hayley asked. She was still hugging Rocky close, almost as if she were afraid to let go. Rochelle did the same thing after Rocky's panic attacks.

Rocky took some more deep breaths before answering Hayley. "I'm fine now," she said.

"Rocky, you don't have to perform if you're that anxious," Mrs. Miller said. "You gave us quite a scare."

Rocky was going to take Mrs. Miller up on that offer, but she thought about how disappointed Hayley would be if Rocky backed out at the last minute. Rocky would also be letting herself down by not pushing herself to get over her stage fright. Why couldn't she be bold like Hayley? Why did her anxiety always have to ruin everything? Rocky wiped her eyes, sighed, and shook her head.

"Hayley was so excited to perform today, and I don't want to be the one to ruin it for her," she said softly. "I'll do it."

"Rocky, no," Hayley protested. "After what just happened, I can't let you do that."

"But this is so important to you. I don't want to let you down."

"You're not letting me down. I don't mind not performing today if you're too nervous."

"I also need to get over my stage fright."

"It doesn't have to be right now, though. I want you to feel comfortable so you can do your best."

"I'll just close my eyes and imagine we're in The Studio. Doing that normally calms me down."

"Rocky, are you sure?"

Rocky nodded her head. If she couldn't do this for herself, she wanted to do it for Hayley. Hayley gave Rocky another tight hug. "You know I'll be right next to you the entire time," she whispered.

"I know," Rocky whispered back.

"Okay, ladies," Mrs. Miller said while holding out a box of tissues for Hayley and Rocky. "If you're going to sing, then dry your eyes and get ready. I'm going to announce you guys." She then walked away from the girls and onto the stage.

Rocky and Hayley quickly dried their eyes and looked at each other. "Do my eyes look puffy?" Rocky asked.

"A little," Hayley said. "I'm certain mine are, too, so we can be puffy-eyed together." They both chuckled.

"We'll make it a new trend," Rocky joked.

It felt great to laugh with Hayley and ease her nerves a bit. That moment didn't last long because Mrs. Miller had already announced them, and she heard everyone in the audience go wild. Her heart began to race, and she grabbed Hayley's hand. "Let's get this over with."

The audience cheered again as the girls walked out on stage holding hands. Rocky couldn't believe how many people were out there! Her legs felt like Jell-O as she stood center stage. Aiden and his boys were sitting near the front, but they weren't cheering like everyone else. Their faces were expressionless, making Rocky wonder if they were still upset about not performing today. What if Aiden thought they were trying to be better than them? *Stop it, Rocky! Focus on the performance.*

Rocky then noticed Adam's friendly face, front and center, cheering them on. Having Hayley by her side and seeing Adam supporting them was the relief she needed. The crowd settled down. Rocky still had a firm grip on Hayley's hand, closed her eyes, and pictured herself in The Studio with only Hayley and Adam present. She cleared her throat and began singing the first verse to Extreme's "More Than Words" while Hayley sang the low harmony.

"More Than Words" was one of Rocky's favorite songs to sing with Hayley because of how calming it was. They sang it all the time in The Studio while Adam played the guitar. Hayley's parents always told them how beautifully their voices blended when they sang. Rocky's mom always wanted them to record a cover of that song.

The audience's clapping to the beat of the song momentarily pulled Rocky out of her image of her being in The Studio. She opened her eyes, saw the crowd, and then closed them back. *Get back in The Studio. You're in The Studio.*

Rocky and Hayley were singing in The Studio together. Adam was beside them while playing his guitar. Only their parents were watching them sing, and they were the ones clapping to the beat of the song. Imagining all the familiar faces made her feel more at ease.

Before Rocky even realized it, they were nearing the end of the song. When she and Hayley finally finished, the crowd cheered loudly. Rocky opened her eyes to see everyone on their feet and clapping, much to her surprise. She even saw Adam standing and cheering enthusiastically, which made her smile. Rocky then looked over to where Aiden and his boys were supposed to be, but they were nowhere to be found. Not seeing them made her heart sink, so she ran off the stage with Hayley following behind. Once they were backstage, Rocky sat on the floor and exhaled deeply. She sang on a stage for the first time in her life, *and* she got a standing ovation. Her mom would be so proud.

"You guys were awesome!" one of the other performers said to Hayley and Rocky.

"The crowd is still going crazy," another one said.

Rocky didn't know how to respond because she was still trying to recover from her adrenaline rush. She was also still in awe that she had performed on stage for the first time. Rocky politely smiled while her peers complimented her performance.

The sound of Mrs. Miller clapping and her heels clicking on the wooden floor caught everyone's attention. "Great job, everyone," she said enthusiastically. "You all were fantastic out there! Thank you all for sharing your beautiful talents with your peers. Like I promised, there's pizza back in my classroom if you guys want something to eat before you go to your next class. Just pop on in, have a bite to eat, and I'll write you a late pass for your class. If you don't want to join us for pizza, that's also fine. I will *not* be writing you a pass if you don't show up, so make sure you get to where you're supposed to be."

The sound of the school bell ringing interrupted Mrs. Miller speaking.

"For those joining us for lunch, follow me," she continued. "If not, then get to class, and I hope to see you perform again real soon!"

Rocky and Hayley decided to go to Mrs. Miller's room for pizza. Rocky didn't realize how hungry she was until all her nerves finally settled after the performance. She still couldn't believe she sang on stage. What a huge accomplishment for her! When they got to Mrs. Miller's classroom, three large boxes of pizza were waiting for them in a separate room in the back. Since Mrs. Miller had a class at the time, all the performers had to eat their pizza there, so they wouldn't disrupt her class. She placed a small pile of hall passes next to the pizza boxes.

"These passes already have everything filled out except your name and the time," Mrs. Miller explained. "Fill them out once you're finished, and you should be good to go. I trust you all won't stay back here for too long and won't be too disruptive. You can leave through the back door when you're ready. Thank you all so much again for performing today."

Once Mrs. Miller closed the door, everyone devoured those pizzas. They finished all three boxes in about five minutes, but nobody wanted to leave right away. They all started some friendly conversations.

"Everybody did a great job today," one guy said. "My favorite was the a cappella version of 'Stand by Me' and you girls," he said to Hayley and Rocky.

"I know," one of the a cappella girls said. "You girls were born to sing together."

Hayley laughed. "Thanks, but you were amazing, too. It takes some real talent to make music with only your voices."

"Are you and Rocky going to sing again next week?" someone else asked.

Hayley looked at Rocky, and Rocky looked down at her lap.

"We haven't decided if we wanted to yet," Hayley said.

"You totally should. Everyone loves you guys."

"Rocky has stage fright," Hayley told them softly. "And I don't want to push her to sing again if she's too anxious."

"Oh, I understand the struggle," one of the students said to Rocky. "I used to hate being on stage my freshman year, but I had to allow myself to feel uncomfortable enough times if I wanted to be a performer. It's a process, but you'll get better over time."

Rocky smiled. "Thank you for the advice," she said. "I'm just really tired of being afraid to sing in front of people."

"I get it, girl. I have faith you'll be more comfortable being on stage by the end of the year. Doing this performance today was a big step, and it's up to you to keep it going."

Rocky thought it was nice how these strangers believed in her more than she believed in herself. She appreciated those encouraging words. They made her feel better about herself and her ability to overcome stage fright.

Although staying in Mrs. Miller's classroom for the rest of the day was tempting, everyone decided to do the right thing and go to their own classes. After leaving through the back door, Hayley and Rocky strolled to their class together.

"I know I probably said this a lot already, but I'm so proud of you for singing on stage today," Hayley gushed. "You were so brave."

Rocky laughed. "Thanks, girl. Despite the overwhelming nerves I had, it was actually kind of fun."

"It was so much fun! When would you want to sing again?"

"Hmm, I'm not sure yet. Maybe in like a few weeks?"

"I don't think it's a good idea to wait too long," Hayley warned her. "You'll be even more anxious about performing the longer you wait.

"I guess you're right. How about every other week?"

"We can talk more about it."

Hayley and Rocky made it to their classroom and took their seats after giving their teacher their late passes.

Rocky, Hayley, and Adam decided to hang out at Hayley's place for a bit after school. Miyoko was so excited about Rocky and Hayley's first performance at school, so she made some delicious cupcakes! After eating, the three of them went upstairs to The Studio to make some music.

"You girls were amazing today," Adam told them. "And I'm so proud of you for finally singing on stage, Rocky."

"Hayley has been telling me that all day," Rocky joked. "Even Hayley's mom made cupcakes to tell me how proud she is of me."

"Because it's a huge deal," Hayley laughed.

"That's right," Adam said. "Now accept the compliments and cupcakes already," he joked.

"Hey man, I didn't say it was a bad thing."

"How did it feel being on stage for the first time?" Adam asked Rocky.

"Honestly, I was so nervous," Rocky looked down at the keyboard she was sitting at and started playing a scale. "I had a panic attack before going out there, and I almost backed down."

"Oh, I'm so sorry, Rocky," Adam said.

"I knew how important it was to Hayley, so I just had to pull myself together and do it."

"And you did wonderful," Hayley said as she smiled at Rocky.

"Everyone's dying to hear more of you guys," Adam told them. "I hear so many other students talking about how much they loved your singing."

"Really? That's so exciting!" Hayley said.

Rocky had to admit it felt nice having more people around the school know who she was.

"Do you think you could write a song for us to sing next time we perform, Adam?" Hayley asked.

"It depends," Adam said. "Sometimes, I have my good days when I can write an entire song in a day. Other times, I have my bad days when it'll take months to finish one."

"Are you working on anything now?"

"Sort of. I started it not too long ago, and I guess it's coming along okay."

Rocky giggled. "Let us hear," she said. "Maybe we can help?"

Adam picked up his guitar and started strumming some chords. "I only have like an intro and a part of a verse. I don't even have a title yet."

"That's totally fine," Hayley said. "Play it."

Adam began playing and singing while the girls swayed along to the beat. Rocky enjoyed the smooth midtempo of the song, and his words beautifully described his love for music. After being unable to come up with any more lyrics, Adam hummed the melody until he finished.

"That sounds so good, Adam!" Hayley said while clapping excitedly.

Adam put his guitar back down and laughed. "Uh, I guess it's okay."

"Hey, don't doubt yourself," Rocky told him. "That's my thing, not yours.," she joked.

"Neither of you can doubt yourselves," Hayley told them with a slight giggle. "But seriously, Adam, that song is fire. All you need to do is finish the verse and come up with a chorus, and then you should be good."

"And possibly have some female vocalists?" Adam suggested.

"Who us?" Hayley asked while doing a dramatic hair flip. "Oh, how thoughtful of you to ask."

"If you're done being a diva," Rocky joked. "Adam, play the song again. I think I might have an idea for the chorus."

"Ooh, this should be good." Adam picked up his guitar again. "I'll start from the bridge."

Rocky cleared her throat. She was no songwriter, but she was more than happy to help in any way possible. When Adam began playing, she channeled her passion for music and tried to come up with some lyrics to describe it. Rocky felt a little weird singing gibberish but knew it would sound better once Adam could come up with more lyrics to the melody.

"I love it!" Hayley exclaimed.

"Me too," Adam agreed. "I think I can work with that."

Rocky shrugged. "It's okay, I guess."

"Hey, no doubting," Adam joked.

The three of them continued to work on the song until it was time for Rocky and Adam to go home. They enjoyed how well it turned out in the end.

"Hey, thanks for helping me with the song," Adam told Rocky as they were on their way out of Hayley's house.

"No problem," Rocky said. "That's what I'm here for."

"Maybe you might end up writing your own songs one day."

Rocky laughed. "No way. I can't come up with lyrics as easily as you."

"Sure, you can! You just did."

"Yeah, but that was today. I don't even think I have the patience to sit and write an entire song. How do you do it?"

"Passion. It's all about the passion."

Rocky and Adam soon had to part ways to go to their own houses.

"I'll see you tomorrow," Rocky said while giving Adam a hug.

"See you," Adam said.

***

On Tuesday, Rocky, Hayley, and Adam decided to eat their lunch outside. Adam brought his guitar to school that day, and after they finished eating, he softly began playing some chords. Rocky recognized the song and perked up.

"Is that 'Oceans'?" she asked excitedly.

"Yeah," he said with a smile. "The church asked me to learn it for an upcoming service. You know it?"

"Of course! I love that song. Hayley, you remember when we first heard it?"

"Oh yeah, I remember," Hayley giggled. "We loved how calming the song was, and we were so determined to learn the lyrics as soon as possible. I think we even considered singing it at a church service, remember?"

"Maybe *you* thought about that," Rocky laughed. "I would never suggest such a thing."

Adam chuckled and continued strumming. Rocky started singing along with him once he got to her favorite part of the song.

"That's good, Rocky," Adam said. "Keep going."

Rocky continued singing, and Hayley joined in perfect harmony with her alto voice. This was the first time Rocky felt completely comfortable singing in public and didn't worry about other people hearing her. Maybe something about singing gospel made her feel more at ease? She didn't even notice the other students were tuning in to listen.

As Rocky and Hayley continued harmonizing, Rocky felt like someone was standing behind her. She turned around and, to her surprise, it was Aiden! And just like that, her heart started racing, her face was flushed, and she forgot the lyrics to the song she knew perfectly by heart. Adam noticed Hayley and Rocky had stopped singing, so he stopped playing his guitar to see what had happened. He glanced at Aiden, scoffed, and then started strumming again.

"You don't have to stop," Aiden said cordially. "Keep going. You sound great."

Hayley and Rocky looked at each other with wide eyes and big smiles. Aiden was the most talented person at Lennox, and he complimented Rocky's and Hayley's singing. This was so unreal!

"Oh, that?" Rocky said nervously. "That wasn't anything special. We were just being silly."

Aiden chuckled. "Well, if you sound that amazing when you're silly, then I'd love to hear you when you're serious." He looked directly into Rocky's eyes and smiled at her.

Rocky broke eye contact with him and looked down at the grass beneath her. "We're not as good as you, though," Rocky said as she began pulling grass blades from the ground.

Hayley and Adam stared at Rocky in disbelief. *I can't believe I said that out loud*, she thought.

Aiden chuckled again. "Well, I beg to differ," he said. "And apparently, most of the school does, too."

Rocky's heart started beating rapidly in her chest as she wondered what would happen next. Aiden just acknowledged how most of the school thought she and Hayley were talented. Does this mean she and Hayley would be the next big thing while Aiden's group were now has-beens? She couldn't stop thinking about what could happen now that Aiden saw them as a threat.

"Anyway," Aiden continued. "I came over here to ask you guys something."

"Whatever it is, the answer is no," Adam spoke up.

Aiden looked down at Adam for the first time since he arrived and laughed. "Oh, Adam. You finally decide to speak to me, and that's all you have to say? You could've at least said 'hello' first."

Adam rolled his eyes. "Just get out of here. We're not doing you any favors."

Aiden disregarded Adam and continued to speak to Hayley and Rocky again. However, it seemed like he had his eyes on Rocky the entire time. "My boys and I were talking the other day, and we all agreed that we're not as good as we used to be."

Rocky looked at Adam, who was tuning his guitar and paying Aiden no mind, then she turned to Hayley, who was just as flabbergasted as Rocky was.

"We were great last year, but I guess since it's a new school year, it's time to try something new," Aiden continued. "Long story short, we thought it would be cool to have some female vocals in the group."

Hayley gasped and grabbed Rocky's hand as she squirmed with delight. Was he asking what they thought he was asking?

"Seriously?" Hayley gasped.

"Seriously," Aiden answered with a smile.

Aiden wanted Hayley and Rocky to sing with him and his group! The most talented singers in all of Lennox. It was way too good to be true. Before Rocky or Hayley could respond, Adam stood up and approached Aiden.

"You think you can come over here and charm your way into having these girls join your stupid little group?" he asked, exasperated. "You're just mad because people are paying attention to them instead of you and your boys. Why can't you accept that there are people out there who are better than you?"

Aiden rolled his eyes. As the two boys stood face to face, Aiden towered over Adam. Rocky had never seen Adam so upset, and she was worried he might do something absurd. She couldn't understand what it was about Aiden that ticked Adam off so much.

"I'm sorry, but I don't think I was speaking to you," Aiden retorted. "Besides, I don't want both of them."

Hayley, Rocky, and Adam all exchanged confused looks. What did he mean he didn't want them both? Aiden looked at Rocky and smiled at her. "I want her."

Rocky's eyes widened, and she felt her heart pounding. "Me?"

Adam spoke up again. "Rocky and Hayley sing *together*," Adam protested. "They're a package deal, and they sound fantastic together. Rocky's not going to sing with you, so forget about it."

"Why don't you let her speak for herself?" Aiden asked almost impatiently. "She has a voice." He looked over at Rocky again. "Which, by the way, is a lovely voice."

Rocky looked down again as she felt her face getting warm.

"No wonder she's always so timid," Aiden continued. "You treat her like a child."

"I treat her like a best friend," Adam fired back. "And she doesn't want to sing with you, Aiden."

"Adam, I think he's right," Hayley spoke up.

"Hayley!" Adam cried.

"You are treating Rocky like a child. It should be her decision, not yours."

Everyone then looked at Rocky to see what she was going to say. She felt pressured to give Aiden an answer and didn't know the right choice. Rocky was infatuated with Aiden and would do anything to get the chance to sing with him. At the same time, she didn't want to abandon her best friends. Also, Rocky knew how perfect she and Hayley sounded when they sang together. How would she sound singing with Aiden and three other guys?

"Um," Rocky stuttered. "I don't know." She looked at the ground and started pulling more grass blades. She was afraid she might have another panic attack and did not want Aiden to see her like that.

"No worries," Aiden said calmly. "I know it's sudden, so take some time to think about it. When you decide, you know where to find me." Aiden smiled at Rocky once more before walking away.

"Rocky, don't do it," Adam told her after Aiden was gone. "He's just trying to stop you and Hayley from singing together because he thinks you guys are a threat. He doesn't want you to be in his group." He looked to Hayley for support. "Back me up here."

"Well," Hayley said uneasily. "It might benefit her to be in Aiden's group."

"Are you seriously telling her to do it?" Adam asked.

"I mean, he knows people in the music industry who could get her noticed by professionals."

"But I don't want to do it if you're not there with me," Rocky told her.

"If an opportunity like that comes, you should take it and run with it," Hayley said.

"But what about you?"

"I'll be fine. I think you should join Aiden's group and get the experience."

"Hayley!" Adam protested.

"It'll be good for her," Hayley said. "Maybe this will be what helps her break out of her shyness."

Rocky shrugged. "I don't know," she said softly.

Adam looked at Rocky. "Don't do it," he repeated. "He's using you."

The sound of the school bell ringing interrupted their conversation. Rocky picked up her backpack, and the three of them walked to their different classes. Throughout the rest of the day, Rocky could only think about whether being part of Aiden's group was a good idea.

5

Later that night, Rocky tried to finish some homework in the living room but couldn't concentrate. She was too busy thinking about whether she should join Aiden's singing group. Rocky had been racking her brain about it all day, causing an overwhelming amount of stress. Her thoughts were then interrupted when her mother came home from work. "Hey, sweetheart," she said. "How was your day today?"

"It was okay," Rocky sighed. "You?"

Rochelle dropped her bags on the floor and plopped on the couch next to Rocky. "It could've been worse," she admitted. "I'm ready for a nap. What are you up to?"

"I'm supposed to be doing homework, but I can't concentrate."

Rochelle stood up. "Oh, I'm so sorry, Rocky," she said. "I didn't mean to distract you. I'll let you finish."

"Wait, Mom," Rocky called before her mom could leave. "You're not distracting me. Sit back down."

"What's the matter?" Rochelle said as she sat next to Rocky again.

"Well, there's this guy," Rocky started.

"Oh, man," Rochelle laughed. "I was afraid this day would come."

Rocky laughed along with her mother. "It's not exactly like that," she explained. "He's the lead singer in this boy group at school, and they're amazing. Like, the best in the entire school."

"Wait a minute. Is this the same group of singers you were telling me about before? The one where they 'pull some strings' to get people expelled if they think they're getting shown up?" Rochelle laughed again.

Rocky looked down at her lap. "Yes," she said, slightly embarrassed.

"What happened? Did they somehow get you expelled? Are they plotting on how to steal your voice next?"

"Mom, please."

"Okay, I'm sorry. Go on."

"During lunch today, the lead singer asked if I wanted to be in his group, and I don't know if I want to or not. Hayley says I should do it, but Adam says not to."

"Well, what does Rocky say?" Rochelle asked.

"I don't know. Rocky's confused," she giggled a little. "Singing with Aiden and his group would be a great opportunity because he knows people in the music industry who could get me noticed."

"That's great!"

"But I don't want to do it if I don't have Hayley and Adam by my side."

"Then don't do it."

"But this is too big of an opportunity to turn down! And this might make me popular for once in my life. Not to mention it'll be a great start to my singing career."

Rochelle smoothed down Rocky's hair. "Hun, if you think joining this singing group is best for you, and you know this is what you want to do, then go for it. You can't always please everyone."

"I always sing with Hayley, though. This would be the first time I'd be singing with someone else, and just the thought of it feels so weird. I don't want her to think I'm ditching her."

"Hayley would understand you're not ditching her, and you know she'll be there to support you every step of the way like she always does. Besides, change might be a good thing. You never know."

Rocky sighed. "Maybe this is a calling or something that'll get me out of my shyness. I don't know."

"Well, the only thing I can tell you is to give it some serious thought before deciding. Think of some ways this group could benefit you and some ways it might not. Whatever you choose, just know you have my full support."

"That makes a lot of sense. Thanks, Mom."

"No problem." Rochelle stood up and yawned. "Now, if you would excuse me, I need a shower, then I'm probably going to bed early tonight."

"Wow, it's not even 8 yet," Rocky joked. "Today must've been one heck of a day."

"Do not get me started," Rochelle laughed. "Everyone seemed to want to get sick and come to the hospital today. And it didn't help that we were short-staffed, so I was driving myself crazy doing administrative and clinical duties."

"That sounds rough. I'm sorry today was so hard for you."

"It was pretty rough, but I still enjoy what I do. It pays the bills."

Rocky and her mom both laughed.

"The fact that you can have bad days at work and still come home and be a mom is incredible," Rocky admitted. "Thanks for always being there for me through it all. I appreciate it."

"Aww, you're too kind," Rochelle said before kissing Rocky on the head and leaving.

Rocky laid back on the couch and sighed. What would be the best decision for her? Should she join Aiden's group, have real-world experience with music, and finally become popular? Or should she not join Aiden's group, continue to sing with Hayley, and only hope they would make it as big as Aiden one day?

Rocky realized she still hadn't finished her homework, so she sprang up and grabbed her worksheets. She briefly contemplated waiting until the next morning to finish it but decided it would be best to get it out of the way now.

***

It had been three days since Aiden asked Rocky to join his group. She'd purposely avoided him for those three days because she worried he would become impatient. Rocky wrote down the pros and cons of singing with Aiden, but she always focused too much on the cons, which triggered her anxiety. Overall, Rocky still felt conflicted and just wanted to make the right choice.

That morning before the first-period bell rang, Rocky, Hayley, and Adam sat together in the courtyard talking about it.

"Have you decided if you wanted to sing with Aiden and the guys yet?" Hayley asked her.

"I'm still not sure," Rocky replied. "I really don't want to feel like I'm making a mistake."

"Don't sing with them then," Adam told her.

"Adam, would you leave her alone!" Hayley snapped. "It's her choice to make, not yours."

"She says she doesn't want to make a mistake. Joining forces with that arrogant bastard would be a huge mistake."

"Adam, be nice," Rocky told him.

"What is it about Aiden you hate so much?" Hayley asked.

"What is it about him you guys *love* so much?" he retorted. "Besides the fact that he thinks he's a better singer than everyone else."

"I mean, have you seen the guy? He's smokin' hot," Hayley giggled.

"Oh, my God," Adam groaned as he put his hand to his head and rolled his eyes.

"Seriously, Adam," Rocky said. "Why do you hate him so much?"

Adam sighed and looked down at his feet. "We used to be friends when we were younger."

"Seriously?" the girls asked simultaneously, bewilderment in their voices.

"Yeah," Adam said. "We were great friends throughout elementary school, and we even sang in the children's choir together at church."

"Aww, that's so cute," Hayley teased.

"I can imagine little Adam and Aiden singing at church together," Rocky giggled at the thought of it.

Adam rolled his eyes again but stifled a small laugh. "Anyway, when I was about ten, and he was eleven, the children's choir was preparing to sing 'Mary Did You Know' for a Christmas concert. The choir director was deciding who would sing the lead, and Aiden typically led the choir."

"That figures," Rocky said quietly.

"Yeah, I'm not going to lie. The dude can sing," Adam said. "But even back then, he was so arrogant about it. He automatically assumed he would be leading the choir like he always does, but the director wanted to change things up a little. So, she asked me to do it.

"I was excited about leading the choir for the first time, but Aiden wasn't thrilled about it. He always complained about it during every rehearsal and tried to convince the choir director to let him sing the lead. He even tried to make me tell her I didn't want to do it anymore. I wanted to lead the choir for once, so there was no way I would let him take that opportunity away from me.

"After a while, the choir director got sick of Aiden's nonsense and punished him by not letting him sing at all for the Christmas concert. That ticked him off. He had this huge meltdown and was going on and on about how untalented I was and how he was a better singer than everyone else in the choir. He quit, stopped coming to my church, and hasn't spoken to me since."

"That's wild," Hayley said in shock.

"Yeah, it is," Adam said.

"Well, you said he was eleven when that happened, right?" Rocky asked. "I'm sure he's matured a lot since then."

Adam stared at Rocky in disbelief. "Are you seriously that naïve?" he asked.

"I'm just saying," Rocky said, almost questioningly.

"Well, *I'm* just saying you'd better watch him, Rocky. He's no good."

"Speaking of Aiden," Hayley said while cocking her head to the side.

The three of them turned to see Aiden and his boys walking toward them. Rocky's heart began to race.

"What if he wants an answer right this minute? What do I do?"

"Do what you think is right," Hayley told her.

"I don't know what's right!"

"Follow your heart, Rocky. Whatever decision you make, Adam and I will be there to support you. Right?" Hayley asked as she nudged Adam.

Aiden and his boys had already approached them before Adam could say anything. Rocky thought all four boys were gorgeous, but Aiden's smile melted her heart.

"Hey, I've been looking for you all week," he said in a friendly way. "Are you avoiding me or something?"

Rocky nervously laughed and started fiddling with her fingers. She saw Adam shake his head out of the corner of her eye.

"I wanted to check in about you joining my singing group. Have you thought about it yet? I'm eager to know."

Rocky's heart was beating so hard in her chest that she was afraid everyone could hear it. She suddenly had no idea how to speak and wished she had a water bottle. How could Aiden choose her, the shy and awkward girl with stage fright, over Hayley, the beautiful and confident girl who loves an audience? Once she became aware of the deafening silence, Rocky knew she had to say something. As everyone looked at her, waiting for an answer, she felt warm and lightheaded. Her breathing became more shallow. *Please don't pass out.*

"Rocky?" Hayley asked, concern in her voice. "Are you okay?"

"I'll do it," Rocky blurted. She sat down on the bench behind her before her legs gave out. There was no way she would let Aiden see her in that state. "I'll sing with you, Aiden."

"That's great news!" Aiden exclaimed.

Rocky looked up and noticed Aiden's boys, who'd been standing quietly behind him the entire time, were now smiling. Rocky couldn't also help but notice that something about their smiles seemed off. Were they taking pity on her? Did they see how dangerously close she was to having a panic attack? Rocky looked over at Hayley and Adam. Hayley looked thrilled, but Adam didn't even attempt to hide the disappointment on his face.

"We're happy for you, Rocky!" Hayley said excitedly. "Don't forget about us once you're famous, though."

Rocky nervously laughed and then looked back at Aiden.

"You have no idea how excited I am that you said yes," Aiden said happily. "Rocky, this is going to be such a great experience." Then he chuckled. "I guess now people can't call us 'Aiden and the boys' anymore."

Rocky stifled another laugh.

"Are you free after school today?" Aiden asked.

"Um, yeah, I'm free," Rocky said.

"Why don't you come to my house, then? The guys and I will be there to give you a proper welcome. That's also where we practice every day."

Practice every day? Did that mean no more hanging out after school at The Studio with Hayley and Adam anymore? This was going to take a lot of getting used to. "Okay," Rocky quietly responded.

"Perfect. Let me give you my address." Aiden took a pen and paper from his backpack, kneeled in front of Rocky, and started writing. "My house is about a block away from school on Waverly Drive. Oh, and I put my number on there, too. In case you need to call me for any reason."

As Aiden handed Rocky the paper, his fingers lightly brushed against hers, which sent intense chills down her spine. Aiden looked at Rocky, and she noticed they were at eye level because he was kneeling. He smiled at her again. "So, I'll be seeing you later?"

Rocky couldn't think straight, let alone speak properly. She nodded her head and said, "mm-hmm."

"Great. I'm looking forward to it." Aiden stood up and walked away while his boys followed behind.

Rocky looked down at the paper with Aiden's address and phone number and couldn't stop smiling. *This is unreal,* she thought to herself. *This is completely unreal!* Usually, the popular and good-looking guys would look past Rocky. But Aiden noticed her. He smiled at her a lot. He even wanted her to be part of his singing group. Rocky was over the moon right now!

As soon as Aiden and his boys were gone, Adam sat next to Rocky. "You're really doing this?" he asked. "After everything I told you about him, you're still going to sing with him?"

Hayley sat on the other side of Rocky. "Come on, Adam," she reasoned. "Don't be like that."

"I mean, seriously, Rocky. Did you not hear anything I said about how arrogant he is?"

"He doesn't seem so arrogant now," Rocky told him. "And I had to give him an answer, so I just went for it. Did you see how excited he was when I agreed to join his group?"

"Rocky, you have to trust me. He's a mean person. Please don't do this."

"Adam," Hayley said again.

Adam threw his hands up in frustration. "Fine! Don't listen to me then."

"Come on, Adam. It's not like that," Rocky tried to explain. "I promise if he starts acting up, I'll leave, and you can say, 'I told you so.' Just be nice to him for now, pretty please? For me?"

Adam had his arms folded across his chest and didn't say anything. More than anything, Rocky couldn't stand it when Adam was frustrated with her. All she wanted was for him to understand that she was doing this to help herself.

Adam sighed and looked at Rocky. "I still don't trust him, and I still don't like him," he said. "But for you, I'll tolerate him."

Rocky squealed and gave Adam a tight hug. "Thank you, thank you!" she said happily. "I appreciate you looking out for me, Adam, but I think this will be good for me."

"It will be good for you," Hayley agreed, leaning her head on Rocky's shoulder. "You're finally learning to spread your beautiful wings and fly."

The bell rang, and it was time to start the school day. Rocky, Hayley, and Adam all stood up and went their separate ways. Rocky was pumped to be singing with the hottest and most talented guy in school, but she was also anxious about it. She didn't know what to expect, and unfamiliarity worried her. Rocky had to keep reminding herself that great things would happen to her once she took this leap of faith. No more letting fear stop her from living her dreams.

After her last class, Rocky went straight to the restroom to see how she looked before walking to Aiden's house. Today was mostly humid, and she had P.E. today, so her hair was a bit frizzy, and she thought she smelled a little. *I wonder if I could run home to freshen up before going to Aiden's house.*

Rocky pulled out her phone to call Hayley and ask if her mother could give her a ride home and then to Aiden's house. *What if I show up too late? I don't want to be late on the first day of rehearsal.* She put her phone away.

The longer Rocky stared at herself in the mirror, the more she hated how she looked. She turned the faucet on, wet her hands, and smoothed her hair down as best as she could. She then put on lip balm and sprayed herself with vanilla-scented perfume. This was about as fresh as she could get.

Rocky took a few deep breaths before leaving the bathroom and walking to Aiden's house. It didn't take long to find the street Aiden lived on since it was so close to Lennox. Rocky thought about how she could wake up an hour before the first bell rang and still make it to school on time if she lived this close. Of course, her mom would never let Rocky do that!

Once she found Aiden's house, her heart started racing. She stood at Aiden's front door but couldn't bring herself to ring the doorbell. Rocky had never been to anyone's house except for Hayley's and Adam's. How was she supposed to react? What if his parents were home? How was she supposed to greet them? How was she supposed to introduce herself? The more questions that popped into her head, the more anxious she grew. Rocky turned around to head back home but stopped herself. *I said this was the year I would break out of my shyness,* she thought to herself. *I'm doing this. I can do this.*

Rocky took one final deep breath before turning back to Aiden's front door and ringing the bell. As she stood waiting for someone to open the door, she kept her head held down, and her knees were shaking like it was 40 below.

A few moments passed, and there still wasn't an answer, so Rocky rang the doorbell again. *He's probably not here yet,* she thought. Then her heart started racing again. *Or maybe this is the wrong house!* Rocky pulled the paper with Aiden's address out of her pocket to verify she was at the correct place. A second later, Aiden opened the door, welcoming Rocky with that gorgeous smile of his.

"Hey, you're here!" he greeted. "Come inside."

Rocky smiled back at him, and as soon as she got inside his house, she noticed how meticulously organized everything looked. All the pillows, bookshelves, and everything on the coffee table looked like they were precisely placed. The neutral colors made his home look welcoming, and Rocky enjoyed the touch of green from the couch pillows. She felt like she was in a house on an interior design show.

"You have a lovely home," Rocky said in awe.

"Thank you," Aiden replied. "My mom is an interior designer, and she always wants to make sure the house looks 'picture ready.'"

Rocky giggled. "Well, she did a great job. Your house looks like something you'd see in a magazine."

"You're too sweet, Rocky. I know my mom would appreciate you saying that." Aiden lightly placed his hand on Rocky's shoulder. "Let's head out to the garage. The guys are already there."

Rocky allowed Aiden to take the lead, and she followed him into his garage. She was secretly relieved Aiden couldn't see her smiling like an idiot after he touched her. Rocky was amazed at how Aiden's garage looked like a much more advanced version of The Studio. However, there weren't nearly as many instruments. There was only a keyboard, a guitar, and a snare drum, but it also had all the equipment a real recording studio would have. Rocky felt as though she were in a dream.

"Welcome to my garage-turned-music studio," Aiden said. "Every day after school, the guys and I practice our songs here."

Aiden's boys seemed to be in their own little worlds, Rocky thought. One of them was playing some chords on the keyboard. Another one was texting and humming along, and the guy who had Rocky's chorus class was playing some cool beats on a snare drum pad. They all stopped as soon as Aiden and Rocky came in.

"Let me introduce you to them," Aiden said. He motioned over to the one who was texting and humming. "That's Angel, and he's our tenor."

"Hi," Angel said politely. Rocky smiled and waved at Angel.

Then Aiden motioned to the guy on the keyboard. "That's Renaldo, baritone."

"Nice to meet you," he said. He had a thick Spanish accent.

Finally, Aiden motioned to the guy on the snare drum pad. "And that's Marcus. He sings bass."

"He has my chorus class," she said quietly.

"Ah, he never mentioned that," Aiden said. "That's cool."

Not knowing what else to say, Rocky smiled.

"So, we meet at my house every day after school and chill for a bit in the living room before we start practicing. Practice usually takes no more than an hour, but it depends on whether we're having a good day. For the most part, it's pretty chill."

"That's cool," Rocky nodded. She still couldn't get over how professional Aiden's studio looked. "This is seriously a cool place you got here."

Aiden chuckled. "Thank you. My dad set it up for me. We record my originals in here, too."

"Originals? You write songs?"

"I do. We mostly sing my songs at real concerts and do covers at school."

"That's so amazing," Rocky said in awe. She glanced over at the boys again. None of them said anything, and their silence almost intimidated Rocky. "The guys don't really say much," she said softly.

Aiden shrugged. "I don't know why they're so quiet today. Guys, don't be rude to Rocky. Let's make our newest member feel welcome."

Marcus put his drum pad and sticks down and stood up. "Welcome to the group, Rocky," he said politely. "I hope you enjoy singing with us, and this should be a lot of fun. I guess. Okay, then." Marcus awkwardly sat back down, which made Rocky giggle. Renaldo and Angel were also holding back their laughs.

"Okay, we'll work on that," Aiden said. He turned to face Rocky again. "So, we have a performance coming up in two weeks. We're going to be singing the national anthem at the Dolphins game."

"Oh, wow, really?" Rocky asked in shock.

"I know, it's amazing. I can't even imagine what my parents did to score us such a great opportunity. Have you been to the stadium before?"

"I haven't."

"It's incredible. You're going to love it there. As the performers, we get hooked up with free tickets and great seats."

Rocky was never a huge sports fan. She never watched football because it was always difficult for her to understand what was happening during the game. However, Rocky was more than happy to have the opportunity to go to a Dolphins game. And for free? Even better!

"My parents will drive all of us there in our SUV. The stadium is about an hour away, the game starts at 1, and they want us to be there by 10. So, we'll have to meet at my place no later than 8 a.m. Is that okay?"

"I'll probably be a zombie, but I'll definitely be there," Rocky joked.

Aiden laughed, which made Rocky feel great about herself. "Don't worry. We'll all be zombies, but I'll make sure we have plenty of coffee."

"Bless!" Marcus called out.

"What day is the game on?" Rocky asked.

"Sunday the 19th. Mark that day on your calendar."

Rocky nodded. There was so much to process. Rocky just joined Aiden's group and had her first real performance in two weeks.

"Oh, before I forget," Aiden said. "I made cookies as a little welcome gift for you."

Rocky smiled and kept her head down. How sweet of Aiden to make her cookies!

"We never got any cookies on our first day," Angel said. Marcus and Renaldo laughed.

"Rocky is special," Aiden replied. He looked at Rocky and smiled again. "I'll get them from the kitchen, and then we'll get started."

Rocky still had her head down, and she couldn't stop smiling. Aiden said she was special! It was so thoughtful of him to go out of his way to make her feel welcome. Aiden seemed like the total opposite of what Adam said he was. He was charming, respectful, and polite. His positive qualities made Rocky like Aiden even more.

When Aiden returned with the cookies, the five of them ate and then began practicing.

"So, how will this whole thing go?" Rocky asked. "You know, four guys and one girl? Do you think we'll sound weird?"

"I don't think so," Aiden answered. "We'll make it work. I've always wondered what female vocals could do with the group. And you have such a fantastic voice, so I'm sure it'll be great."

Rocky smiled again.

"Alright, let's do this!" Aiden said enthusiastically. "Renaldo?"

Renaldo pressed a key on the keyboard, and Aiden hummed it. "One, two, three, one, two..."

Aiden started the song, and then she and the boys joined right after. Rocky was amazed at how well their voices blended. She thought they sounded fantastic!

"Not bad, not bad," Aiden said once they ran through the song once.

"I like the five-part harmony," Renaldo said. "I think it makes us sound fuller and better than before."

"I think you're right," Aiden agreed. "I knew what I was doing when I brought Rocky on."

Rocky looked down again, smiled, and crossed her arms across her torso. Aiden was the sweetest! His compliment made her feel better about herself.

"Let's run through it again, guys," Aiden continued. "Rocky, I need you to be a little bit louder this time. We don't want to drown out your beautiful voice."

The five of them continued rehearsing for about twenty more minutes before Aiden decided to call it a day.

"I'd say we had a great day of rehearsal," Aiden said happily. "We sound bomb, and we're going to kill it at the game on the 19th. See you next time."

Angel, Marcus, and Renaldo all said goodbye to Rocky before leaving. Before Rocky could go, Aiden stopped her.

"Hey, Rocky," he said. "I wanted to tell you how proud I am of you. I know you're shy, but you're doing a great job stepping out of your comfort zone and singing with us. You sounded incredible today."

"Aww, thank you, Aiden," Rocky said shyly.

"Why do you always look down when I talk to you?"

Rocky picked her head up to look at Aiden but put it back down. Keeping eye contact has never been easy for Rocky because she didn't want to seem like a strange person staring at someone. With Aiden, it was even harder because he was too gorgeous, and he made her feel even more anxious. She definitely didn't want him to think she was a freak or something for staring into his eyes.

"I'm sorry," Rocky said. "I guess it's just my shyness. I'm sorry." She felt like a complete idiot.

Aiden chuckled and gently lifted Rocky's head up to look at him. Her heart started pounding as she stared into his eyes, his fingers under her chin.

"Hey, you don't have to be shy around me," he told her.

Rocky smiled, and Aiden smiled back at her. She wasn't used to guys like Aiden treating her like this. It felt different, but she loved feeling this way. Getting compliments from cute boys helped her with her self-esteem.

"I don't want to keep you too long," Aiden said. "Let's get you home. I'll walk you to the front door."

Now Rocky didn't want to go home! She desperately wanted time to stop and had a sudden desire to stay and get to know Aiden better. Sadly, Rocky knew she had to leave before it got too late. Besides, her mother would flip if she stayed at a boy's house until dark!

Rocky followed Aiden to the front door, and he held it open for her as she walked outside. *He's such a gentleman,* Rocky thought to herself.

"Thank you, Aiden," Rocky said. "I guess I'll see you Monday, then."

He smiled at her again. "Get home safely."

Rocky turned around and began walking home with a big grin on her face. She was so excited about seeing Aiden again.

Rocky couldn't wait to tell her mom about her first rehearsal at Aiden's house and her upcoming performance. She was so eager that when Rochelle came home, she ran to her and tried to jump on her. They both almost fell to the floor.

"Rocky, what is it?!" Rochelle asked impatiently. "You almost knocked me over."

"Sorry, Mom," Rocky chirped. "I'm just so happy, and I couldn't wait to tell you the good news."

Rochelle went to put her bags on the table and sit on the couch. "What's up?"

"I decided to join Aiden's singing group," she told her mom. "I went to my first rehearsal with the group at his house today."

"Wait, you were at his house?" Rochelle asked seriously.

"Well, yeah," Rocky said, slightly embarrassed she forgot to mention it to her mom before. "But it wasn't anything like that. It was only to practice our singing."

"And you didn't think to tell me about this, Rocky? I'm not comfortable with you being at a boy's house you just met. I haven't even seen this guy yet. Were his parents home, at least?"

"I'm so sorry, Mom," Rocky said. "I guess I was so excited about it that I completely spaced on telling you about it."

"That's no excuse."

"I know. At least you know now."

Rochelle gave Rocky her stern "mom stare" with narrowed eyes and a slight frown. She knew she messed up whenever her mom gave her that look!

"We're singing the national anthem at a Dolphins game on the 19th," Rocky said, trying to lighten the subject.

"Oh, really?"

"Yeah. His parents are going to drive us there."

Rochelle stood up and looked at Rocky as if she were insane. "I'm sorry, what?" she asked.

Rocky sighed. She understood Rochelle was only being a mom. Still, she thought she would be more excited about her daughter finally breaking out of her shell and performing.

"Are you out of your mind?" Rochelle asked. "I'm not letting my fourteen-year-old daughter get in a car with some boy and his parents without me meeting them first."

"You can meet them Monday," Rocky said. "I promise Aiden is a nice guy. You know I wouldn't be doing this with someone you would disapprove of."

Once again, Rochelle gave Rocky that "mom stare." *Note to self*, Rocky thought to herself. *Never forget to tell Mom about these things.*

"Did I mention we're going to sing at a Dolphins game?" Rocky awkwardly brought up again. "Front row seats. Free tickets."

Rochelle sighed and shook her head. "Monday, okay?"

"Okay," Rocky said.

"They'd better be good people."

"I haven't actually met his parents yet," Rocky admitted. "But I'm sure they're good people."

"Rocky!" Rochelle cried in outrage. "You were going to get in a car and drive to Miami with some people you haven't even met?"

"*Yet*," Rocky said. "I said I haven't met them *yet*."

"Monday," Rochelle repeated before leaving to go into the kitchen.

Rocky couldn't wait for her mom to meet Aiden. She knew her mom would love him. How could she not? He was polite, talented, and good-looking. Aiden was the guy every mother dreamed their daughter would end up with! For the first time, Rocky felt confident about her decisions.

6

Rocky arrived at school on Monday morning in a great mood when she met up with Hayley and Adam in the courtyard. She was smiling from ear to ear and was itching to tell them about her great experience with Aiden. Noticing Rocky's excitement, Hayley and Adam both grinned when Rocky approached them.

"Hey, how did it go with Aiden's singing group?" Hayley asked her.

"Aiden is the absolute sweetest guy I've ever met," Rocky blurted in delight. "And did you know he has a recording studio in his garage? Like, an *actual* recording studio with all the equipment and everything. He uses it to record songs he writes himself. Can you believe he's a songwriter, too? The boys are also sweet. One of them plays the piano, just like us. And there's a Dolphins game in two weeks, and we're going to be singing the Star-Spangled Banner, and I'm so nervous but so excited at the same time. Aiden is such an amazing singer, and he's so cute and so nice, and I'm so happy!"

Rocky's giddy feeling was building up inside her, and she couldn't help but explode in happiness. There was no doubt in her mind that joining forces with Aiden would help her after all.

Hayley laughed and gave Rocky a tight hug. "I'm glad you're happy," she said. "And yay for you having your first real performance. This is huge."

"I know, and I'm so scared," Rocky admitted. "That stadium is gigantic. There's going to be so many people."

"I believe in you, Rocky."

"Well, I'll be singing backup with the guys, so I guess it won't be too bad."

"Wait. Aiden has you singing backup?" Adam asked.

"Yeah," Rocky said.

"Unbelievable," he sighed.

"Come on, Adam. Don't start," Hayley pleaded.

"Do you honestly think a voice like Rocky's should be singing backup?"

"Of course not, but..."

"But nothing, Hayley," Adam snapped. "Rocky's incredible talent doesn't deserve to be overshadowed by that clown." He turned to face Rocky. "I think you need to leave Aiden's group and go back to singing with Hayley."

Rocky lightly placed her hand on Adam's shoulder to calm him down. "It's okay, Adam," she said. "I just joined his group. I don't think he would let me have a solo right away."

"You know his boys have been singing with him for almost a year," Adam said. "Have you seen any of them with a solo? He doesn't care about anybody but himself, Rocky. Please understand I'm not hating or anything. I'm only trying to protect you."

"I appreciate it, but I think I know what I'm doing."

Rocky genuinely appreciated that Adam was trying to look out for her. Still, she felt like she was making the right decision. Aiden was always polite to her, and it seemed he'd matured a lot since his fit about the church choir lead. Rocky firmly believed that anybody could change if they wanted to, and she knew Aiden had changed.

"Like I said before, if he starts getting out of hand, then I'll leave him," Rocky assured Adam. "I'll be okay. I promise."

Adam still seemed uncertain about the whole thing. How is it that Adam wasn't seeing the same Aiden that Rocky was seeing? Not wanting to continue this subject, she decided to lighten the mood.

"Would you guys be able to come to the football game?" she asked them.

"If my parents are willing to buy the ticket and drive me to the stadium, then absolutely," Hayley said. "If not, then we'll be sure to watch it on TV. We wouldn't miss your first real performance for anything."

"I'm going to be so scared," Rocky admitted. "What if I mess up? Like, what if I get so nervous that I forget the words? Or what if I start singing off-key and ruin the harmonization?"

"Don't worry about it," Hayley assured her. "You'll be wonderful like you always are."

The sound of the school bell interrupted their conversation, and the three of them went their separate ways to their classes.

Rocky's mom wouldn't allow her to return to Aiden's house until she met him and his parents, much to Rocky's annoyance. She told Aiden about her situation. Luckily, he understood and worked out a deal with one of his music teachers to practice in his classroom for the day. Rocky's mom and Aiden's parents would come to pick them up from school once Rocky's mom got off work.

When Rocky got to the classroom for practice, the boys were inside chatting. Aiden wasn't there, so she stayed at the door.

"Hey, you're here," Marcus said.

Rocky shyly smiled. "Hi," she said. "Where's Aiden?"

"He had to step out to take an important call," Angel said. "He said it shouldn't be too long, though."

"Come and sit while we wait for him," Marcus said.

Rocky made her way into the room and sat closer to the back, leaving two desks between her and the guys.

"Why are you so far from us?" Renaldo asked. "We're like family here."

"Girl, scooch on closer," Marcus joked. "We don't bite."

Rocky giggled and moved to the desk closest to Marcus. Something about his carefree energy made her feel less anxious. "Are you guys nervous about singing at the Dolphins game?" she asked to start a conversation.

"Not really," Angel shrugged. "It's no big deal."

"So, you don't get stage fright at all?"

"Nope."

Rocky looked down and embarrassingly said, "I wish I were more like you guys."

"You'll get over your stage fright," Renaldo said. "I was shy like you once. Since joining this group, I've gotten over it a lot."

"And as a backup singer, nobody pays much attention to you anyway," Marcus said. "You can be in the background chilling while all eyes are on the lead singer. That makes it much easier to get over your stage fright."

"And Aiden's, uh, perseverance will help your stage fright in no time," Renaldo said.

"It seems like he wants to help us get over performance anxiety," Rocky said.

"Yeah, something like that," Angel said. "You can't afford to have stage fright when it comes to singing with Aiden."

"How is it like singing with Aiden?" Rocky asked out of curiosity. "It must be really fun, huh?"

Renaldo, Angel, and Marcus all exchanged looks. There was a long pause before one of them answered, which made Rocky uneasy.

"Like any job, there are some good moments and some not-so-good moments," Marcus admitted.

"But it definitely has its advantages," Angel said. "Like having the privilege to sing the national anthem at a Dolphins game."

"I have another question," Rocky asked, already knowing the answer. "Do you guys ever get solos?"

They all laughed.

"You know people call this group 'Aiden and the boys,' right?" Renaldo asked. "That's pretty much all we are. Just 'the boys.' Aiden gets all the attention, and we're here to make him sound better."

"Oh," Rocky said. "Have you ever asked to have a solo part?"

"Actually, no," Angel admitted. "I guess it's because we're his backup singers. Like Renaldo and Marcus said earlier, we don't get as much recognition as the lead singer."

"But that doesn't mean we aren't as important," Marcus said. "I mean, we're creating such a wonderful harmonic foundation to complement Aiden's voice. That takes some real talent."

"Marcus, what are you going on about?" Angel laughed.

"I noticed the disappointment on Rocky's face, and I wanted to make sure she knew her worth," Marcus defended himself. "Excuse me for being a decent human being, Angel."

Rocky giggled again, now not knowing what else to say. When she and Hayley sang together, they usually alternated who sang lead. Sometimes Rocky would lead while Hayley sang the low harmony; other times, Hayley would lead while Rocky sang the high harmony. Rocky didn't understand how it would work for a five-person group and figured it might not be as easy to have interchangeable leading roles.

When Aiden walked into the classroom, the guys instantly sat up straighter.

"Okay, guys. Let's do this," he said enthusiastically. "I know it's a little different since we're used to rehearsing in my garage. But once I win Rocky's mom over, we'll be back to rehearsing in there."

Rocky looked down embarrassingly. "I'm sorry again for the inconvenience, guys," she said quietly. "My mom can be a little overbearing at times."

"You don't have to keep apologizing," Aiden said with a slight laugh. "She's only being a mom."

"Shoot, if I had a teenage daughter hanging out with a bunch of guys..." Marcus started, but Aiden's glare shut him up quickly. "So, are we practicing or what?" he blurted out.

They all began rehearsing and continued for about twenty minutes. Rocky didn't know what it was, but they were all in great harmony with one another — even she couldn't believe how perfect they sounded. After a few successful takes, they all began talking.

"Great work today, guys," Aiden said happily. We sounded so perfect. We could sing tomorrow!"

"Are we?" Rocky asked, mildly panicking.

Aiden laughed. "No, we're still singing on Sunday. I was saying we're so good that we could perform tomorrow if we wanted."

Rocky felt foolish for asking such a silly question. She giggled nervously, hoping Aiden didn't think she was a complete idiot.

Angel stood up. "If practice is over now, I'm going to head home," he said. "I have a big project due soon, and I haven't had much time to do it."

"You can go if you need to," Aiden said. "I think we've had enough practice today."

Soon the guys left, and Rocky was alone with Aiden. Her mom and Aiden's parents wouldn't arrive for at least another 30 to 40 minutes. Rocky noticed Aiden looking at her, which made her heart race and her neck hot.

"You seem nervous," Aiden laughed.

Rocky didn't know how to respond, so she laughed too. What was she supposed to say? She was freaking out on the inside! Rocky had never been alone in a room with a perfectly handsome guy.

Aiden decided to break the ice. "So, I can't wait to meet your mom," he said. "When will she be here again?

"She's coming straight after work. She gets off at 5: 00 today and works about 15 minutes from here."

"Okay, so we have some time before she comes." Aiden sat down and smiled at her. "Why don't you tell me a little about yourself while we wait?"

Rocky returned the smile but stood awkwardly on the other side of the room. "What do you want to know?" she asked.

"The simple stuff like your hobbies, likes, dislikes."

"Um, well, you know I love music and singing." Rocky tried to think of other simple things about herself to tell Aiden but couldn't come up with anything. Why was it so hard for a person to talk about themselves? "I'd rather learn more about you," Rocky finally said. "Nothing about me is exciting anyway," she joked.

Aiden laughed. "Oh, I bet that's not true. How about we play 21 questions?"

Rocky admired how Aiden made an effort to get to know her better. She thought it was sweet of him, and it made her like him even more.

"Okay," Rocky said shyly.

"Come sit down, and we'll play," Aiden said.

Rocky was way too nervous to sit next to Aiden, but she didn't want to sit at the desk farthest from him and distance herself. She made her way across the room and sat at the desk behind Aiden. Rocky's face began to feel warm, and her heart rate increased rapidly.

"I guess I'll start," Aiden said.

Rocky could not get over how thoughtful Aiden was. And he was hot! She couldn't fathom how someone like him could be interested in plain old Rocky.

"What do you usually do in your spare time?" he asked.

"I normally hang out with my best friends," Rocky answered. "My friend Hayley has a room full of instruments, and we all get together to make music there."

"That's cool. You seem passionate about music."

"I live and breathe music. I don't know how I'd survive without it."

Aiden chuckled. "I know exactly how you feel. I have a musical family, and we all are passionate about what we do. Your turn to ask me a question."

Rocky tried to think of a good question to ask him. She didn't want to ask him something too simple that didn't spark a conversation, but she was afraid of asking something too complex or personal. She decided to keep things going with music since it was something they had in common.

"Um, do you have a favorite artist?" she asked.

"Oh, it's too hard to pick only one," he laughed. "But if I could pick one, it would probably be Whitney Houston."

Rocky's face brightened up. "I love Whitney Houston! She's, like, my idol."

"My mom used to listen to her songs all the time when I was growing up, and her music sort of grew on me. What's your favorite Whitney Houston song?"

"It's so hard to pick just one," she laughed. "I'd probably say 'I'm Your Baby Tonight' is my favorite."

"Ooh, what a fun song."

"It's one of my favorite songs to jam out to when I'm getting ready in the mornings."

"I can't imagine you jamming because of how timid you are," Aiden laughed. "You'll have to let me see it one day."

Rocky shyly giggled. "What's your favorite Whitney song?" she asked him.

Aiden thought about it for a moment. "'I Wanna Dance with Somebody.' Now that's the song I would definitely jam out to."

"Oh, that's such a great song, too."

"What's your favorite love song?" Aiden asked. "It doesn't have to specifically be a Whitney song."

Aiden's question caught Rocky off guard. Her heart started racing.

"Um, I really like 'Bleeding Love.' Hayley and I enjoy singing that song together a lot."

"That's sweet. I'm sure you sing it beautifully."

Rocky looked down in her lap so Aiden wouldn't see her blushing.

"Mine is 'Suddenly' by Billy Ocean," Aiden said. "I first heard it at a family member's wedding a few years ago, and I've loved it ever since."

"Aww," Rocky giggled. "That's a beautiful song."

"I've always pictured myself singing it to the one special girl in my life, wherever she is right now."

Rocky smiled. She would die if anyone, especially Aiden, were to sing a love song to her. It would be so romantic, like in the movies. Rocky thought caring and good-looking guys didn't exist in real life, but one was sitting right in front of her.

"That's sweet," Rocky told him. "She would be one lucky girl."

"I feel like I'd be the lucky one once I find her."

Rocky's face felt hot again, and she couldn't stop fidgeting her fingers. She decided to ask another question to ease her anxiety. "What made you decide to come to Lennox?"

"Because it's the best performing arts school in the city!" Aiden laughed. "A lot of Lennox alumni end up having successful music careers, so I knew I had to go to school here."

"My mom went to Lennox and sang professionally before meeting my dad and having me," Rocky said.

"That's so awesome. Lennox is known for making people successful in the entertainment industry. All I want is to be big in music, and I won't let anything stand in my way of accomplishing that dream."

Rocky thought of the rumors she had heard about Aiden and wondered if she should ask him about them. It would ease her mind by getting some clarity on exactly what happened and why the rumors spread.

"Aiden, can I ask you something else?"

"Ask away," Aiden said.

"Do you know of these rumors about you and this other student who tried to show you up? I heard you pulled some strings to get him expelled and hired people to hurt him so that he couldn't sing again."

Aiden laughed. "People love to share these stupid stories," he said. "He got expelled because he was constantly harassing me."

"For real?" Rocky asked, surprised.

"Yeah, people thought I was jealous of him, but it was the other way around. He felt threatened by me, so he wouldn't leave me alone. He was bullying me online and threatened to come to my house and hurt my family and me. That was when I decided to take it to the principal, and he got expelled because of it."

"I'm sorry that happened to you," Rocky said sadly. "I can't believe people are spreading wrong information."

"I know about the rumors, but I don't let them bother me. I know what really happened, so I'll let other people believe what they want."

"What about his throat injury?"

"I would never hurt anyone," Aiden said. "His injury was probably bad karma or something, but I had nothing to do with it." Aiden looked at Rocky, a bit disappointed. "Do you think I hurt that guy?"

"No," Rocky blurted. "You don't seem like the type of guy to do that. I was just curious to know what happened. I'm sorry if I made it seem like I thought you were a bad guy."

Aiden laughed again. "It's okay, Rocky," he said.

It felt great to get some clarity and not have to worry about Aiden getting her expelled. It was all some misunderstanding, and the student got what he deserved for bullying Aiden – minus the throat injury.

Rocky and Aiden didn't get a chance to ask 21 questions because after they gave their answers to one question, an entire conversation started, and they almost forgot about the game. Surprisingly, Rocky grew less timid around Aiden as she got to know him better and invested more in their conversations. Rocky loved him even more now that she had learned how much they had in common.

Rocky received a text from her mother saying she was outside the school, and her heart started beating faster. She didn't know what it was that made her so nervous about her mom meeting Aiden and his family. Maybe Rochelle wouldn't like them and forbid her from singing with Aiden again. But what reason would she not like them? They seemed like decent people.

Rocky cleared her throat to ease her nerves. "My mom is waiting outside," she told Aiden. "Are your parents on their way here?"

Aiden pulled his phone from his pocket to check it. "I haven't heard anything from them," he said. "I can call them and let them know your mom is here."

"Do you want to come outside and say hi to her while we wait for your parents?" Rocky asked timidly.

"Of course," Aiden answered with a smile. "I'll have to let Mr. Walker know we're about to leave first, so he can lock up the classroom. I'll meet you out there in a bit?"

"Sure," Rocky said.

Rocky went to meet her mom, who was outside the student drop-off and pick-up area. She was sitting in her car with the passenger side window down.

"Hey, Mom," Rocky called out when she got to the car.

"Hey, Rocky," Rochelle said. "Where's the guy I'm supposed to be meeting?"

"He had to let his teacher know we were done using his classroom. Aiden was also going to call his parents to see where they were. He should be out in a few minutes to say hello."

"Okay. Hopefully, his parents don't take too long to get here. The couch at home is calling my name."

Rocky and her mother both laughed.

"Well, get in while we wait for them," Rochelle said.

Rocky opened the passenger door and sat inside. "Another rough day at work?" she asked her mom.

"Don't even get me started," Rochelle said. "I don't want my work stress to ruin my mood when I meet these people."

"Oh, look! Here comes Aiden." Rocky got out of the car to wave at Aiden. He walked over to the car when he noticed her.

"Hello," he greeted Rochelle. "It's so nice to meet you, Mrs. Coleman. My name is Aiden."

Rochelle reached over to shake Aiden's hand. "It's nice to meet you too, Aiden," she said. "Rocky's told me quite a bit about you."

"Mom!" Rocky whispered, embarrassed.

Aiden chuckled. "Hopefully, it was all good things," he joked.

"She's just excited about joining your singing group," Rochelle said.

"Any word from your parents yet?" Rocky asked.

"So, funny story," Aiden said. "The family car is in the shop being serviced for when we drive to the game this weekend, and our other car has a dead battery. They're stuck at the house until my older sister gets home later tonight."

"Oh dear, that's unfortunate," Rochelle said.

"They did say you and Rocky are welcome to come to our house, and we can all get to know each other there," Aiden said. "Or we can try again tomorrow. It's up to you."

"They live right down the street from the school, Mom," Rocky said. "Let's go to his house to meet his parents. It'll be a lot easier than waiting until tomorrow."

Rochelle sighed. "If it'll be easier, then sure," she said. "You can get in the back and direct me to your house, young man."

"Absolutely," Aiden said as he got in the back seat of Rochelle's car. "I appreciate the ride home."

Rocky returned to the passenger seat, and her mom was on her way to Aiden's house. Rocky couldn't stop her leg from shaking as her anxious thoughts began taking over. *Everything will be fine,* she thought to herself. They made it to Aiden's house about a minute later.

"Wow," Rochelle said, surprised. "That took no time at all."

"Yup, living this close to school is amazing," Aiden said. "Let's head inside. My parents are excited to meet you guys."

As they got out of Rochelle's car and followed Aiden to his front door, she whispered to Rocky, "he's gentlemanly."

Rocky kept her head down, praying Aiden wasn't close enough to hear what her mom said.

Aiden held the front door open for Rocky and her mom to enter; his parents were already waiting in the living room. They stood up the moment the three of them walked in.

"Hi, it's so nice to meet you ladies," Aiden's mom said, shaking Rochelle's hand and then Rocky's. "I'm Aiden's mom, Kaycee, and this is my husband and Aiden's father, Edward."

"Rochelle," Rocky's mom introduced herself. "And I must say you have such a beautiful home. I love how much detail you've put into the design."

"Thank you, Rochelle," Aiden's mom said. "I'm an interior designer, so I have to make sure my home looks its best."

"You sure are great at what you do."

"Oh, you're too sweet!" Kaycee laughed. "Can I offer you ladies anything to eat or drink?"

"No, thank you, I'm fine," Rochelle answered.

"No, thank you," Rocky said timidly.

"Aiden has been telling me so much about Rocky and how lovely her singing voice is," Kaycee continued. "He can't stop talking about how much his group has improved since she joined."

Rochelle looked at Rocky and smiled at her. "Well, that's a nice thing for him to say," she said.

"It's the truth," Aiden said. "Rocky is truly gifted."

Rocky stared at her hands in her lap so nobody could see the shyness on her face. She wasn't used to having that much focus on her, and she wished they would start talking about something else — anything else but her.

"I hear your son is quite talented as well," Rochelle said. "Rocky talks about him a lot."

Rocky sank lower into her seat. *Why would she say that?! She's going to make it seem like I'm obsessed with him!*

"Oh, Aiden makes us proud every day," Kaycee said as she looked at him admiringly. "He's been singing ever since he started talking. He loves what he does."

"Sounds like Rocky," Rochelle said. "Even when she was a newborn, her cries were so high-pitched and melodic. The doctor told me I had just given birth to a singer."

"Aww, I love that," Kaycee said. "So, I'm sure you're aware of the Dolphins game the kids will be singing at this Sunday."

"Yes, I am aware."

"We're getting our SUV serviced so Edward can drive us down to the stadium. I hear you're a bit concerned about this?"

"Well, it's because Rocky is so quiet, and I only want to make sure she's okay. She's also my only daughter, so I'll admit I can be a bit overprotective."

I think you mean a lot overprotective, Rocky thought.

"I also have a daughter, so I know what it's like to always want to protect her," Kaycee told her.

"She's all I have, and since her father passed..." Rochelle's voice trailed off. Rocky held her mom's hand. "I want her to be okay."

"I'm so sorry to hear about your husband's passing," Edward said.

"I understand how much you want to protect her," Kaycee repeated. "I can assure you your lovely daughter will be in great hands with us."

"I am a safe driver, and I drive on the highway all the time," Edward mentioned. "You won't need to worry about anything happening."

"Oh, I wasn't doubting your driving competence," Rochelle said. "All I wanted was to meet and get to know you guys. I wasn't going to let my young daughter get in a car and drive to Miami with some people I haven't met."

"I understand, and I admire how much you care for your daughter," Kaycee said.

"You're more than welcome to join us if it eases your mind," Edward suggested.

"Unfortunately, I'm not even fully certain I'll be able to make it."

Rocky looked at her mom. "I thought you were taking that day off," she said.

"I put in my request to take off, but it seems as though a lot of other medical assistants are requesting that day off, too. I'm asking around to see if anyone would be willing to cover my shift if my request gets denied."

Rocky's heart sank. She was going to have her first real live performance, and her mom possibly wouldn't be there to watch. Knowing that made her feel even more anxious.

"I really wanted you to be there," Rocky said sadly.

"I'm doing everything in my power to make sure I'll be there," Rochelle reassured her. "The hospital sometimes makes it so hard to request days off, but I'm trying my hardest."

"I'm sure they'd understand if you explained your situation," Edward offered.

"You can't miss your daughter's first performance," Kaycee added.

"I wouldn't want to miss it for anything," Rochelle said. "Anyway, I also wanted to ask about Aiden's rehearsals here."

"Oh, yes," Edward said. "We turned our garage into a recording studio, so the boys like to practice there."

"That's lovely," Rochelle said. "But, I'd like to know if either you or your wife would be home while Rocky and the boys are rehearsing."

"I'm generally home when they're rehearsing," Kaycee said. "I'm usually in my office finishing up what other work I have left to do. There are also times when I'll be out for most of the day."

"I would feel a little better knowing that one of you would be home with the kids," Rochelle admitted.

"If my parents aren't home during our rehearsals, I can ask my teacher if we can use his classroom again to practice," Aiden said. "But most of the time, my mom will at least be here."

"I was also wondering if I could have someone I know come to rehearsals with Rocky."

"Mom, I don't think that's necessary," Rocky whispered.

"Whatever you need to do to ease your mind, we're okay with it," Kaycee said. "As a mom, I understand wanting to know your kid is always safe."

"I appreciate your understanding," Rochelle said.

Aiden and Rocky sat quietly as their parents continued to talk. They agreed that one of Aiden's parents had to be home during rehearsals, and if neither could be home, they had to rehearse at school. Rocky was glad they could reach an agreement quickly and were getting along well. At the same time, Rocky was a little annoyed that her mom made her feel like she always had to be supervised like a child. After a while, it was time for Rocky and Rochelle to go home.

"It was nice meeting you guys," Rochelle said, shaking Aiden's parents' hands.

"It was nice meeting you, too, Rochelle," Kaycee said. "We'll keep in touch?"

"Sure, I'd like that," Rochelle said.

"Hopefully, we'll see you at the game on Sunday," Edward said.

"I'll do everything I can to make it. I can't miss my baby's first performance."

Rocky rolled her eyes. She hated it when her mom called her "baby" in front of other people. She was even more embarrassed that she was doing it in front of Aiden!

"I'll walk you ladies out," Aiden offered.

"Thanks, Aiden," Rocky said shyly.

"No problem," he said. He shook Rocky's mom's hand after walking them both outside. "It was wonderful getting to know you, Mrs. Coleman. My parents and I enjoyed having you over."

"Oh, you're too kind," Rochelle said. "It was nice getting to know you and your parents as well."

"And thanks again for the ride home from school," he said. "Get home safely."

"Thank you, Aiden. And good luck with the performance on Sunday."

"Thanks, but with your daughter singing with us, I know we'll crush it on Sunday."

Rocky held her head down while Rochelle chuckled. Aiden went back inside his house after Rochelle pulled out of the driveway. Rocky stared out the window and didn't say anything during the ride home.

7

As Rocky and her mom made it inside the house, Rochelle started trying to spark a conversation.

"Why so quiet?" she asked.

"No reason," Rocky said shyly. Rochelle knew Rocky had a crush on Aiden and was being nosey.

"That boy's parents seem cool," she said.

"Yeah," Rocky fake yawned. "I'm beat. I'm going to go to my room. Goodnight, Mom."

"Hold on," Rochelle called out before Rocky could make it to the stairs. "We're not done talking, little lady. Come here."

"But Mom," Rocky whined.

"Sit."

Rocky slumped over to the couch and sat next to her mother. She was in no mood to talk about her crush on Aiden with her mom.

"I understand you joined this singing group because you wanted to get over your shyness," Rochelle started. "But I'm not too comfortable with you being the only girl in this group."

Rocky sighed, afraid her mom would force her to leave the group. Wasn't she supposed to be supportive of Rocky breaking out of her shell? This was the first step she was taking to do that, and her mom was already being difficult.

"Mom, it's nothing bad," Rocky tried to explain. "The guys are all nice. Please don't make me leave the group. This is my one chance to break out of my shell."

"I'm not making you leave the group."

"You're not?" Rocky asked. "But you just said you weren't comfortable with me being the only girl."

"I know how important this is for you, and this guy and his parents seem like they love music as much as you do. Is there any way Hayley could be in this group with you, too?"

Rocky would love the idea of Hayley being in Aiden's singing group with her. The thought of it brought a smile to her face.

"I would feel much better knowing she was there with you," Rochelle explained. "Or at least some more girls, so you aren't the only one."

"I can talk to Hayley and Aiden about it to see what they think," Rocky said. "I would love for Hayley to sing with us."

"Is there any reason why he didn't ask both of you to join his group? It seems odd to have an all-boy singing group with only one female vocalist."

"I'm not too sure," Rocky admitted. "I think he might like the idea of adding more singers to his group, though. I'll ask him as soon as I can."

"I'd appreciate that, Rocky. Thank you."

"You're welcome. If that's everything, I'm going to head upstairs now." Before Rocky could get up from the couch, her mom placed her hand on Rocky's leg to keep her seated.

"Wait, wait," Rochelle said with a smile. "Tell me a little bit more about this guy. Do you like him?"

"Mom," Rocky moaned. "Come on."

Rochelle laughed. "Okay, fine, I'll let it go for now. But if you want to date him, I approve. He's cute, and he seems like a nice guy."

Rocky smiled to herself. "Yeah, he is a nice guy," she said quietly.

"He's quite the gentleman, too."

"He really is," Rocky gushed. "He's nice to me and wants to get to know me. Every time I'm around him, I get butterflies. He's just perfect."

Rocky didn't mean to say that out loud. She was so infatuated with Aiden and couldn't help but go on about how wonderful he was. She felt embarrassed about telling her mom all her thoughts. Rochelle smiled at her.

"Wow," she laughed. "Someone's crushing hard."

"I'm going to my room now," Rocky said as she ran upstairs.

In the middle of the week, Rocky's mom finally heard back from her job that her request to take off for Sunday had been denied, but they allowed her to take a half-day. That means she would still make it to see Rocky's performance! Unfortunately, Rocky's mom also decided she would rather have someone she knows drive Rocky to the game. She still wasn't too familiar with Aiden's parents and wanted a chance to get to know them better. A family friend was heading in that direction on Sunday, so she agreed to drive Rocky.

"Mom, wouldn't it be easier if I went with Aiden and his parents?" Rocky protested. "I thought you said you liked them."

"My mind is made up, Rocky," Rochelle said. "I still don't know them well enough to let them take you on a road trip while I'm not around. Pauline is taking you to the game."

"But I have to be at his house for a final rehearsal at 8 a.m."

"And she'll pick you up there."

"Mom..."

"Pauline is taking you to the game, and that is that," Rochelle said.

Rocky sighed in frustration as she went upstairs to her room. What would it take for her mother to trust her? Why couldn't she let Aiden's parents take her to the game? Rocky wished her mom wasn't so difficult.

***

Early Sunday morning, Rochelle dropped Rocky at Aiden's house before driving to work. They rehearsed for about twenty minutes before Pauline arrived, and then they all left for Miami. Rocky didn't know Pauline too well, but she and Rocky's mom were close friends in high school. They lost touch after Rochelle started singing professionally and reunited shortly after Rocky was born. Now and then, they reached out to each other.

The hour-long drive to the football stadium was awkward as Pauline tried to initiate a conversation with Rocky a few times, and Rocky didn't speak much. There was too much on her mind: it was early, Rocky didn't know how to hold a conversation, and she couldn't take her mind off the fact that she was only a few hours away from her first major performance.

When they arrived at the stadium, the crew was setting up the microphones and speakers for their performance. Rocky's legs started shaking as she saw how *huge* the stadium was. In less than three hours, it would be filled with thousands of people staring at her as she sang. Rocky began taking deep breaths to calm herself down before she had an anxiety attack.

Once everything was set up, the crew led Rocky, Aiden, and the rest of the guys to the bottom bleacher. Aiden's parents sat behind them. They waited while the stadium started filling up a little at a time. The more people that arrived, the worse Rocky's anxiety grew. Terrified couldn't even begin to describe how she felt about going on that field and singing in front of over 70,000 people. The game was also internationally broadcasted, so basically, everyone in the world would be watching her — which meant she'd be singing in front of *billions* of people. Before Rocky could process all her thoughts, the game was starting.

"They're going to announce us pretty soon," Aiden said enthusiastically. "Everyone ready?"

"Aiden, I don't think I can do this," Rocky said with a shaky voice. "There are way too many people out there looking at me."

"We've been practicing for weeks and sound exceptional," he told her. "We can't back out now. We have to give the people what they want."

Rocky's breathing started getting more labored. *I know this will fade away*, Rocky thought to herself. *I know this will fade away. I know...oh, God. There are so many people out there!*

"What's the matter with you?" Aiden asked, sounding confused.

"I just can't do it," Rocky put her head in her lap so Aiden couldn't see her crying. She felt ashamed for chickening out at the last minute and thought Aiden was upset with her. The thought of Aiden being mad at her intensified her anxiety.

Aiden sighed. "Rocky, I thought you wanted to break out of your shell," he told her. "This is the perfect opportunity for you to do that. I guarantee you'll never get anxious about performing again once you sing in front of this many people."

Rocky couldn't concentrate on what Aiden was saying because she was working hard to stop her anxiety attack. She desperately wanted her mom to hold her and tell her everything would be okay. She didn't want Aiden to see her like this. She didn't want billions of eyes to be on her. Rocky was struggling to get her breathing under control and was feeling lightheaded. *I know this will fade away. I know this will fade away. Please just fade away already!*

"Come on," he said, almost impatiently. "Please don't do this to me, Rocky. Not now."

Rocky felt someone pat her on her back reassuringly. She thought it was Aiden but heard Renaldo's voice.

"Take it easy on her, man," he told Aiden. "Can't you see she's panicking? It's scary to perform in front of so many people."

"Would you let me handle this?" Aiden snapped. He forced Renaldo's hand from Rocky's back, took her by the hand, and pulled her to an area behind the bleachers. They were alone and facing each other when he gently put his hands on her shoulders and caressed them. Rocky looked up at Aiden with tears in her eyes and her breathing still not under control.

"Tell me more about how much you love Whitney," Aiden suddenly said.

"What?" Rocky said between breaths.

"Whitney Houston. What do you love the most about her?"

It was hard for Rocky to think straight. "Um," Rocky stuttered.

"Come on, she's your idol," Aiden continued. "There has to be a whole list of things you love about her."

"She's talented," Rocky said.

"That she is. What else?"

"Um, she has an amazing vocal range."

"Oh yeah, her range is phenomenal. Keep going."

The more she started thinking about things she admired about Whitney Houston, the more she could control her breathing. "She's influential to a lot of other singers."

"Such as yourself, right?"

Rocky nodded her head.

"And I'm sure your mother loves Whitney's music, too, right?"

"Oh, yeah," Rocky said.

Aiden wiped away Rocky's tears, which made her smile.

"How are you feeling?" Aiden asked.

"A little better," Rocky said.

"I'm sorry if I seemed a little mean before, but I know how important it is for you to break out of your shell. You have to go out there and sing. If you don't, it's like all that hard work you've been doing will go to waste, and nobody will ever hear how incredibly talented you are."

"You think I'm incredibly talented?"

"Of course. Why else would I choose you to sing with me? You have a gift, Rocky. Everyone should be able to hear how talented you are."

Rocky couldn't stop smiling. That was the sweetest thing Aiden had ever said to her.

"Now stop being selfish with your gift. Go out there and give it your best shot," Aiden said.

"I'm just so nervous," Rocky admitted.

"I'll be right there with you," Aiden told her. "You won't be alone. You're never alone."

As Rocky and Aiden both looked into each other's eyes, she felt like she was in a romantic movie, and this was the scene where the cute guy kissed the girl. She wanted Aiden to kiss her so badly! If Aiden kissed Rocky, it would make her entire life. She felt like it was so close to happening until Marcus came from around the corner, startling Rocky.

"Guys, we're about to go on now," he said. He noticed Aiden and Rocky together and cleared his throat. "Did I interrupt something?"

Rocky tried to mask her embarrassment with a giggle, and Aiden rolled his eyes.

"Okay, let's do this," Aiden said. He gently placed his hand on Rocky's shoulder. "Remember, you got this," he told her.

Rocky smiled and followed Aiden and Marcus back to the bleachers. They picked up their microphones as she and the guys were being announced.

"Ladies and gentlemen, put your hands together for Aiden and Company with the National Anthem!"

Rocky's heart started pounding so hard in her chest that she could hardly move, but she forced herself to follow behind Aiden and the boys as they walked to the football field center. The sound of everyone's cheering was deafening. Rocky kept her eyes glued to the ground, so she wouldn't have another panic attack.

When she glanced up to adjust her microphone stand, she noticed a relatively large pink and purple sign in the bleachers. She had to squint to read it. "GO ROCKY!!" was written on it in giant bubble letters. That was when she recognized her mom, Hayley, and Adam cheering her on. She'd never been happier to see them! The crowd silenced, and it was time to sing.

Aiden started the song with his beautiful baritone voice. Rocky felt chills run down her spine because of how phenomenal he sounded, but she had to focus. Once they got to the lyrics, *what so proudly we hailed,* she and the boys joined Aiden in perfect harmony. Rocky had to admit she was impressed at how wonderful they all sounded.

During the entire performance, Rocky kept her head down and her eyes closed. She imagined being in The Studio with only her family and friends watching, which helped ease her mind. Before she knew it, the song was over, and the crowd went wild. Rocky opened her eyes and noticed many people standing up and cheering loudly, making her feel proud. She saw the "GO ROCKY!!" sign again and smiled widely. Rocky sang in front of thousands of people, something she never thought would happen in a million years.

After they got back to their seats, Rocky couldn't keep still.

"I can't believe I just did that," she said in amazement.

"I knew you could," Renaldo told her.

"I actually performed in front of all those people," Rocky said, still awestruck. "This is so surreal. I feel like I can do anything now! I did it!"

"You were great, Rocky," Aiden said. "You and the guys came through and made me sound fantastic."

Aiden's comment discouraged Rocky a bit. Was that more of a compliment for her or himself?

Rocky tried to ignore it because she had finally conquered her stage fright and felt like she was ready for more. She felt like she was on top of the world!

Rocky barely watched the game because she didn't understand football and was still astounded by her performance. She would always remember it for the rest of her life. Pretty much all Rocky got from the game was that the opposing team won by only two points.

As they were getting ready to exit the stadium, Rocky heard someone shouting her name. After turning around and seeing the "GO ROCKY!!" sign again, she ran over to her mom, Hayley, and Adam and hugged them tightly.

"I didn't know you were bringing Hayley and Adam with you," Rocky told her mom.

"We wanted to surprise you!" Hayley said.

"How did you have the time to get them?"

"It turns out they didn't need me to stay the entire 4 hours, so they let me leave even earlier," Rochelle said. "I thought it would be nice to bring your best friends along to cheer you on."

"I'm so happy you guys came!" Rocky said, hugging Hayley and Adam again.

"We wouldn't miss it for anything," Adam said.

"I can't believe you sang in front of all those people!" Rochelle said excitedly. "You all sounded amazing, and I'm so proud of you!"

"Thank you so much," Rocky said.

"You were so great," Hayley exclaimed. "How did you feel standing there in front of thousands of people?"

"I was so totally beyond nervous."

"You kind of looked it," Adam laughed. "But at least you didn't sound it. From the times we could hear you, at least."

"Yeah, we had to listen extra hard to hear you, Rocky," Rochelle said. "Your voice was drowned out by all the extra bass from the boys."

Aiden and the guys walked up, and Rocky saw Adam ball his fists.

"It's nice to see you again, Mrs. Coleman," Aiden said to Rochelle. "I'm glad you got to see your daughter's first major performance."

"I told you this was something I couldn't miss," Rochelle said. "You all were wonderful."

"Thank you," Aiden said. "Rocky was nervous at first, but after I calmed her down, she pulled through and tackled that performance."

"I'm so proud of her!" Rochelle said as she gave Rocky another tight squeeze.

"My parents were going to take us all out to eat at a nearby restaurant to celebrate," Aiden said. "We'd love for you to join us, Mrs. Coleman."

"Okay, sure. I don't see why not," Rochelle replied.

"Can Hayley and Adam come, too?" Rocky asked.

"The more, the merrier." Aiden never even acknowledged Hayley or Adam. Rocky wondered if he didn't want them to tag along. Or at least he didn't want Adam to tag along.

"I think I'll pass," Adam spoke up.

"Oh, come on, Adam," Hayley said. "It's not like you have a choice anyway. You have no other way home."

"I can call my parents."

"It'll take them over an hour to get here," Rocky said. "Don't inconvenience them. Come with us, please."

Adam sighed. "I need a license and car," he said under his breath. "Fine, I'll go since I don't have a choice."

Rocky jumped up and hugged Adam again. "It'll be fine," she reassured him. "You don't even have to talk to him."

"Trust me, I won't," Adam told her.

"So, you can follow behind my parents then," Aiden told Rochelle. He looked at Rocky and asked, "Rocky, did you want to ride with us to the restaurant?"

Of course, Rocky wanted to ride with Aiden to the restaurant! She had already missed the opportunity to ride with him to the game. At the same time, she couldn't wait to tell her mom, Hayley, and Adam about everything relating to her performance.

"I'll drive her there," Rochelle answered for her. Rocky sighed and rolled her eyes.

"No worries," Aiden said. "See you there in a bit." He then walked away, and Rocky followed her mom to the car.

8

Rocky had a great experience singing at the football game. She took a big step in breaking out of her shyness and felt better about herself now that she'd done something so major. Aiden was fun to be around, and Rocky thought they had a great time at the restaurant after the game. She just wished he and Adam would get along.

As Rocky, Hayley, and Adam walked into the school's courtyard that Monday, a small group of girls ran up to Rocky and crowded around her. They were all excitedly talking over one another, and Rocky started feeling anxious from all the commotion.

"I saw you and Aiden and the boys singing on TV at the Dolphins game last night!"

"You guys sounded perfect!"

"You're so lucky you got to sing on TV!"

Rocky started backing away from the antsy girls, but they kept moving closer and going on about yesterday's performance. All of them continued to talk at once, making it difficult for Rocky to understand any of them. She soon began to feel overwhelmed and desperately needed some breathing room.

"Girls, give her some space, please," Hayley said. However, the girls didn't listen and continued to crowd Rocky.

"Rocky, you're the luckiest girl ever. You got to sing with Aiden!"

"Everybody in the world got to see you guys sing!"

"You're totally going to get famous now!"

Rocky smiled politely and tried backing away again. The girls continued to crowd her.

"Everybody back up!" Hayley shouted loud enough to get the girls to settle down. "I'm sure Rocky appreciates you guys for watching her performance, but she doesn't like being crowded. We'd like to be left alone if you please."

The fanatic girls all smiled and said goodbye before leaving. Now that Rocky was finally alone with Hayley and Adam, she felt like she could breathe again. *Is this how Aiden and his boys live every day?* she thought.

"Way to stick it to them, Hayley," Adam laughed.

"When you grow up with four brothers and sisters, yelling to be heard is the norm," Hayley giggled.

"I appreciate you doing that, Hayley," Rocky said. "They came out of nowhere."

"I got you, girl."

"How are you enjoying being the popular girl?" Adam said, playfully nudging Rocky.

Rocky looked down. "I don't know. I guess it feels different. I'm still used to being the girl nobody notices."

"Well, everyone's noticing you now," Hayley mentioned. "That's what you wanted, right?"

"I didn't think it would be this crazy," Rocky admitted.

Before anyone could get another word out, Aiden showed up, nearly pushing Hayley and Adam out of his way to get to Rocky.

"Hey, there you are," he said. "Would you mind if I spoke to you alone for a minute?"

Rocky looked from Hayley and Adam back to Aiden. "Um, okay," she murmured.

"I'll just borrow her for a moment," Aiden told Hayley and Adam. "But I promise to give her back." He took Rocky by the hand and led her to a spot farther away from her friends.

"You did a great job last night," Aiden told her when they were alone.

"Thanks," Rocky said. "I'm sorry about almost backing out, though."

"You're fine," Aiden said reassuringly. "I understand it was your first major performance, and you had to do it in front of a large crowd. You were great, though, and everyone loved us."

Rocky smiled as she started fidgeting with her fingers.

"How would you feel about performing at the local amphitheater next week?"

Rocky looked at Aiden in surprise. They just had a performance yesterday. How was there another one coming up so soon?

"We have to sing again already?" she asked meekly.

"Well, yeah. I'm trying to get us noticed, and we have to perform a lot to get noticed. We'll be singing one of my originals, and this performance has choreography that I want you guys to learn."

Rocky felt her heart race again. Rocky was no good at dancing and would make a fool of herself during that performance. But how could she tell him no? She had just joined the group and didn't want to wimp out again.

Rocky laughed nervously. "Um, I'm no dancer," she admitted.

Aiden smiled at her. "No worries. The choreography isn't too complicated, so you'll be fine."

Rocky tried to act calm, but she knew Aiden could see the worry on her face.

"You'll be fine," he told her again. "Come to the rehearsals and practice. I promise there's nothing to worry about."

"Do you really think I'll learn everything by next week?"

"I know you can do it, Rocky. Like I said before, it's not that complicated. I'm sure you'll have it down pat in no time."

It was sweet how Aiden saw so much potential in Rocky that even she couldn't see. If he thought she could do it, then she would try. Anything to make Aiden happy.

"Okay then," she said.

Aiden smiled at Rocky. "Perfect. Make sure to come to all the rehearsals this week. We'll be practicing on the weekend and the morning before the show. Since it's choreographed, I wanted to have extra practice to get it perfect."

"That's fine."

"I should let you get back to your friends. I'll see you after school today. Be prepared to dance."

Rocky laughed. "I'll try my best," she said.

"Oh, you'll be great. I'll see you later." Aiden gave Rocky's arm a light tap before walking away. Rocky sighed and smiled as she watched Aiden walk away from her. She didn't notice Hayley and Adam were standing behind her until she heard Hayley speaking.

"What were you guys talking about?" Hayley asked.

"We have to perform at the amphitheater next week," Rocky told her.

"Wow, another performance already?" Adam asked.

"Yeah. The worst part about this performance is that it's choreographed. I can't dance at all. How will I pull this off without making myself look like an idiot in front of everyone?"

"Why would he only give you a week to learn an entire dance routine?" Adam asked.

"I don't know. He says it's simple, but I'm still scared of messing up."

Hayley shrugged. "I guess just practice a lot?" she suggested.

"He's going to be holding a lot of rehearsals this week because we have to learn the dance moves. But what if I don't get it right by the time we're supposed to perform?"

"Rocky, you can't always be so negative," Hayley told her. "What if you *do* get it right by the time you're supposed to perform?"

"I already can see the show ending in disaster," Rocky said, ignoring Hayley. "Aiden's going to hate me. He's probably going to kick me out of the group if I don't get this choreography right."

"Oh, please," Adam said while rolling his eyes. "He can't blame you for something like that. Choreographed songs should be planned way in advance. He's such a..."

"Adam, let's not start this," Hayley jumped in. "We're happy for Rocky, remember? She's getting more onstage experience, and it's helping her break out of her shyness."

"Whatever, Hayley. He's all nice now, but his true colors will show."

"Adam, he's not like that," Rocky said. "He's genuinely sweet. I told you he's matured since his fit at church."

"Whatever you say, Rocky."

Hayley laughed and put her elbow on Adam's shoulder. "Is someone maybe jealous?" she teased.

"Jealous of that sorry excuse for a human being? Absolutely not."

Rocky found it hard to believe that Aiden was as corrupt as Adam made it seem. All she saw was greatness and kindness in him. There couldn't have been one mean bone in his body.

"Oh, come on, Adam," Rocky pleaded. "Aiden is a good guy. And you promised you'd be nice."

"I said I would tolerate him," Adam said. "I said nothing about being nice to him, especially not with how he's treated me in the past."

"Can't you let the past stay in the past?" Rocky asked. "Forgive and forget. Holding on to resentment is only going to make you bitter. You should know this, Preacher's Son."

Adam rolled his eyes while suppressing a laugh. "You know I don't like being called that."

"And I don't like you bad-talking Aiden," Rocky said as she lightly shoved Adam.

Adam put his hands up in surrender. "Okay, fine," he said. "I won't say anything bad about Aiden."

The school bell rang, and Rocky, Hayley, and Adam parted ways to their classes.

***

During the rehearsal at Aiden's house after school, Rocky became more anxious about the upcoming performance. The routine wasn't nearly as simple as Aiden made it seem. After practicing for almost an hour, neither Rocky nor any of the guys were getting it. Aiden tried to mask his frustration, but Rocky thought he would explode on them any minute.

"Come on, you guys," Aiden sighed after many failed attempts. "It's not that hard."

"It's not that hard for you because you're a dancer, unlike us," Marcus told him.

"Seriously," Angel agreed. "And you're only giving us a week to learn all this."

"You don't need to be a dancer to learn something as simple as this routine," Aiden retorted. "Even a monkey could get it quickly. Now quit complaining, and let's try this again."

"Can we please take a break?" Renaldo asked. "I have no more energy left."

Aiden rolled his eyes at him. "We haven't even been practicing for an hour yet, and you already want to take a break? And you never do anything at rehearsals anyway. How could you possibly have no energy from doing nothing?"

Renaldo sighed as he slumped his shoulders.

"But seriously, can we take a break?" Marcus asked. "I'm kind of hungry anyway."

Aiden looked at Rocky, who hadn't spoken yet. "Can you believe these guys?" he asked her. "Always complaining about something."

Rocky still didn't say anything. She also wanted a break because she wasn't getting the dance routine either and was afraid Aiden might get angry with her.

"Fine. Take a break," Aiden said. "I need to make a phone call anyway."

Rocky and the guys went to wait in Aiden's living room while Aiden was talking on the phone in his bedroom. Marcus was looking for a snack in the kitchen, and Rocky awkwardly stood with Angel and Renaldo.

"Why does he make us do this when he knows we're not great dancers?" Renaldo asked.

Angel shrugged. "Maybe he enjoys making us miserable."

After a moment of silence, Angel turned to Rocky and said, "You're so quiet today."

Renaldo laughed. "She's quiet all the time," he said in a friendly way.

Rocky smiled, thinking about how much she appreciated the guys' friendliness toward her. "I don't know what to say," she admitted. "I'm just trying to do my best not to look stupid on stage next week."

Marcus came from the kitchen with a large bag of barbeque chips. "Did you not see the train wreck that went on earlier?" he asked with a laugh. "We're *all* going to look stupid on stage next week."

"How do you expect to sing and dance after you eat all that?" Angel took the chips from Marcus and got some for himself.

"One bag of chips won't affect anything, Angel," Marcus replied, taking them back. "I don't even feel like rehearsing anymore. I want to go home and sleep for like ten years."

"Honestly, same," Renaldo said with a laugh. "I don't care what Aiden says. We're not going to learn that entire dance before the show."

"If he doesn't want to get embarrassed, he should simplify the routine," Angel said.

"Or take it out completely," Renaldo said.

"I second that," Marcus said.

"This is too much."

Rocky continued to stay quiet. Even though she completely agreed with the guys, she didn't want to talk about it. She didn't want Aiden to think she complained about everything, so she thought it was best to keep quiet and listen to the guys.

When they began rehearsing again, there was no improvement. Rocky doubted they would get it together by next week, which intensified her anxiety.

"Okay, this isn't going to work," Aiden finally said. "What can I do to make you guys get it? I mean, it seriously isn't that hard."

Marcus sat down on the couch. "Don't you think, since all four of us aren't getting the routine down, that maybe it's not us? It could be the dance routine isn't as easy for us as it is for you."

Aiden sighed and shook his head. "Is it actually that difficult?" he asked.

The guys nodded their heads in silence. Aiden then looked at Rocky, who still hadn't said anything.

"So, now you have one of three options," Marcus said. "Continue this routine and look ridiculous on stage because your backup singers can't dance. Change or simplify this routine, so we'll look less ridiculous. Or take the dancing out entirely."

"I vote to take the dancing out entirely," Renaldo chimed in.

"I'm not going to do that," Aiden told him. "I'll see if I can make the routine simpler since none of you guys can get it right."

It took a while for Aiden to create new, more straightforward dance moves for Rocky and the guys to learn before the show. Even though this new routine was easier, Rocky was still anxious about performing on stage. She felt as though her shyness would get the best of her, and she would end up messing up the entire routine, making everyone look bad. Thinking about that made her not want to perform anymore.

Rehearsals ended later than usual because of the sudden change in plans. As Rocky was getting ready to leave, she noticed Aiden sitting on the couch with his head in his hands. He seemed bummed out, so she thought she should check on him.

"Are you okay?" Rocky asked.

"I will be," Aiden answered with a sigh.

"Are you sure?" she asked. "If you need to talk, I'd be happy to listen."

Aiden picked his head up and looked at Rocky. "I think I've kept you here long enough already," he told her. "Besides, you haven't said one word all day today. I almost forgot you were here at one point."

Rocky laughed. "I'm sorry," she muttered.

"Don't apologize."

Rocky kept her head down as she spoke to Aiden. What good would it be talking to him anyway? She was still timid around Aiden and felt like she would waste both of their time trying to talk with him.

"Okay," Rocky said. "You seemed down, and I wanted to make sure everything was all right."

"I wanted this performance to be amazing, you know?" Aiden admitted. "I didn't want to simplify the entire dance routine, but it is what it is. I'll get over it."

"I'm sorry you feel that way. I think the performance will still be amazing with the simpler routine."

"Did I maybe overestimate you guys? Answer honestly."

Rocky shrugged. "You couldn't have known we all were lousy dancers," she joked.

Aiden laughed. "Now that I know, maybe I should just let you all stick to singing."

Rocky laughed, too. Deep down, she hoped Aiden would let them only stick to singing because she didn't think she could handle learning a song and choreography again.

"Have you ever thought about getting backup dancers for the group?" Rocky asked. "You know, who can actually dance? That way, you won't have to simplify your routines because the guys and I can't dance."

"That's not such a bad idea." Aiden paused, stood up, and looked at Rocky with a big smile. "That's actually a *great* idea. Why didn't I think of that before?"

Rocky shrugged again. "Well, you go to a school full of talented people. I'm sure you can find a good group of dancers in no time."

"This is perfect," Aiden said happily. "I'll start looking for some dancers as soon as possible. Thank you for the idea, Rocky. I should've gotten dancers from the start instead of stressing you and the guys out."

"No problem," she said with a smile. "I'm happy to help you look, too. You know, if you want."

"I'd appreciate that." Aiden went over to Rocky and hugged her, much to her surprise. As Rocky hugged Aiden back, she couldn't stop smiling. She loved every second of being in Aiden's strong embrace.

"Can I ask you something else?" Rocky asked after she and Aiden finished hugging.

"Sure, what's up?"

Rocky figured since they were on the subject of adding new members to the group, she thought it would be a great time to ask if Hayley could be another backup singer. Rocky had been putting it off for a while because she wasn't sure how to bring it up and was scared to ask him. She was afraid Aiden would think Rocky was asking for too much change as the group's newbie and didn't want him to think anything bad about her.

"When you first met my mom, she said she was a little concerned about me being the only girl in the group," Rocky said. "And she thought it was worth asking if you considered adding more girls to the group."

"Of course," Aiden said. "I imaged my backup dancers being female anyway, so now you and your mom won't have to worry about that anymore."

That was easier than I imagined! Rocky thought. "Wow, thanks for being so considerate, Aiden," she told him.

"No problem. It would be nice to diversify the group a bit and see where it takes us."

"What if we added more female singers, too? My best friend Hayley could be your alto, and we can look for another mezzo-soprano, and..."

"Whoa, slow down, Rocky," Aiden laughed slightly.

Oh no, was Rocky overstepping now? She should've just kept quiet.

"I'm so sorry," Rocky said. "I didn't mean to...I'm sorry." Rocky hung her head in shame.

"No, it's fine. I see you have a lot of great ideas you want to get out, but let's focus on one change at a time."

"You're right. I just thought it would be fun if Hayley was singing with us, too. My mom gave me the idea."

"I can keep your suggestion in mind," Aiden said. "Let's worry about finding some dancers to join the group for now."

"Sounds great."

"I seem to be on your mom's good side right now, and I'd like to *stay* on her good side," Aiden joked. "So, we should get you home soon."

Rocky giggled. "Smart thinking," she said.

"Let me walk you outside."

Rocky followed behind while Aiden walked her to his front door. Aiden's mom was in the living room watching television when they passed by.

"Have a good evening, Rocky," she called out.

"Thanks, Mrs. Benjamin," Rocky said. "You too."

Rocky and Aiden lingered outside, not saying anything for a moment. It was incredibly awkward, and Rocky soon felt embarrassed. Should she say something? Should she wait for Aiden to say something? Should she leave? Aiden ultimately broke the awkward silence between the two of them.

"I'll see you tomorrow," he said.

"Yeah, tomorrow," Rocky said. "And when you start looking for dancers, I'll be here to help you."

"Thanks again, Rocky," Aiden told her. "You're a kind-hearted person. Don't ever change."

Rocky smiled and looked at the floor. "Thanks."

"You're welcome. Get home safely."

Rocky turned around and began her short walk home.

Aiden told Rocky and the guys that he wanted to start looking for dancers to perform at this weekend's concert as soon as possible. They spent most of the day asking dance students if they were interested in joining the group. Those who wanted to join were given the dance routine to watch and had until the end of the week to learn it and show Aiden. He would then pick his top three favorites after school on Friday to perform at the concert the following day.

Between the last-minute scrambling to find backup dancers and Aiden being extra hard on the group, the entire week was stressful for Rocky and the guys. They all were frazzled by everything going on so quickly, which made them not perform their best during rehearsals. Even at the slightest mistake, Aiden lost his mind. Rocky felt bad for Aiden because she saw how stressed he was about the upcoming performance and finding backup dancers. Rocky thought it was best to stay behind a few moments after rehearsal every day that week to make sure Aiden was okay. Every time she stayed, he always expressed how much he appreciated her.

On the evening of their concert, Aiden, Rocky, and the guys were standing backstage watching a pop band perform. Aiden picked three talented dancers to join his group the day before — two girls and a guy. Aiden felt that they had the routine down the best and wanted them to perform with the group. Rocky was still amazed they could learn the routine in a matter of days and be comfortable enough to perform it at a concert soon after.

Although the audience and atmosphere were lively, Rocky was paralyzed in fear. This performance was extra nerve-racking for her because Aiden said a talent agent would be watching. That explains why he wanted the performance to be perfect. Because of the stressful week they had, Rocky was worried about messing things up and upsetting Aiden. She would never forgive herself for messing up in front of a talent agent! Rocky had to clear her mind before she had an anxiety attack. She couldn't let Aiden see her like that again.

"Hey," one of the female dancers greeted Rocky. "Is everything okay?"

"I'm not used to performing on stage," Rocky sighed. "I get so scared when I have to go out there, and I hate letting my stage fright get the best of me."

"I have something that might help." She pulled out a small amber bottle from her pocket. "Hold out your arm."

Rocky did as she was told, and the dancer dabbed some of the oil from the amber bottle onto Rocky's wrist. She wasn't expecting the herbal, floral scent to be so powerful.

"Now, rub your wrists together," the dancer said.

"What is this?" Rocky asked as she rubbed her wrists together.

"It's lavender essential oil. The scent should help you feel calmer. If you're ever feeling nervous during the performance, take a quick whiff of your wrists."

Rocky sniffed her wrists and exhaled. Once she got used to the scent, it wasn't too bad. It helped her feel calmer. Where has this essential oil been all her life?

"Thank you," Rocky said. "I appreciate it."

"Absolutely," the dancer said with a smile. "We're going to do great out there."

The band on stage was finishing their song, and Rocky's face began to feel warm. She knew she couldn't afford to be nervous at that moment, so she sucked it up.

"We're up next," Aiden said. "Put on your best performance, and don't make me look bad." Aiden glared at Renaldo as if he were speaking directly to him. "Got it?"

Lately, Aiden had been hard on all the guys, but he was even worse with Renaldo for whatever reason.

"*Pendejo*," Renaldo mumbled under his breath as soon as Aiden turned his back.

As soon as the announcer introduced Aiden and Company, they all took their places on stage. Rocky's heart began racing as she thought about how much she didn't want to ruin the song and have Aiden hate her. They were going to perform "Turn it Up," an original, catchy club-pop song that made you want to get up and dance. That explained why Aiden wanted it to have choreography.

As soon as the song began playing, Rocky closed her eyes and imagined herself in The Studio. Rocky and the other guys sang backup while Aiden was front and center, killing his dance moves and the song. The backup dancers were behind him. Rocky occasionally stole some glances at Aiden and kept thinking about how perfect he was. She was amazed at how well he could sing and dance at the same time. He had it all: great looks *and* great talent!

When they finished the song, the audience cheered loudly and wildly. Even after they were no longer on stage, the audience still cheered for them.

"You guys were awesome out there!" one of the other performers told them.

"Thanks, man," Aiden said. "I think we could've done better, though. It wasn't one of our best performances."

Rocky, the guys, and the dancers all exchanged looks. What did he mean it wasn't one of their best performances?

"No way," the other performer said. "You guys killed it out there. I don't think there's anything else you could've done to make it better."

"Well, there's always room for improvement."

Aiden made it clear that their performance didn't meet his expectations, discouraging Rocky. She thought they did well despite all the last-minute changes. What could she have done differently to make Aiden love the performance?

***

Rocky had been in Aiden's singing group for a little over a month, and what an eventful month it had been for Rocky! Pretty much every weekend, Aiden had a show booked for them. Rocky started getting used to performing on stage since she'd done it every weekend for a month, but she was still incredibly nervous before getting on stage. Her panic attacks weren't as bad. She had them under control and even bought her own lavender essential oil to use before performances.

Ever since Rocky joined the group, Aiden and the guys hadn't been singing much at school. They hadn't signed up for any lunch concerts because they usually had other performances to prepare for. Every so often, they would do an impromptu performance in the courtyard. Rocky still wasn't used to all the attention she was getting, but she was proud of herself for starting to break out of her shell.

Practice after school on Monday got cut short because Angel was home with the flu. They tried practicing without him, but the group didn't sound the same without its tenor.

"I don't know about you guys, but I'm not feeling it," Aiden said about 10 minutes into the rehearsal. "Let's continue tomorrow; hopefully, Angel will be doing better then."

Marcus was lying comfortably on the couch with his drumsticks in his hands. Then, he stood up and stretched. "Cool," he said casually. "I'll go over by Angel's to check on him."

"I'll come with you," Renaldo said, getting up from the keyboard.

"I should probably head home," Rocky said. "Tell him I said to get well."

"Will do. See you tomorrow," Marcus said.

Rocky waved goodbye to Marcus and Renaldo and got up to leave. Aiden lightly touched her arm.

"Rocky, wait," he said. "Do you have a minute?"

"Uh, sure. What's up?" Rocky sat back down next to Aiden.

He rubbed the back of his neck and couldn't make eye contact with Rocky. "Um, I'm sure you've noticed by now, but I've been a little stressed lately. And it seemed like I'm taking my stress out on you and the guys."

Rocky nodded her head. "Yeah, I kind of noticed that."

"I wanted to say sorry if I came off as rude to you, and I promise I'm not that kind of guy. We usually have a great time during our rehearsals. Booking all these concerts and trying to perfect our sound has been driving me crazy."

"I understand that. I mean, success doesn't come easy."

"You don't have to tell me that twice," Aiden said with a slight snicker.

"You have a lot of talent and potential, though. I know you can get through this, and your hard work will pay off."

Aiden sighed. "I don't know. Trying to make everything perfect is such a burden, and I feel like the guys aren't taking it seriously anymore. It was all fun and games when we used to sing at school talent shows and all, but now we're experiencing real-world stuff." Aiden looked down at his lap. "Sometimes, I wonder if I'm even good enough."

"Of course, you're good enough. You wouldn't have been chosen to sing at real concerts or pro football games on national TV if you weren't good enough. And if you want, I can talk to the guys about taking things more seriously."

Rocky couldn't understand how someone as talented as Aiden could doubt his skills. Everybody loved him, and he was so popular at school. It came as a surprise to Rocky that Aiden felt the way he did.

"You're talented, Aiden," Rocky said. "And you're so good at what you do. Your hard work and determination will pay off in the end, and all that stress will be worth it when you reach your dreams."

Aiden looked at Rocky and smiled, which made her face feel warm. She was used to always receiving encouraging words. It felt different now that she was saying them to someone else. She was proud of herself.

"Thank you, Rocky," Aiden said. "I needed to hear that. Nobody's ever said anything like that to me before."

"Seriously?" Rocky asked in shock. "Maybe it's because you're, like, the best at what you do, and people assume you have everything made. But even the best deserves someone to lean on and words of encouragement from time to time. You can count on me to support and motivate you when you need it."

"That means a lot to me. Thank you." Aiden put his hand on top of Rocky's and looked into her eyes. Rocky stared back into his dark and mesmerizing eyes but quickly broke eye contact and looked down. That bit of confidence she had when she was encouraging Aiden suddenly vanished.

"I'm sorry," he said. He moved his hand from on top of Rocky's and placed it in his lap.

"Sorry for what?" Rocky asked softly.

"Being an awkward dud," Aiden chuckled. "You're...you're beautiful, and I wanted to admire you for a bit. I know I probably sound so stupid right now."

"No, you don't." Rocky blushed again and kept her head down. She was way too nervous to look at Aiden. "You really think I'm beautiful?"

"Of course. Hasn't anyone ever told you that before?"

"No," Rocky admitted. "I honestly never thought I was attractive."

"Are you kidding?" Aiden asked in disbelief. "You're so beautiful, Rocky."

Rocky was so overjoyed that she could've cried. After being practically invisible to all the attractive guys in her life, someone finally called her beautiful. Aiden thought she was beautiful! She felt more than butterflies in her stomach. She felt the entire zoo.

Rocky finally looked up at Aiden and smiled at him. "Thank you for telling me that, Aiden."

"Anytime." Aiden took a deep breath. "Can I tell you a secret?"

"Sure."

"I've been thinking about us a lot lately."

Rocky giggled in an attempt to seem cute, but it came out more like a nervous chuckle. "Oh?" was all she could manage to say.

"Yeah, I think we could make a cute couple. Don't you think?"

Was Aiden saying what Rocky thought he was saying? There was no way this was happening. Not possible. Rocky thought she might have been dreaming or maybe even hallucinating. She blinked her eyes a few times to make sure.

"Um, I don't know," she blurted out. *Why am I so stupid?!* She nervously giggled again. "When did you, um, start thinking this?"

"When I first saw you singing on stage, I knew I had to have you. I was just too nervous to tell you how I felt."

"Really? No way."

"Why is that surprising to you?"

"Because you're all popular and good-looking and have lots of confidence. Meanwhile, I'm just a Plain Jane with low self-esteem. You could get any girl you want. How could you possibly be nervous about asking *me* out?"

"Don't talk so badly about yourself, Rocky. Like I said before, you're gorgeous. And I would love for you to be my girlfriend."

Rocky was fiddling with the loose thread on the sleeve of her shirt. She tried to look at Aiden, but her shyness forced her to keep focusing on that loose thread. If this was a dream, it was one she did not want to wake up from.

"Would you want to be my girlfriend?" Aiden asked with hope in his voice.

He didn't have to ask Rocky that twice! "Okay," she said excitedly.

Aiden breathed a huge sigh of relief.

It was official: Rocky and Aiden were boyfriend and girlfriend. This was a day Rocky never dreamt would happen. She bit her lower lip. *So, I guess I have a boyfriend*, she thought. *Now what?*

"So, Rocky," Aiden said. "My girlfriend, how do you feel right now?"

"Nervous," Rocky admitted.

"Still? I thought you would've been used to me by now."

"Now that we're dating, I guess it makes me feel even more shy to be around you."

Aiden chuckled. "How come?"

"I've never had a boyfriend before," Rocky embarrassingly admitted. "I don't understand how relationship stuff works."

"Well, I'm honored to be your first. But don't overthink how relationship stuff works. Just be your cute little self, and things will be fine."

Rocky couldn't get over the fact that Aiden was now her boyfriend. She couldn't wait to tell Hayley about the exciting news.

"I know you said you wanted to get home, so I'll let you go," Aiden said after a moment of silence. "I'm sorry for keeping you so long."

"No, it's fine." Now Rocky didn't want to leave! At the same time, she didn't want to seem obsessive. She'd been in a relationship for less than a minute and couldn't ruin it already. This may never happen again.

"I'll walk you out," Aiden offered.

"Okay," Rocky said quietly. She and Aiden walked to the front door together, where they lingered outside on the porch. She suddenly forgot how to speak to him.

"I'll see you tomorrow," Aiden said, breaking the silence.

"Yeah, tomorrow," Rocky said. She turned to walk away, but Aiden lightly took her by the shoulder, turned her back around, and gently pulled her into a hug. She rested her head on his chest while his chin was on her head. His cologne smelled subtle yet spicy, making Rocky want to stay wrapped in his arms all day. Unfortunately, all good things must come to an end. Aiden let go, said goodbye, and Rocky walked home with a smile on her face.

9

As soon as Rocky got inside her house, she jumped for joy and squealed. She and Aiden were dating! She still couldn't believe it was happening. Rocky ran to her bedroom and jumped on her bed while giggling like a kid in a candy store. As soon as she settled down, she took out her phone and called Hayley.

"Hey, Rocky," Hayley answered. "What's up?"

"Hayley, you'll never guess what happened!" Rocky exclaimed.

"What is it?" she asked eagerly.

Rocky began getting excited again, and she started jumping up and down while giggling uncontrollably.

"Tell me, Rocky!"

"Okay, okay. I'm so excited." Rocky tried to calm herself down so she could speak. "Oh, my goodness. So, you'll never believe what Aiden did today."

"What? What?"

"He asked me to be his girlfriend! Can you believe it?"

Hayley shrieked on the other line. Rocky screamed and started jumping up and down again.

"No way!" Hayley cried. "Are you for real?"

"Yes, I'm for real."

"Did you say yes?"

"Of course, I said yes! Only an idiot wouldn't agree to be Aiden's girlfriend."

"Oh, my gosh, Rocky. All the good things are happening to you, and it's not fair!" Hayley joked.

"Hayley, no boy has ever asked me out before. Now, a hottie like Aiden wants to be my boyfriend? This is so unreal."

"Tell me everything that happened, and don't leave out a single detail."

Rocky sighed happily. "Okay. After we finished rehearsing at his house, he said he wanted to talk to me for a minute. So, he told me about how he was stressed from all the performances we have coming up, and I told him I'd be his support system whenever he needed it."

"Go on."

Rocky started smiling. "Then he said he thought we'd make a cute couple and that he was nervous about asking me out."

"Oh, my goodness! I'm so jealous of you right now!"

Rocky laughed. "Hayley, he told me I was beautiful."

"Aww, he's right. You are beautiful, girl, and I'm glad he told you that. Then what happened?"

"Um, I left."

"Are you serious?" Hayley asked in shock. "Did he kiss you or anything?"

"No," Rocky said. "We hugged, and that was pretty much it. He smelled so good. I wanted to bury my face in his chest and stay there forever."

"Aww, my little Rocky is growing up. I think I'm going to cry!"

Rocky laughed again. "I'm so nervous about how our first kiss will go, though. Like, when and where will it happen? What if he does it unexpectedly, and I have bad breath? What if he tries to tongue me during the kiss?"

Hayley laughed. "Just relax, and always be prepared with breath mints and flavored lip balm. And don't be afraid to tell him no if he tries to take things too far. I'm happy that you're happy."

"Thanks, girl." Rocky heard the front door open. "Hey, my mom is home. Let me call you back."

After Rocky hung up the phone, she skipped downstairs and hugged her mom.

"Hi, Mom," she said happily. "How is everything?"

"Hey, sweetheart," Rochelle said. "Everything's good. Are you okay?"

"Oh, I'm wonderful."

"Well, what's gotten you in a wonderful mood?" Rochelle smiled at Rocky. "Is it a boy?"

"Maybe," Rocky said mysteriously.

Rochelle laughed. "Is it that same boy you're in the singing group with?"

Rocky couldn't stop the grin from forming on her face. "Possibly."

"Oh, my baby girl is turning into a young lady!" Rochelle exclaimed, giving Rocky a tight hug.

"Mom!" Rocky laughed.

"Now, here comes the dreaded moment where I have to have 'the boyfriend talk' with you."

"Oh, my gosh." Rocky plopped on the couch behind her and rolled her eyes.

Rochelle sat down next to Rocky. "It had to happen one day, and it looks like that's today."

"I already know what you're going to say, Mom. Don't let a boy pressure me into doing something I don't want. Don't let him touch me inappropriately. Don't have sex. All the usual stuff."

"I only want you to be happy. And I refuse to let you be a guy's easy target for a 'hit it and quit it' because he might as well forget it."

"I know when to say no."

"Well, at least I've met him and his parents already, so that's out of the way. We have to plan another time to meet again soon. And I think I kind of like this guy. He seems decent."

Rocky smiled. "I like him, too."

Rochelle laughed. "Aww!" she said, giving her another tight hug. "I'm glad you're happy."

"Does this mean you won't be as strict about me being at his house to practice?"

"Oh, honey. I'm going to be even *more* strict about it now that you two are dating. You're definitely not allowed to be alone with him if no adults are around."

"Great," Rocky sighed.

Rocky and her mother spent the next hour together on the couch watching television before Rochelle fell asleep, and then Rocky went upstairs to her room. She was still excited about dating Aiden and felt popular. Rocky couldn't be happier about how her freshman year of high school was turning out for her.

The next morning at school, when Rocky looked for her friends in the courtyard, she saw Hayley walking over to her. Adam was nowhere to be found.

"Hey there, Mrs. Benjamin," Hayley teased.

Rocky shyly laughed and looked down at her feet.

"So, when's the wedding? I call dibs on being the maid of honor."

"Leave me alone, Hayley," Rocky said with another laugh.

"You know I'm messing with you," Hayley told Rocky. "I'm so happy for you."

"Thanks, I guess. Where's Adam?"

"I don't know. He's usually here before I come, but I didn't see him."

Rocky didn't get a chance to respond because another one of Lennox's outstanding impromptu courtyard performances was beginning. A group of girls dressed in red and green sweaters and Santa Clause hats gathered in the courtyard and started singing "Carol of the Bells."

"There's never a dull moment at Lennox," Hayley said in amazement.

"I know," Rocky agreed.

As Rocky and Hayley continued to watch the girls' performance, Rocky couldn't help but get excited about the Christmas season. She got to bake cookies with her mother, Christmas carols played everywhere, and places were decorated with gorgeous lights and ornaments. It was the most wonderful time of the year! Rocky remembered when she was little and first heard "Carol of the Bells." Her church's choir sang it during a Christmas concert, and she loved it. Rocky enjoyed it when "Carol of the Bells" played on the radio and sometimes even sang it to herself during holiday season.

After the girls finished, they bowed as the other students applauded them. They left the courtyard in a single file line.

"I can't believe it's almost Christmas," Hayley said once everything calmed down. "It feels like it was August yesterday."

"I know, right," Rocky laughed. "The school year is flying by. Before we know it, we'll be graduating."

"Tell me about it. What are you doing during winter break?"

"Singing," Rocky sighed. "We have a Christmas concert to sing at two days before Christmas and a New Year's concert on New Year's Eve."

"How exciting! Make sure I get front-row tickets to both concerts."

"Of course. It's fun having all these concerts to sing at, but it's also a lot of work. Sometimes, I wish I could just be home watching TV."

"You're almost like a professional singer with all these performances. Do you think one day you guys might go on tour?"

Rocky shrugged. "He's never really talked about going on tour, but it'll be so cool if we did."

"Right! It would be so much fun. You should convince Aiden to do that."

"I'd want to bring you and Adam and my mom with me if we ever do."

The school bell rang, and the two girls went their separate ways. Rocky sighed as she walked to class. Lately, she'd been stressed for multiple reasons. It was almost time for Christmas break, and she worried about her upcoming exams. Not to mention the two concerts that were a week apart from each other. Rocky couldn't find the time to study because she was constantly rehearsing or singing at concerts. She was beginning to get overwhelmed. On top of that, her throat was getting sore from all the singing. That made things worse because she had to sing a song for her chorus exam, too!

Later in the day, during chorus class, Rocky spotted Marcus and waved. They became much closer as friends since Rocky joined Aiden's group. Rocky loved how adorable and goofy he was, and she soon became comfortable talking to him. Rocky started coughing as soon as Marcus sat next to her.

"Oh, no," he said. "Coming down with something?"

"I hope not," Rocky sighed. "I can't afford to fail this exam and not be able to sing at the Christmas concert."

"Hey, if you need to go on vocal rest, then go for it. I'd rather you miss a few performances than risk damaging your vocal cords."

"I don't want that either. But what can I do?"

As soon as the final bell rang, Ms. Rose stood in front of the class, and everyone stopped talking.

"Good afternoon," she said. "I wanted to remind you all that your semester exam will be next week. Then we won't be seeing each other until after winter break. As you know, you're required to perform a song of your choice, but only if it meets the requirements I've listed on the rubric I gave you all last week. I hope you're using your time wisely. If there are no questions, we'll begin our vocal exercises."

Nobody raised their hand to ask questions, so they started with the vocal warm-ups. During the warm-ups,

Rocky kept coughing, and her voice cracked. This wasn't good.

"Raquel," Ms. Rose called out after they finished the vocal warm-ups. "Are you feeling okay, dear?"

"I just have a little cough," Rocky said after a short coughing fit.

"That sounds like more than 'just a little cough.' You need to rest up, dear. We don't want you ruining that beautiful voice of yours. And if you still aren't feeling better by exam week, bring me a doctor's note, and I'll exempt you from the exam. Deal?"

"Okay," Rocky said.

Ms. Rose smiled at her and went back to her desk.

"I hope I'm better by next week," Rocky told Marcus in a panic. "I don't want to miss the semester exam and the concert."

"Relax," Marcus told her. "Your health is more important than missing an exam and a concert. You should be fine if you take the teacher's advice and rest up. Whenever Angel gets sick, he eats a lot of citrus fruits to feel better, and Renaldo usually makes an herbal tea whenever he's sick. You should probably try something like that."

"I'll do anything to get better quick," Rocky laughed. "Do you know what song you'll be singing for the semester exam?"

"Not a clue. You?"

"I have no idea. Ms. Rose said we could sing duets or in groups, right?"

"Yeah. You want to do a duet?"

"Sure. I don't want to even think about standing up there by myself in front of everyone."

Marcus laughed. "No worries. It's not that bad."

"Yeah, for you. You're so carefree, and nothing seems to bother you."

Marcus shrugged. "What do you want to sing?"

"I don't know. It has to be an old-school song, and I know tons of them. I just can't decide on one."

"Why don't you search for some boy/girl duet songs and let me listen? I'm sure we'll find something."

"Well, is there a specific genre you prefer?"

"It doesn't matter to me. I'm open to anything."

Rocky took out her cell phone and searched for male and female duets from the 80s. "There's so much to choose from," she said. "These are all great songs, and I don't know which one I want to sing."

"Eenie, meenie, miny, moe?" Marcus joked.

Rocky laughed. "Seriously, Marcus?"

"Hey man, I'm just trying to help you choose something for us to sing for the exam."

"Tell me which one you like," Rocky said, handing Marcus her phone. He gave it back to Rocky without looking.

"I told you I'm open to whatever you want. Pick whatever song your little heart desires, and I'll go along with it."

Rocky laughed again. "Marcus, if I choose something you don't like..."

"I promise that won't happen," Marcus said. "I'll sing anything to get a good grade in this class."

Rocky spent the rest of the class period searching for duets for her and Marcus to sing for their semester exam. They eventually decided to go with "(I've Had) The Time of My Life." It was a popular and fun song, but most importantly, Rocky and Marcus already knew the lyrics by heart! They began practicing for about five minutes until the bell rang.

"See you next time," Ms. Rose called out before everyone left. "And don't forget to practice, practice, practice!"

Rocky and Marcus walked out of class together.

"You want to finish practicing today after rehearsal at Aiden's?" Marcus suggested. "Or is that too much singing for one day?"

Rocky coughed again. "It's fine," she said. "I don't mind."

"On second thought, you need to rest up. We'll practice during our next chorus class."

"Are you sure?"

"Of course. Take it easy, okay? And tell Aiden you aren't feeling well and have to miss rehearsal today."

"I don't have to..."

"Raquel." Marcus gave Rocky a funny but stern look, making Rocky laugh.

"Okay, fine. I'll let him know."

"Attagirl." Marcus patted Rocky on the head and chuckled. "Catch you later."

Rocky smoothed her hair down before walking away to her next class.

***

By exam week, Rocky felt a lot better physically; however, she was drained mentally. She'd been studying for her exams and rehearsing her songs nonstop all week and was ready to get everything over with so she could finally breathe. Rocky and Marcus practiced their duet during chorus class and occasionally during Aiden's rehearsal while he wasn't in the room. She rarely heard Marcus sing alone and was amazed at how great he sounded.

On the day of the chorus exam, Rocky felt overwhelmed with anxiety. She thought it was ironic that she managed to sing in front of more massive crowds than her chorus class but was still so worried about this performance.

"Nervous?" Marcus asked her.

"Yeah, very," Rocky said.

"It'll be fine. Ms. Rose already loves you, so you don't have anything to worry about. I can guarantee you already passed this exam."

Rocky giggled, thankful for Marcus's lightheartedness.

"We practiced all week long," he reassured her. "You got this."

Rocky sighed and put her hand on her head. "I wish I could be more laid back like you," she said. "Nothing seems to bother you."

Marcus shrugged. "Well, I guess I like the attention," he chuckled. "Crowds don't intimidate me. And if something embarrassing does happen to me while I perform, I just laugh it off and move on. No biggie."

As the final bell rang, Ms. Rose made her way to the front of the classroom, and everyone stopped talking.

"Exam time!" Ms. Rose cheered. "You all know how you'll be graded on this performance. 50% is if your chosen song meets the criteria I provided on the rubric, and the other 50% is for your performance. Pretend you're at a real concert, and there's a talent agent in the crowd you must impress. I want you all to wow me!"

Why did Ms. Rose have to use that analogy? Now Rocky was even more uneasy about going up there to sing.

"I better not hear anybody chatting while your peers are performing," Ms. Rose continued. "If I hear talking, you'll get an automatic zero. Now, who would like to go first?"

Nobody offered to go first.

"If there aren't any volunteers, then I'll go alphabetically," Ms. Rose said.

Marcus looked at Rocky. "You want to go first and get it over with?" he whispered.

Rocky shook her head. Fortunately, a girl in the front row raised her hand and volunteered to go first.

"Perfect," Ms. Rose chirped. "The stage is yours."

Rocky's classmate went to the front of the class and nervously smiled. "I'm Chrissy," she said quietly. "And today, I'm going to be singing 'Time After Time' by Cyndi Lauper."

Chrissy cleared her throat while Ms. Rose cued up the song's instrumental. Then she began her performance.

"Can we go last?" Rocky whispered to Marcus.

"No way," he whispered back. "Don't wait that long."

Rocky looked toward Ms. Rose's desk to see if she noticed them talking.

"Let's go third," Marcus whispered. "Is that fine with you?"

Rocky sighed. She wanted to say no but agreed because Marcus was right. Rocky would much rather get the whole thing over with than anxiously wait until everyone else finished.

Before Rocky knew it, Chrissy finished her song, and the class applauded her. Although Rocky didn't see much of the performance, she could hear how phenomenal a singer her classmate was. The more she thought about it, the more nervous she was about performing after her.

"Thank you, Chrissy," Ms. Rose said. "That was a beautiful rendition of 'Time After Time.' Who will be performing next?"

"We'd be going after this next person, right?" Rocky quietly asked Marcus.

"Yeah," he replied.

Another brave soul volunteered to go. He and two other boys went up to the front of the classroom. "We'll be singing 'Soul Man' by Sam & Dave," he said. "Hope you guys enjoy it!"

"Ooh, R&B soul," Ms. Rose said excitedly. "This should be good."

Once the song cued up, the three guys began bopping and dancing to the music. Their energy was so infectious that most of the class bopped along for the performance. Even Ms. Rose looked like she was enjoying the show. Rocky secretly envied how well the trio was able to dance and sing at the same time so effortlessly. How would she compete with that? Rocky's heart began to race after watching two impressive performances and realizing she would be up next.

She couldn't just stand there and sing with her eyes closed like she usually did because her grade would reflect that.

Once the trio finished, everyone clapped. A few people loudly wooted, making the boys laugh before they sat back down.

Rocky took some deep breaths when she felt a panic attack coming on. She wanted to do well on this exam and couldn't let Marcus down. She had to do this. "I know this will fade away," Rocky whispered to herself repeatedly until she started feeling calmer.

"Great job, boys," Ms. Rose said, still clapping. "Your energy was truly remarkable. Next?"

Marcus raised his hand, and Rocky froze in fear.

"Wonderful! Come on up, sir."

Marcus stood, but it was as if Rocky's bottom was superglued to her seat. "It'll be fine, kid," Marcus said gently. "I'm here with you, and this is the smallest crowd you'll ever sing in front of. You got this."

Rocky sighed and finally stood up to go to the front of the classroom with Marcus. She hated that everyone was watching her, but having someone with her took some of the anxiety away.

"Hello, class," Marcus said. "I'm Marcus." He turned to Rocky so she could introduce herself.

"I'm Raquel," she muttered.

"And the song we'll be singing is '(I've Had) The Time of My Life' from *Dirty Dancing*."

"Ah, a classic," Ms. Rose sighed. "I'm looking forward to hearing you two sing it."

As Rocky and Marcus picked up their microphones, Ms. Rose started the music, and Marcus began singing the song. Rocky did her best to keep her eyes open during their performance and move to the music. However, anytime she looked at her classmates, she got nervous all over again. Rocky tried to mimic Marcus's moves and keep her focus on him rather than her peers to stay calm. Seeing him get into the song made her feel less anxious as they continued to perform.

As they neared the last part of the song, Marcus tried to recreate the climactic scene from the dancing finale in the movie when Johnny lifted Baby, much to Rocky's surprise. It didn't go quite as smoothly as Marcus probably thought it would since he ended up holding Rocky one-handed over his shoulder while spinning around. It got everyone in the class laughing, including Ms. Rose.

As ridiculous as the two might've looked, Rocky couldn't help but giggle. She was surprised by Marcus's reenactment, but everyone seemed to enjoy their performance.

Everyone clapped when the two finished. They even got a standing ovation from one of their silly classmates, making them both chuckle.

"That was fantastic," Ms. Rose said. "That last bit was, um, different. But wonderful performance overall. Well done, you two."

Rocky smiled as she and Marcus went back to their seats. "I told you it was going to go great," Marcus said once they sat back down.

Rocky giggled and playfully shoved Marcus. "I can't believe you pulled that stunt at the end! That totally caught me off guard."

Marcus started laughing, too. "I guess I was too in the moment," he said with a shrug. "But come on. Everyone loved it!"

"I guess. I'm just glad it's over with."

Now that Rocky had gotten her performance out of the way, she could enjoy the rest of the performances without her anxiety going crazy. Overall, Rocky thought all her peers were excellent singers, but not all of them put on their best performances. Some had more energy than others, and one girl who sang "Un-Break My Heart" nearly left Rocky in tears. Finally, everyone in the class got to perform.

"Well, it looks like that's everyone," Ms. Rose said, standing up. "There were some flawless performances and some that needed a bit of improvement. Overall, I'm extremely proud of you all. Now, we won't see each other again until January, and when we're back, be prepared to work. I hope you all have a wonderful Christmas and a happy New Year. Feel free to talk until class is over."

As soon as Ms. Rose sat down, everyone began chatting.

"I think we did a great job," Marcus told Rocky. "We should sing duets more often."

"I'm down for that. But no more surprise stunts!"

Marcus and Rocky both laughed. They chatted for the rest of class about their winter break plans outside of concerts with Aiden. Generally, he'd been the topic of most of their conversations, but she was glad they could talk about other things. She learned a lot more about Marcus through their chats in chorus class.

10

The holiday break began, but Rocky was hardly on a break. She, Aiden, and the guys still rehearsed every day for their upcoming Christmas concert at the amphitheater and the New Year's concert at a performing arts theater. Since school was out, Aiden held rehearsals earlier in the day, and they lasted longer. Since Aiden's parents wouldn't be home for the most part and school was closed, Pauline supervised their rehearsals. Rocky was so embarrassed, but Aiden was understanding.

Rocky, Aiden, and the boys were backstage waiting for their cue on the morning of the Christmas concert. Rocky felt surprisingly confident about this show. Something about the holiday season brought her spirits up and made her feel like she could conquer anything. Rocky peaked at the audience from backstage and smiled after spotting her mother, Adam, and Hayley. She was grateful they made such an effort to be there and support her at her concerts.

"How is everyone feeling?" Aiden asked once Rocky joined the guys backstage.

"Great," Marcus said.

"Super," Renaldo answered.

"Awesome," Angel said.

Aiden turned Rocky. "Feeling nervous, Rocky?" he asked her.

"I feel great," Rocky exclaimed. "I'm ready to tackle this!"

He smiled at her and put his arm around her. "That's my girl. I knew you'd get over your stage fright. I'm proud of you."

Rocky blushed and looked down at her feet. She loved hearing Aiden praise her. "Thanks," she said shyly.

"Where are the dancers?" Aiden asked. "We're going on soon."

"We're over here!" one of the dancers called from the corner.

"Perfect. We're ready."

Rocky got butterflies in her stomach once they were cued to go on stage.

"Let's do this!" Aiden said enthusiastically.

Rocky took a few deep breaths before following the boys and the dancers on stage. She heard someone from the audience shout her name and saw her mom, Adam, and Hayley cheering her on. Rocky smiled and waved at them.

They sang a pop version of "Do You Hear What I Hear?" that got the audience on their feet, singing and clapping along. This was the most at ease Rocky felt while performing on stage, and she loved every moment. Even the dancers seemed more energetic. Rocky loved the Christmas season!

When the song was over, they got a standing ovation from the audience. Rocky thought this might've been their best performance yet. When they got backstage, Aiden was giving everyone high-fives.

"Great job!" he told them. Seeing Aiden so happy made Rocky feel great. Especially since he was so critical before, Aiden's enthusiasm about their performance made her feel like they were doing better. Aiden picked Rocky up and spun her around; she couldn't stop laughing at his giddiness.

"I'm so proud of you," he told Rocky once he put her back down. "Everything was perfect."

Rocky smiled at him and stared into his dark eyes. For the first time, she managed to keep eye contact with Aiden. It felt like time had stopped, and they were the only two in the room. Was he going to kiss her?

Unfortunately, Rocky's fantasies were cut short by someone calling Aiden's name. She looked down, feeling slightly disappointed by the interruption.

"I'll be back, love," Aiden told her before walking away.

Rocky watched him disappear behind a group of other people and sighed happily. *He called me love!*

***

Rocky wanted some alone time with Aiden, but her mom made that impossible with her constant supervision. On a day when Aiden's mom would be home all day, Rocky decided to arrive at practice early so she could have some time with him before the guys and dancers showed up. Rocky thought things between her and Aiden were going well, and she'd never been happier. They still hadn't had their first kiss, and Rocky was a bit anxious about that. They'd been together for almost a month now. How long was she supposed to wait? Was she moving too fast? Maybe Aiden was just as nervous as Rocky was about it.

"I have a question," he asked, interrupting Rocky's racing thoughts.

"I have an answer," Rocky replied.

"What do you think about getting makeovers?"

"Huh?" Rocky asked, a bit dumbfounded for a moment. "Do you plan on giving me one or something?"

"Well, my sister is in cosmetology school and needs to give someone a makeover for an assignment. I thought you would be the perfect client for her."

"Really?"

"Sure, why not? She's a great esthetician. She'll have you looking flawless. And you know, as my girl, I need you to look your best for me."

Rocky smiled shyly and rubbed her arm. She wasn't too sure about going through with it and was nervous about the whole thing. Suppose Rocky didn't like the makeover? What if Aiden's sister got upset at Rocky for not liking the makeover? What if that made Aiden upset? What if Rocky looked unrecognizable?

"Um, what exactly would she be doing to me?" Rocky asked.

"She's just going to do your hair and makeup. She'll also take some before and after photos for her portfolio."

Nobody other than Rocky's mom had ever styled her hair, and she'd never worn makeup before. This would be so different for her.

"Do you think you could do this for my sister?" Aiden asked. "She needs a client for this assignment, and a lot of the people she knows are too busy."

"Um, can I at least see her portfolio first? I'm not too comfortable letting anyone do my hair."

"You act like she's going to shave your head or something. Come on, Rocky. Do you think I would let her style you if she weren't good?"

Rocky still wasn't sure, but she didn't want to offend Aiden or his sister. If he was certain she was good, then it shouldn't be that bad to let her style her. Since she was in cosmetology school, she was somewhat of a professional. It wouldn't hurt to give her a shot.

"I guess," Rocky said apprehensively. "But I still want to see her portfolio first."

"Fine. You can ask for yourself when practice is over."

After they finished rehearsing for the day, Rocky followed Aiden into his living room, where his sister was waiting. She was going to drive them to her rented salon studio for the makeover. Rocky already told her mom so she wouldn't freak out about it later.

"Hey," Aiden's sister said once they were in the living room. "I'm Kaylah, and you must be Aiden's girl."

Rocky waved and looked down with a slight smile on her face. She got butterflies in her stomach when Kaylah called her Aiden's girl.

"I'm Rocky," she said softly.

"It's nice to finally meet you. Are you ready to get your hair and makeup slayed?"

"Um, can I see your portfolio first? Just to see what you do before you get started?"

Kaylah seemed a bit taken aback by Rocky's question, which worried her. Rocky was afraid she might've angered Kaylah and thought Rocky assumed she was a bad stylist.

"If you want," Rocky added.

"No worries," Kaylah replied. "Can I show you once we get to the studio? My portfolio is there."

"Sure."

Kaylah's studio was about five minutes from Aiden's house, and when they got there, Rocky was amazed at how pretty and professional it looked. The walls were painted pink and had floral designs all around them. In one corner, there was a ring light near a red-carpet backdrop. That's probably where Kaylah took all her client's photos for her portfolio. Aiden decided to stay outside until Kaylah finished so he would be surprised by the result.

"Your studio looks amazing," Rocky said in awe.

"Thanks, girl," Kaylah said. "I wanted to make sure my space had some personality. Ready to get started?"

"Do you have any previous work I can see first?"

"Oh, right," Kaylah said with a laugh. She opened her dresser, pulled out a small tablet, and opened her gallery before handing it to Rocky. "Swipe left to see all my latest work."

All the pictures she saw were breathtaking. Rocky almost thought these clients could be models with how detailed their makeup looked and how silky smooth their hair was. She would be amazed if Kaylah could make plain old Rocky look *that* flawless.

"Wow, you're fantastic," Rocky said.

"Thanks, girl," Kaylah said. "Take your hair down and let me feel it for a bit."

Rocky took her hair out of its ponytail and let Kaylah run her fingers through it. "This is a thick head of hair you have," she said with a chuckle.

"Yeah. It gets a little hard to manage at times," Rocky admitted. "You think you can tame it?"

"Girl, there's nothing I can't do. Before we get started, I want to ask some questions. Are you allergic to any products or ingredients?"

"Not that I know of."

"Have you ever flat ironed your hair before?"

"Rarely. I'm afraid of the heat."

"Are you tender-headed? How's your scalp?"

"I'm not that tender-headed, but after I wash my hair, my scalp gets dry, itchy, and flaky."

"Okay, I have just the thing for that. Unless you have any questions, it's time to get this party started."

As Rocky sat down, Kaylah began combing Rocky's thick hair. There were moments when the comb got stuck in Rocky's hair, and Kaylah had to yank on it, which was painful for Rocky. She tried her best to keep quiet.

"Your hair loves eating combs, doesn't it?" Kaylah said jokingly.

Rocky giggled and then winced as Kaylah combed through another knot. Once her hair became less tangled and easier to comb, Kaylah put a cold cream in Rocky's hair that soothed her scalp. She started feeling a bit more relaxed.

"What are you putting in my hair?" Rocky asked out of curiosity.

"It's a deep conditioner," Kaylah said. "It'll make your hair softer and much easier to manage."

"Looks like it's working already," Rocky said.

After Kaylah applied the deep conditioner to Rocky's hair, she placed a bonnet on her head and let it sit.

"What does this do for my hair?" Rocky asked.

"It needs to sit for about five minutes to penetrate and deep condition your hair," Kaylah explained.

"It won't cause any permanent changes to my hair, will it?" Rocky gasped. Her mom would kill her if she did something drastic like that.

"Is this 21 Questions?" Kaylah asked. Rocky thought there was some edge in her tone, but she started laughing instead. "Relax and enjoy the process, girl. I got you."

Rocky decided to stay quiet for the rest of the appointment. She worried that her many questions offended Kaylah. Rocky was only curious and wanted to know what she was doing. She didn't want Kaylah to think she doubted her cosmetic skills.

After Kaylah rinsed out the deep conditioner, she washed, conditioned, blow-dried, moisturized, and flat-ironed her hair. That deep conditioner truly made Rocky's hair feel much softer, and she loved it! After Kaylah finished Rocky's hair, she did her makeup. The whole thing took almost two hours, and Rocky was facing away from the mirror the entire time, so she couldn't see the process.

"Okay, girl," Kaylah said. "You're all finished, and you look fabulous! Are you ready to see?"

"I'm ready," Rocky said enthusiastically.

Kaylah spun Rocky around to face the mirror. When she looked up, she gasped, barely recognizing the girl staring back at her. Her hair was shiny, sleek, bone straight, and stopped at her mid-back. She didn't even know she had that much hair! The foundation she wore made her skin look smooth and clear for the first time. Her eyebrows looked perfect. The golden eyeshadow and false lashes made her eyes pop. The shimmering lip gloss made her lips look plump and juicy. All she could do was gawk at herself.

"I love it!" Rocky shrieked.

"Aww, I knew you would," Kaylah said.

For the first time in her life, Rocky couldn't stop staring at herself in the mirror. This was the first time in her life she felt beautiful. She couldn't stop running her fingers through her now manageable hair.

"Do you have any samples of all the products you used for my hair?" Rocky asked eagerly.

"Uh, no. Unfortunately, I don't."

"Well, could you tell me where I could get some? These products work miracles!"

"My school gave me these products, so I'm not too sure where they're from. But if you ever want to get your hair and makeup done like this again, you know where to find me!"

"Of course! I'll even recommend you to some other people. I'm in love with how I look right now!"

Kaylah smiled. "You're too sweet," she said. "Let's get these after pictures for my portfolio, grab Aiden, and get you home."

After Kaylah shot a few pictures of Rocky on her tablet, she cleaned up her studio, locked up, and then walked outside with Rocky. Aiden was sitting by the door looking at his phone.

"Introducing the new and improved Rocky," Kaylah announced once they were outside.

When Aiden saw Rocky, he looked just as amazed as she was when she first saw her new, made-over look. "Wow," was all he could say.

Rocky smiled and blushed. "What do you think? Do you like it?"

"I *love* it! I didn't think it was possible for you to be any more beautiful."

Rocky couldn't stop smiling and looking at the ground.

"That two-hour wait was worth it," Aiden whispered.

"Let's get her home," Kaylah said, "so she can show off her new look."

Kaylah dropped Rocky off at her house, and Aiden walked her to the front door. Her mom's car wasn't in the driveway, so she could have some one-on-one time with Aiden without any awkward interruptions. Maybe even her first kiss?

"You look amazing," Aiden said, taking Rocky's hand into his. "I can't stop looking at you."

"Your sister did an incredible job," Rocky said softly. "I love this look."

"Me too." Aiden tucked a lock of Rocky's hair behind her ear and smiled at her. That wouldn't have gone so smoothly if she had her hair in a puff! This moment was too perfect. Rocky smiled back at Aiden.

"I guess this is goodbye for now," Aiden said. "I can't wait to see you again." He kissed her on the cheek before returning to Kaylah's car, and Rocky went inside her house.

Rocky ran to the nearest mirror and gazed at herself once more. She felt her confidence skyrocket. Aiden loved her new look! *And* he kissed her on the cheek. She was on top of the world. For once in her life, everything was going great.

Rocky was excited to show her mom her new look. She never let Rocky wear makeup or straighten her hair, so this would likely be a shock. Maybe after seeing how good Rocky looked with straight hair and makeup, her mom might let her do it more often.

Rocky patiently waited in her room when she heard the front door open and ran downstairs. Rochelle was smiling when she walked in the door, but when she saw how Rocky looked, her smile instantly dropped.

"Rocky, what did you do to your hair?" she asked frantically. "And why are you wearing so much makeup? Did you get a perm after I specifically told you not to?"

"No, it's not a perm. I got it flat ironed," Rocky explained. "That's the favor I did for Aiden's sister. She's in cosmetology school and needed a client to makeover. What do you think?"

Rochelle ran her fingers through Rocky's hair and sighed. "You know I don't like anyone doing your hair."

Rocky was hoping to get a better reaction than the one she was getting now. She should've known her mom would freak out on her like this.

"What did this girl use in your hair?" Rochelle asked. "If she gave you any sort of heat or chemical damage, she'll be hearing from me."

"She put in a deep conditioner before she washed it," Rocky said.

"Wait, she deep conditioned your hair *before* she shampooed it?"

"Why does that matter?"

"Because you're supposed to deep condition after you wash it, or it won't be as productive. Do you know what she put in your hair?"

"I don't know, Mom."

"Raquel Coleman, why didn't you ask this girl what she was putting in your hair?"

"Mom, she's a professional. I think it looks good. Don't you like it?"

Rochelle ran her fingers through Rocky's hair again. "You do look nice," she said. "What I'm worried about is your hair getting heat damaged. Not everyone knows how to style natural hair properly."

"I looked at her portfolio before she did my hair. She's an incredible stylist."

"I wish you would've told me about this beforehand."

Rocky held her head down. "I'm sorry," she said quietly. "I wanted to surprise you, and I thought you would like it."

Rochelle sat down, and Rocky sat next to her.

"Did she at least put a heat protectant in your hair?" Rochelle asked.

Rocky couldn't remember. Kaylah put so many products in Rocky's hair and was already annoyed that Rocky was asking too many questions.

"I'm sure she did," Rocky said. "I promise everything will be fine, Mom. As soon as I wash my hair, it'll revert to the coils you taught me to embrace."

"Oh, it better," Rochelle said. "If it doesn't, then this girl will regret damaging your hair."

Rocky laughed and hugged her mom. Even though Rochelle could be overbearing, Rocky couldn't help but love how much her mom cared about her.

A few days later, Rocky, Hayley, and Adam were all hanging out in The Studio before Rocky had to rehearse with Aiden and the guys. She hadn't been able to see them as much as she wanted to all winter break since she was so busy with rehearsals, concerts, and hanging out with Aiden. Rocky missed being at The Studio and made sure to spend some time with her best friends. This would be their first time seeing Rocky in person with her new hairstyle.

"You look different with straight hair," Adam said. "I like it on you."

"Thanks, Adam," Rocky said. "Aiden's sister did it a few days ago. She also did my makeup."

"Isn't your mom picky about who can touch your hair?" Adam chuckled.

"Oh, yeah," Rocky laughed, too. "She wasn't thrilled about it at first, but I think it's growing on her now. Besides, Kaylah is in cosmetology school, so she knows what she's doing. And I looked at her portfolio before I let her style me. She's a beast."

"Well, she did do a great job. It was nice of her to hook you up. Unlike her stupid brother, she..."

"Could you not?" Rocky cut him off. "You promised."

Adam held his hands up. "I apologize."

Hayley had been at the drum set making a lot of noise.

"I wish we had a drummer in our family," Hayley laughed. "I need someone to teach me how to play!"

"One of the guys in Aiden's group is a drummer," Rocky said.

"That's great! You should have him come over and give me some drumming lessons."

"Hayley, you know you'd just flirt with him if he came over," Adam joked.

Hayley dramatically gasped and placed a hand over her chest. "That's absurd, Adam," she said. "I would do no such thing!"

"Girl, yes, you would," Rocky teased.

"Okay, maybe a little," Hayley laughed.

"Enough boy talk! I want to have a jam session," Adam said. "Go grab your instruments, and let's play something."

"I already have mine!" Hayley said, holding up a drumstick in each hand.

"Hayley, put those drumsticks down and get your guitar," Rocky said. "You're not a drummer."

"Not yet, I'm not." As Hayley got up and picked up her pink guitar, Adam sat at the keyboard, and Rocky grabbed the microphone.

"Testing...one, two, three," Rocky said into the mic. "Freestyle or cover?"

"Ooh, freestyle," Adam said enthusiastically. "Let's get those creative juices flowing and write us a song." He began playing some riffs on the keyboard, and Hayley started playing her guitar shortly after.

Rocky moved to the rhythm of what Hayley and Adam were playing. She wasn't the best at freestyling, so she put together some random lyrics that made no sense.

"I get on with life as a student,

I'm a shy kinda person.
I like watching TV and listening to music.
I like to contemplate yellow.
But when I start to daydream,
My mind turns straight to blue.
Shala la la la la la!"

Hayley and Adam couldn't continue playing because they were both doubled over in laughter at Rocky's nonsensical song lyrics.

"Girl, what the heck was that?" Hayley asked.

"I call it 'Utter Nonsense,' and I'll have you know that was a banger," Rocky joked.

"Maybe I should come up with the lyrics for you to sing," Adam laughed.

For the next fifteen minutes, the three of them came up with a hook and a verse, but Rocky had to rehearse at Aiden's house for the New Year's concert.

"But we were having fun," Hayley said. "Do you have to go now?"

"Yeah, I have the New Year's concert to sing at tomorrow night, remember?" Rocky reminded her. "Will you guys be there?"

"My whole family said they were going to go," Hayley told her. "Isn't that great? They all want to support you."

"That's great." Rocky looked at Adam. "Will you be there?"

"I'm sorry, but I can't," Adam told her. "My dad volunteered me at the last minute to play for my church's Watch Night service."

"Oh no, I really wanted you to be there," Rocky said.

"I promise I'll make it up to you."

Rocky glanced at the clock. "I gotta go, but I'll see you guys later," Rocky said before leaving.

The New Year's concert was at the performing arts theater instead of the outdoor amphitheater they usually perform at, so the crowd was much larger. Kaylah would also be styling Rocky and the other dancers for this performance, so she got her hair straightened again and was glammed up. Aiden wanted this to be the concert of the year, so he wanted everyone to look their best. They performed another one of Aiden's originals called "New Days," which was the perfect contemporary R&B song for the New Year. It was about growth, leaving behind the old, and going after the new. After the performances ended at around 11: 50 p.m., the countdown to the new year started. They all celebrated once the clock struck midnight.

11

After a holiday break full of excitement, Rocky was a little bummed about going back to school. At least freshman year was officially halfway over. And more people got to see her with straight hair! When Rocky arrived at school on Monday morning, she got a lot of compliments on it. She still had to get used to people other than Hayley and Adam talking to her.

"I can't get over how gorgeous your hair looks," Hayley said in the courtyard.

"Thanks," Rocky said. "I already had so many people compliment me, and school hasn't even started yet! I wonder if I could convince my mom to let me get it straightened more often."

"What did Aiden say about it?"

Rocky smiled. "He loves it. He tells me every day how beautiful I am and runs his fingers through my hair."

"Aww, you guys are too cute!" Hayley laughed.

Rocky also laughed, and then she looked at Adam. He was unusually quiet. "No snide comments about Aiden today?" she joked.

Adam rolled his eyes but laughed. "It seems like no matter what I say about him, you never hear, so what's the point?"

"Come on, Adam. I keep telling you he's not a bad guy. Maybe if you would get to know him better..."

"Trust me, Rocky. I know what kind of guy he is."

Rocky tried everything she could to convince Adam that Aiden wasn't corrupt. She couldn't understand why Adam would think otherwise. Aiden was the kindest gentleman Rocky could ever ask for, and nothing, not even Adam's pessimism, was going to change her mind about that.

Rocky had gotten numerous compliments on her hair throughout the day and enjoyed every moment. Her new look gave her a level of confidence she never thought she could achieve. Some people hadn't even recognized Rocky without her signature puff. However, things quickly began to take a turn for the worse.

A week later, Rocky's hair was falling out in clumps every time she combed it. She also noticed her hair wasn't reverting to its natural kinky-curly texture, even after she washed and conditioned it. Rocky feared her hair might've gotten horrible heat damage from getting it straightened twice in two weeks. Or worse: whatever Kaylah put in her hair might not have been what she said it was. Rocky almost didn't want to tell her mom because she knew an "I told you so" would follow. However, this was too horrible to be left alone, and she didn't know what else to do.

When Rochelle came home, Rocky ran to the front door teary-eyed.

"Mom, I think something's wrong," she sobbed. "My hair is breaking like crazy, and it's not curling like it used to."

Rocky's mom closed her eyes, tightened her jaw, and exhaled heavily. She did that when she was infuriated and ready to snap at someone.

"What did that girl put in your hair?" she asked, trying to keep her tone calm.

"I don't know," Rocky admitted. "She told me it was a deep conditioner but never said the name. She said she got it from school."

Rochelle carefully examined Rocky's hair. "Did she ever complain about how 'nappy' your hair was?"

Rocky wiped her eyes. "I wouldn't say she complained, but she was surprised at how thick my hair was."

"Do you remember what the deep conditioner smelled like?"

Rocky sighed and tried to think about it. "It had kind of a funky smell to it. Why?"

"I think I know what that snake did. She mixed a relaxer with the deep conditioner before putting it in your hair. She secretly permed your hair, Rocky."

Rocky couldn't stop crying. What kind of hairstylist would perm their client's hair without their consent? She trusted Kaylah; why would she do something so cruel? Rocky felt angry, stupid, and betrayed.

"Rocky, nobody is allowed to touch your hair except me, okay?" Rochelle said. She was just as angry as Rocky. "This is going to take forever to fix."

"What are we going to do?"

"I'll tell you what *I'm* going to do. I'm going to have a talk with this girl because she messed with the wrong one. I swear nobody has respect for curly hair."

Rocky held her head down and couldn't stop crying. "I'm sorry, Mom," was all she could say.

"Don't cry, Rocky," Rochelle said, hugging Rocky. "She should've told you what products she put in your hair. A professional hairstylist doesn't do these kinds of things.

What's this girl's name? I never want to see her working in an actual salon."

"Her name is Kaylah," Rocky said. "I recommended her to a lot of girls at school."

"Find all those girls and tell them not to let that witch touch their hair. Do you know what school this girl attends? I'll get her expelled if I have to. So help me, I'll make sure she never gets a cosmetology license."

"Mom, please just relax," Rocky cried. She loved her mother dearly, but she could turn into a lunatic when it came to her family. Rocky wanted to focus on repairing her hair, not ruining Kaylah's career.

"I'm calm."

Rocky looked at her limp hair and sighed. "Will I have to cut it all off?" she asked her mom.

"I want to say no, but the damage looks irreversible. I'll try everything I can to help, but you might have to cut it."

Rocky had long hair all her life. It made her feel somewhat decent looking, so it terrified her that she might have to cut it all off.

Over the next few days, Rocky and her mom tried different treatments to get her hair healthy again. She tried protein treatments, hair masks, and moisturizing more, but her hair continued to fall out. Rocky brought up the situation to Aiden during rehearsal one day after school, hoping for an explanation. She expected him to at least show her some sympathy, but instead, she got the opposite.

"Do you seriously think my sister would do something like that?" he asked defensively.

"Well, yeah, because she did it," Rocky explained. She took her hair out of its bun to show Aiden her stringy locks. "See? She mixed relaxer with the deep conditioner, and now it's damaged."

Aiden rolled his eyes. "I can't believe you would accuse Kaylah of doing something so awful."

"Aiden," Rocky tried to explain.

"She's a professional and would never do anything like that to her clients. Everybody who sees her gives her positive feedback. Why do you have to be the only negative one?"

Rocky held her head down. Why didn't Aiden believe her?

"Your sister is a good stylist," Rocky began. "It's just the fact that she...."

"She would never do that, Rocky!" Aiden snapped. "Your hair was fine after she styled it. Maybe you did something wrong and damaged your hair."

Rocky couldn't believe what she was hearing. Aiden didn't even try to hear her out. Did he seriously think she would give his sister a bad name for the heck of it?

"But I'm telling you the truth," Rocky whimpered. She was starting to get teary-eyed. "I wouldn't try to make your sister look bad if I didn't have a real reason. I can't let her get away with this."

"So, what are you going to do? Tell everyone not to go to Kaylah because you messed up your own hair? Cosmetology means everything to her, just like how music means everything to you. Would you want to do that to her? To me?"

Rocky was silent for a moment. She wanted to empathize with him, but she couldn't. If cosmetology meant so much to Kaylah, why would she do something this wicked and try to get away with it? If cosmetology meant so much to her, she should know better than to secretly put a relaxer in her client's hair.

Rocky sighed. "She can't get away with this," she repeated.

Now Aiden was silent. He couldn't even look at Rocky, and that killed her on the inside.

"I think you should go," he told her.

Rocky didn't get up right away. She didn't know what else to say or do. Why was Aiden acting like this?

"Now," he said.

Rocky finally got up and left, feeling worse than she did before.

After trying every possible hair treatment with no success, Rocky had to cut off all her hair. Rochelle helped Rocky cut off her limp locks, and she broke down in tears after seeing all her hair on the floor. She was only left with about two inches of hair. Looking at her teeny-weeny afro made her feel even worse about herself. There was no hair to hide her chubby face and imperfections. Rocky was also afraid having shorter hair would make her look like a boy.

Rochelle stood behind Rocky and smiled at her in the mirror.

"It'll grow back full and healthy in no time," Rochelle reassured her.

Rocky felt like a giant weight was sitting on her chest and couldn't stop the tears from falling. "I'm not going out like this," she said.

"I know it's a drastic change, but you can't let it stop you from going out."

"I don't want anybody to see me like this."

"Oh, Rocky."

"I look even uglier than I did before!"

"Raquel, do not talk about yourself like that. You know that's not true. You're so beautiful."

"Mom, look at me!" Rocky cried. "I don't have any hair. My face is fat, my nose is huge, and not having hair makes it stand out even more. I'm not beautiful. I'm hideous!" She ran to her room, locked her door, and cried into her pillow.

Her confidence was so shattered that she stayed in her room for the past two days. Rocky was determined to remain in hiding until her hair grew back to the length it was before Kaylah damaged it. She didn't care about missing school or rehearsal. She didn't want to talk to anyone, even Hayley or Adam. Nothing her mom said helped cheer her up. Rochelle had to go out and buy some wigs to get Rocky out of the house.

"Even though I think you're way too young for wigs," Rochelle started. "If it'll help you get out of this funk, you can wear some of these until your hair grows long enough for box braids. Then we can keep braiding it until it gets to your desired length. You don't have to go out with short hair if you don't want."

Rocky turned over in bed to see the wigs her mom had bought.

"Rocky, I also need you to understand that hair doesn't define beauty," Rochelle continued. "You were beautiful before you cut your hair, and you're still beautiful now. And I'm not just saying that because I'm your mom."

"I don't feel beautiful," Rocky said, her voice a bit hoarse.

"Being beautiful is more than about how you look. And society always puts these unrealistic beauty standards on women. A perfect body, clear skin, long hair, and whatnot don't make a woman beautiful. Having a good heart and how you carry yourself is what counts." Rochelle placed a hand on Rocky's back. "And I know it sounds like I'm spewing a bunch of clichéd stuff, but it's true. I don't ever want to hear you call yourself ugly again. Do you hear me, Raquel?"

"Okay, Mom," Rocky said.

"I mean it. You're beautiful on the inside and the outside. I want you to keep saying that to yourself."

"I'm beautiful on the inside and the outside," Rocky mumbled unenthusiastically.

"Say it like you mean it."

"But I don't mean it."

"The more you say it, the more you'll start to believe it. Trust me, it works."

Rocky sighed.

"We need to work on your self-esteem," Rochelle said. "It broke my heart to see you feeling this bad about yourself. Why don't you take a shower, get dressed, and we can go out to dinner tonight? I can invite the Marin and Wolfe family if you'd like. What do you say?"

"Where would we go?" Rocky asked.

"Your favorite restaurant in the whole world."

Rocky sat up. "Uncle Mike's Steakhouse?" she eagerly asked.

"That's the one," Rochelle said with a smile.

Rocky's dad used to take them to Uncle Mike's Steakhouse, and they had the juiciest, tastiest steaks Rocky ever had. The restaurant was rather pricey, so they only went on special occasions.

Rocky finally got out of bed, showered, and brushed her teeth for the first time in two days. She barely ate anything during that time, so she was ready for some steak!

After spending the evening with her mom, Hayley's family, and Adam's family at her favorite restaurant, she felt better. She was thankful to be surrounded by people who loved her and made her feel good about herself.

***

The next morning at school, Rocky told Hayley and Adam about what happened. She didn't want to get into it while they were having a good time at Uncle Mike's Steakhouse. Rocky told them about Kaylah, Aiden not believing her, and her low moment when she didn't want to get out of bed.

"I'm so sorry you had to go through that, Rocky," Hayley sighed. "Gosh, and I can't believe Aiden didn't believe you when you said his sister messed up your hair."

"His entire family is corrupt," Adam said.

"Stop it, Adam," Hayley hissed.

"Let's be real here. You've been doing your hair your entire life, and it was perfectly healthy. You go to his sister once, end up with chemical damage, and it's not her fault?"

"He insisted his sister would never do such a thing," Rocky said. "He seemed upset that I accused her of damaging my hair."

"I don't know what to say about that," Hayley said. "I understand it's his sister and everything, but you're his girlfriend. He should've at least talked to his sister about the whole thing instead of shutting you down."

"I guess what got him the most upset was my mom going to his house and cursing his sister out about the whole thing."

Adam and Hayley burst into laughter, but Rocky remained serious. A few days after Rocky went to her mom about the chemical damage, Rochelle went to Aiden's house without Rocky's knowledge and gave Kaylah a piece of her mind. Rocky's mom demanded Kaylah apologize for what she did. Of course, Kaylah denied everything, and from how Rocky's mom and Aiden described, things got a little heated before Rochelle finally left. Even though Rocky wasn't there when it happened, she was utterly embarrassed her mom did that.

"Your mom really cursed out Aiden's sister?" Hayley asked in between laughs.

"It's not funny, guys," Rocky said. "Aiden and I haven't spoken much since then. What if he breaks up with me because of it? What if he kicks me out of the group, and I go back to being a nobody again?"

"Rocky, you can't be serious right now," Adam said, outraged. "Aiden's sister damaged your hair so badly that you had to cut it all off, and you're worried about him dumping you and kicking you out of his group? You hadn't left your room for two days because of her, and he believed her over you. How could you still take his side after all you've been through?"

"It's not that I'm taking his side," Rocky explained. "I know what his sister did was wrong, and I wish he would believe me. I don't want him to think I'm blaming his sister for my damaged hair just to be mean."

"How will you convince him what his sister did to you, though?" Hayley asked.

Rocky shrugged. "I don't know. Maybe I can try to look for the deep conditioner she put in my hair and show him that it was mixed with perm product."

"I don't think you should be trying this hard to get him to believe you," Adam said. "This only proves what kind of guy he is."

Rocky didn't have anything to say to that. She would believe Aiden was a nice guy, no matter how much Adam tried to convince her otherwise.

On her way to her last class of the day, Rocky ran into Aiden in the hallway. It was her first time seeing him since she tried to tell him about what his sister had done to her hair. He kept his hands in front of him, similarly to how Rocky stood when she was nervous about something.

"Hey," he said softly.

"Hi," Rocky said with her head down.

"Your hair looks good. It looks different. What did you do to it?"

"I'm wearing a wig."

"Oh."

The last time Rocky had seen Aiden this timid was when he told her he wanted her to be his girlfriend. She wondered what was on his mind now.

"Has your natural hair recovered yet?" Aiden asked. "You know, from the last time you got it done?"

Rocky shook her head. "No. I had to cut it all off. That's why I wasn't at school for the last two days. And why I'm wearing a wig."

"I'm so sorry about that," Aiden said with his head down. "Is there anything I can do to make it up to you?"

Rocky figured Kaylah had finally confessed to what she had done. Or he realized her absence meant something was seriously wrong. Rocky never understood why Aiden didn't believe her in the first place and shrugged her shoulders. "Not unless you know of any products that will make all my hair grow back overnight," she joked.

Aiden stifled a laugh. "Unfortunately, I don't." He put his head down again and sighed. "I can't believe she did that to your hair. It's so unlike her."

Rocky didn't say anything. She kept her head down too.

"I'm sorry I didn't believe you," Aiden said.

"It's okay."

"Are you sure?"

Rocky nodded silently. She appreciated the apology. It showed how much he cared, which made her feel better.

"I hate seeing you down like this," Aiden told her. "It makes me feel bad."

"Well, it's not like *you* did this to me," Rocky said.

"But I feel like it's my fault. I sang her praises, and she turned around and damaged your hair. I feel terrible about this."

"You couldn't have known she would do this." Rocky couldn't help but notice the troubled look on Aiden's face. She could tell he felt awful about his poor reaction to Rocky a few days ago. "It's okay, Aiden," she reassured him.

"I swear to you, this is the first time something like this has happened with one of her clients," Aiden said. "I don't understand why she would do that to you."

Rocky took Aiden's hand into hers. She was touched that he was now showing how much he cared. She only wished he had done so when she first told him about the incident. But better late than never.

"Aiden, it's fine," she told him again.

"You're not mad at me?"

"I'm not mad at you."

Aiden sighed with relief. "That's great. I really am sorry about what she did. I'm sure your hair will be long and healthy in no time."

"That's what I'm hoping for," Rocky said.

"Long hair, short hair, wig, or whatever, you're still the same beautiful Rocky I fell for."

Rocky smiled and tried not to look down, but she couldn't help it. It was just a natural reflex!

"Thanks, Aiden," she said. "That means a lot to me.

Aiden gently pulled Rocky into a bear hug. She could've melted in his arms right there.

"I promise I'll make it up to you," Aiden told her softly.

Rocky sighed happily, enjoying every moment in Aiden's warm embrace. Her doubts and worries faded away every second she was in his arms. For the first time in a while, she was starting to feel better about herself.

The next day between classes, Angel stopped Rocky in the hallway before Rocky could walk to her classroom.

"Hey, Rocky, wait," he called out. "Do you have a second? I want to ask you a quick question."

"Yeah, what's up?" Rocky said.

Angel's face turned bright red as he began shifting his weight from one foot to the other. "Um, so you know your friend, right?"

Rocky giggled at his question. "Which one?"

"Hayley's her name, right?"

"Yeah, what about her?"

"Does she have a boyfriend? Or does she like anybody at school or anything?"

Rocky giggled again. She had to admit Angel's awkwardness was too adorable. She was also used to guys talking to Rocky only to ask about Hayley. Since Angel was her friend, she didn't mind giving Hayley a good word about him. Rocky thought they would make a cute couple!

"Nope," Rocky said. "No boyfriend and no crush that I know of. Is there somebody interested in her?"

Angel rubbed the back of his neck and awkwardly chuckled. "Um, yeah," he said. "That someone is me."

Rocky couldn't stop herself from gushing. "Aww, that's so sweet!"

"Do you think you could talk to her for me and let her know I like her? Whenever I try to talk to her in between classes, I get tongue-tied and super nervous. Then I chicken out."

"Of course, I can tell her you're interested! But I should let you know she likes it when a guy pursues her. She probably won't believe me until you tell her how you feel about her."

"Every time I look at her, I freeze up. I don't want to make myself look stupid in front of her."

"Oh, trust me. You won't."

The second bell rang, and students hurried through the hallway to make it to their classes before the final bell rang.

"How about this? After school, I can help you come up with the right things to say when you're ready to profess your love for Hayley."

Angel laughed at Rocky's joke. "Sounds like a good idea."

"I can't wait! I would love to see you two together."

"Rocky, you're a lifesaver. Thank you."

"No problem. Now get to class before you're late," Rocky joked.

Angel laughed. "Alright, I'll see you soon. And thanks again!" Angel waved before hurrying off, and Rocky went to her class.

12

Aiden, Rocky, and the guys had an upcoming performance, so they all met up that afternoon with the dancers for one last practice before the show. They were performing another one of Aiden's originals called "Dangerously," which featured a reggae-pop beat. It was a fun song about going after what you want by taking risks and living "dangerously."

While Aiden was outside on the phone, Rocky, the guys, and the dancers were all in Aiden's garage waiting for him to finish up. Renaldo made some herbal tea and brought it to practice for everyone. He generally made tea and provided some for everyone before a concert because Renaldo says it's great for soothing the throat. Rocky thought it was nice of him to go the extra mile for everyone. As everyone drank their tea and waited for Aiden to come back inside, they entertained themselves by joking, laughing, and having a good time.

"You know what irritates me?" Angel asked. "Why does Aiden still make us dance even though we have the dancers now?"

"Honestly, who knows why Aiden does some of the stuff he does?" one of the dancers joked.

"I mean, Aiden always complains about how I have no rhythm but continues to make me dance — even though we have actual dancers in the group now! Like, what is this?"

Rocky laughed. "I feel you on that one," she agreed. "I have no rhythm, either."

"No big deal," Marcus said. "Everyone will be looking at him instead of us anyway."

"Also true," Rocky said.

Marcus took another long sip of his tea. "Renaldo, this is some good stuff."

"I know," Angel agreed. "After drinking a cup of your tea, I feel so relaxed. My throat feels so great, and I feel like I can hit those opera notes."

Angel's joke made everyone laugh.

"You dare me to try?" Angel asked.

"Please don't!" Renaldo said.

"No, Angel!" Marcus said at the same time. "Last time you tried to show out, you nearly blew my eardrums."

"Hey, I've expanded my range since then," Angel joked.

Rocky couldn't stop giggling at the boys' silliness.

"Rocky, you wouldn't believe what this fool did," Marcus said. "A couple of months ago, Angel tried to hit a whistle tone."

"No way," she said in disbelief. "Can Angel's voice go that high?

"Of course not," Renaldo laughed. "He tried to hit that note in "Emotions" and failed epically."

"He sounded more like a screaming chick in a horror film about to get slaughtered," Marcus said.

Angel laughed. "Oh, come on. It wasn't that bad."

"No, it was bad," Marcus said. "Please don't ever try to sing that song again, dude. Leave it to Mariah."

"Whatever. You're just hating on my mad vocal range," Angel joked.

"Rocky, I wish you could've been there," Renaldo said. "It was too funny."

"I can imagine," Rocky said.

This was the most fun Rocky had during rehearsal. Sure, they barely rehearsed. Nonetheless, Rocky had a blast with the guys. She enjoyed the close bond they had with each other. Their mellow personalities made them easy to talk to, and their goofiness made them a lot of fun to be around.

After a while of joking around and laughing, Rocky almost forgot they had all gathered to rehearse. She and the guys were having so much fun that it almost didn't feel like they had a concert to perform at in a few hours.

"No offense to him or anything, but rehearsals aren't this fun when Aiden's around," Rocky said. "Like, he's always so serious, and you guys like to have a good time."

The three boys nodded in agreement.

"Yeah, we understand," Angel said. "It's never this chill while Aiden's here."

"He's also pretty brutal at our dance rehearsals," one of the dancers commented. "It's like we can never get things right."

"We thought your rehearsals were like this all the time," another dancer commented.

"Nope, Aiden sucks the fun out of the rehearsals with his seriousness and harsh criticism," Marcus said.

"Maybe that could be why he's so stressed and hard on us all the time," Rocky said. "He probably just needs to let loose for once, and maybe he'll be a lot nicer."

The guys shrugged, then the garage door swung open. Everyone went from chill mode to work mode in a matter of seconds before Aiden made his way into the garage.

"Sorry for taking so long," he said. "I hope you all were being productive while I was gone." He poured himself a cup of Renaldo's tea.

Rocky swore the environment got less lighthearted now that Aiden was back.

"Okay," he said. "Let's not waste any more time. We have a show to do tonight."

Without hesitation, they began practicing. After about fifteen minutes of rehearsing, things already started getting tense. They couldn't get through the entire song because Aiden kept stopping them and pointing out things that were wrong. After their fifth take, Aiden grew increasingly frustrated.

"What's wrong with you guys?" he asked in exasperation.

"What do you mean?" Angel argued. "We got it right."

"No, you guys aren't getting it right. You're going too high, and Marcus, you're singing off-key. Don't even get me started on the choreography being all wrong. You're all doing terrible right now."

"Aiden..." Angel tried reasoning with him, but Aiden wasn't hearing any of it.

"You guys better not make me look bad in front of all those people tonight," Aiden continued. "This is serious, so act like you care already."

"*Que cabrón*," Renaldo mumbled under his breath. It wasn't soft enough because Aiden heard.

"Speak English or get out!" Aiden hollered.

"Listen, man," Marcus said. "It's hard to try to sound our best when you always criticize us. Maybe if you would lighten up a bit..."

"I'm losing my patience with all of you," Aiden interjected. "Can you not screw up this one performance?"

Rocky didn't think they sounded too bad for Aiden to yell at them the way he was. Since he was usually on his worst behavior right before a performance, Rocky assumed the stress from preparing for the concert was getting to him, and he needed to relax for a bit.

"Let's take a break," he sighed. "Go outside and do something. I'm sick of all of you."

Everyone went to Aiden's living room without hesitation, but Rocky stayed behind to make sure Aiden was okay. He sat down on the couch with his head in his hands, and Rocky went to sit next to him. She placed a comforting hand on Aiden's back, but he pushed her away.

"I told you to go outside," he snapped.

"You just seem tense, and I wanted to make you feel better," she said meekly.

"You can make me feel better by disappearing."

Rocky stared at Aiden with wide, confused eyes. She didn't expect him to be this harsh to her when she was only trying to help. "Okay," she said. "If that's what you want." Rocky was halfway to the door when Aiden spoke up, stopping her in her tracks.

"And about your little comment from before," he said. "If I'm not serious, then we won't be able to function. This group needs someone who's serious about this."

Rocky was confused at first but then remembered her comment earlier about rehearsals being more fun without Aiden. Her heart hammered in her chest.

"I didn't think you heard that," Rocky stammered over her words. "I thought you were outside, Aiden, I'm so sorry."

"I only take this so seriously because you guys don't. All you do is joke around, and it's affecting our performances. Don't you realize how important this is for me?"

"I know how important it is for you," Rocky said apologetically. "I'm sorry."

"No, you're not," Aiden said coldly. "You don't care, and you know it. It's all supposed to be fun and games for you." Aiden stared into his lap. "Maybe it was a mistake letting a girl into the group."

Rocky was close to tears. She felt like she let Aiden down when all she wanted to do was make him happy.

"I do care," she said tearfully. "I really do care. I'll take things more seriously now. I'll talk to the guys for you if you need me to."

"You said that last time."

"I mean it this time. I promise. I won't play around anymore. I'll do my best at rehearsals. Please don't be mad at me. Please."

Aiden seemed to calm down a little after seeing how hysterical Rocky was. He looked at her and sighed. "Alright, I'm not mad at you. Just stop crying."

Rocky quickly wiped away her tears, and Aiden gave Rocky a warm hug.

"I don't mean to be hard on you," Aiden said into her hair. "This is so important."

"I know," Rocky said.

"Tonight's performance has to be great. I can't afford for it to go badly."

"I understand."

"You say you understand, but do you?"

"Of course. I like giving great performances too."

"Then could you act like it, please?"

"Okay, Aiden."

Aiden kissed Rocky on the forehead. She then went to the living room to meet up with the guys.

"What's his problem?" Angel asked. "He's grouchier than ever."

"I know, right," Marcus said. "He's always quick to point out what we do wrong but never compliments us on the good things we do."

"I don't think anything was wrong with our singing," Renaldo told them. "We sounded perfectly fine to me."

"You guys sounded great," one of the dancers said. "I don't know what his issue is."

"He needs to check himself before complaining about us."

The guys stopped talking when they noticed Rocky was in the room. They sat quietly until Rocky finally spoke up.

"Guys, he's not acting like this on purpose," Rocky said to them. "He's really stressed out. He wants the concert to be perfect, and he thinks we're not taking things seriously anymore."

"He thinks we're not taking things seriously?" Angel asked in outrage. "Do you know how many sacrifices we make to sing with him? We're at practice all day and then have concerts every weekend. I can't even get my schoolwork done with everything going on, and he thinks we don't take things seriously? How much more serious does he want?"

"I think he's mad because we were goofing around today," Rocky told him. "We just have to prove to him that we are serious about this, like you said."

Angel rolled his eyes and went to sit down on the other side of the living room.

"Do you notice how easily Aiden can manipulate you?" Renaldo asked Rocky.

"What are you talking about?" Rocky replied.

"He knows how much you like him, and he's using that to his advantage. He can get you to believe anything he says and do whatever he wants. I don't want to see you get hurt by him."

"He won't hurt me," Rocky said.

"Please just be careful," Renaldo warned.

"Let's go back inside and try to do better," Rocky said, brushing off what Renaldo told her. "He's normally the most stressed right before a concert, so let's try to be more serious during those times."

None of the guys said anything.

"When he's not stressed out, he won't be so mean," Rocky explained.

Silence again. It seemed like they didn't understand Aiden the way Rocky did.

"Can someone say something?" Rocky asked. "Anyone? Please?"

"Please be careful, Rocky," Renaldo repeated.

They all went back into the garage to practice. Later that evening, they had an excellent performance at the amphitheater. At least Rocky thought it was excellent, considering they received a standing ovation from the audience! She and the guys were in perfect harmony, and the dancers didn't miss one beat during the show. However, Aiden didn't believe their performance was up to par and was upset about it. When they returned to his house, he kept going on about how they needed to start taking things more seriously. His constant complaining and criticizing wore Rocky and the guys out.

***

When Rocky came home from the concert, she was exhausted and wanted to sleep. It was after 9 p.m., and her mother wasn't home yet. Since she was working overtime, she wouldn't be back until around 11 p.m. While waiting for her mom to come home, Rocky went into the kitchen and helped herself to some leftovers from the night before. While she was eating, Hayley called her cell phone.

"Hey, Hayley," she said after swallowing a mouthful of food.

"Hey, Rocky! How was the concert?"

"It was okay."

"Just okay?"

"Yeah, pretty much."

"You seem down. What's up, girl?"

"Not much. I'm just tired. We have so many concerts, and then there's school, having a personal life, and all that.

It's a lot to take in." Rocky didn't mention the part about how Aiden's screaming and criticism wore her and the guys out.

"I would figure. With all the concerts comes more recognition. Joining Aiden's group kind of made you famous!"

Rocky laughed. "Not quite."

"But you're getting there."

There was silence for a while. Rocky wasn't sure what else to say.

"I'm glad you did this," Hayley said, breaking the silence. "I know how much it meant for you to be popular, and you finally stepped out of your comfort zone. How do you feel?"

Rocky thought about it for a moment. "Honestly, I don't know how I feel about it," she admitted. "It's exciting and everything, but also overwhelming."

"I feel you."

"I also miss when it was only me, you, and Adam."

"What do you mean? We all still hang out together."

"I know, but not as much as I'd like since I'm always busy with Aiden."

"Well, making some time to hang out with us is better than you completely ditching us for him. That's what I love about you. You still remember your friends even though you're a celebrity now."

Rocky laughed again. "Hayley, I'm not a celebrity."

"You're almost there, though!"

"Not even close!"

Hayley laughed too. "How is it like being the only girl in a group with all boys anyway? Don't you ever feel weird?"

Rocky laughed again. "It felt weird at first, but I guess I've gotten used to it. And there are some female dancers in the group, so I'm not the only girl."

"I'm not sure I would've been able to handle it, to be honest. I mean, being the only female singer surrounded by all those gorgeous guys? I would die!"

"You're insane," Rocky chuckled. "But the guys are cool and a lot of fun to be around. I want you to hang out with them one day. I think you'll like them." Rocky then realized something and giggled. "Speaking of the guys, you'll never believe which one of them is crushing on you."

"One of them likes me?" Hayley gasped. "Not possible. There's no way."

"Nope, one of them is crushing on you big time."

"Well, which one?"

"His name is Angel. He's the tall one with the green eyes."

Hayley shrieked. "Oh my gosh, he likes me? You're lying!"

"Nope, he wants you, girl! What do you think of him?"

"He's beyond cute. He's a theater student, too, so I see him occasionally. He sometimes talks to me between classes." Hayley giggled again. "I can't believe he likes me."

"Believe it. He's just shy about it."

"But he's also a junior. I've never been with someone who was that much older than me."

"Oh, age is but a number. You should give him a chance. He's such a sweetheart, and we could maybe double date one day."

"That would be perfect!"

"He gets flustered when he tries to talk to you, so next time he does, let him know you're interested in getting to know him better."

Hayley hesitated before responding. "You know I like it when guys come to me first," Hayley joked. "But since he's shy, I'll try talking to him a little more."

"That's the spirit, Hayley!"

"Can you believe we might have boyfriends together?"

"It's so exciting!"

Hayley cleared her throat. "By the way, how are things with you and Aiden?"

Rocky sighed. It didn't feel as though she and Aiden were an actual couple. Things were pretty much the same between them as they were before they began dating. They've never gone out on a date or done anything special with only the two of them. They still hadn't even kissed yet. Is this what it was supposed to be like to have a boyfriend?

Instead of saying what was on her mind, Rocky gave Hayley a vague answer. "We're great," she said. "Besides all the stress from concerts and stuff, we're totally great."

"That's great. Has he taken you anywhere special yet?"

Rocky was afraid Hayley would ask that. She hesitated. "Um, no. Not really."

Things got quiet on Hayley's end of the line, which made Rocky worried about her response. Finally, after what felt like hours of silence, Hayley spoke up. "Seriously?" she said in disbelief. "You guys have been together for over a month, and no date? No anything?"

Even Rocky had to admit how absurd that sounded. She didn't know what having a boyfriend was like and how often they were supposed to do stuff together. She was worried she was doing this whole relationship thing all wrong.

"Are you sure you guys are even dating?" Hayley asked.

"Well, he's just been so busy with concerts and school, and he hasn't had a chance to take me out on a date yet. But it'll happen soon, I'm sure." Rocky knew that had to be the lamest excuse ever, but she didn't know what else to say.

Hayley was once again quiet for another minute. "Okay," she said skeptically.

"I think I'm going to get ready for bed now," Rocky yawned. "I'm exhausted from tonight's concert. I'll see you at school tomorrow."

"Okay. Sleep well," Hayley said before hanging up.

Rocky sighed and thought about her relationship with Aiden. She was new to the dating world but figured Aiden would at least have taken her to see a movie after being together for as long as they'd been. The only time they ever saw each other was at school and during his rehearsals. The only time they were alone together was during the quick breaks at rehearsals. Was this how all relationships were supposed to start? Would they start going out more after a few more months of dating?

After Rocky finished getting ready for bed, it was hard for her to fall asleep. She was worried people would start doubting her relationship with Aiden since they didn't act like a real couple. What if people thought Rocky made the whole thing up so she could seem popular? No matter how hard she tried to put those thoughts out of her head, the whole thing about her and Aiden kept her up for most of the night.

13

After class, Rocky desperately had to go to the bathroom, so she and Hayley walked to the restroom together before going to the cafeteria for lunch. When they got there, all the stalls were occupied, and there was a line almost to the door. Rocky sighed in frustration.

"Why now?" she asked herself. "You can go ahead, Hayley. I'll meet you in the cafeteria after I'm finished."

"Are you sure?" Hayley asked. "I don't mind waiting for you."

"No, go ahead. Buy me something, and I'll pay you back?"

"If you say so. I'll be at our spot."

"Thanks so much, girl. See you in a bit."

Hayley then left, and Rocky fidgeted in place while she waited for the next available stall. *Why is there always a line in the girls' bathroom?* Rocky briefly wondered if the boys' restroom ever had lines like this. Finally, Rocky was next in line and was able to relieve herself.

After leaving the restroom, she took her cell phone out to text Hayley, not paying attention to where she was walking. As Rocky turned the corner, she collided with someone rushing from the other direction. Several sheets of paper fell on the floor.

"I'm so sorry," Rocky said, squatting down to help pick up the papers. When she looked up, she noticed the person who had run into her was Renaldo. "Oh, hey, Renaldo."

"Rocky, hi," he said while hurrying to clean up his mess. "I'm sorry for bumping into you. I was in a hurry."

"Yeah, I can see that," Rocky giggled. "Let me help you." She started picking up the last few sheets left on the floor.

"No, no. You don't have to," Renaldo stammered. He was trying to get everything up before Rocky could get to it first.

"I don't mind." Rocky peaked at one of the sheets and noticed it had some song lyrics that looked familiar. "Wait a minute. Isn't this the song Aiden was writing?" There was a new verse added to it.

Renaldo kept his head down and didn't say anything. Suddenly, he wasn't in a hurry to pick up all his papers anymore.

"Why do you have this?" Rocky asked.

"Um, he let me hold on to it for a bit," Renaldo said.

Rocky scratched her head. "Why?"

"Because..." Guilt covered Renaldo's face as he tried to think of an explanation. He couldn't look at Rocky as he was speaking. "Because he wanted me to look over it. And he wanted my opinion on it."

It was clear Renaldo didn't do well under pressure based on his horrific attempt at lying. Rocky didn't believe his story and thought he was doing something he shouldn't be. Was he stealing Aiden's song and trying to sabotage him?

"Really?" Rocky asked. "Aiden wanted your opinion on his song?"

"He happens to value my opinion."

Rocky shook her head. "Renaldo, why do you have Aiden's song?" she asked again. "Please don't lie to me."

Renaldo finally gave up and sighed. "I was going to finish writing it."

"But this is Aiden's song. Why would you...?"

"It's not his song," Renaldo admitted. "Well, he's going to sing it, but he didn't write it. I did."

Rocky stared at Renaldo with wide eyes. He couldn't have written the song. She didn't believe what Renaldo was saying and was becoming angry.

"What do you mean you wrote it? Aiden's been working on it. Not you."

"No, Rocky. Aiden doesn't write our songs. I do. He just takes all the credit."

"I don't believe you." Rocky crossed her arms.

"Okay. Follow me, and I'll prove it to you then." Renaldo led Rocky outside the back door and into a different building that led to an empty auditorium. The theater department usually used this auditorium for practicing or performances.

"Are we supposed to be back here?" Rocky asked.

Renaldo didn't say anything as Rocky followed him backstage and down a narrow hallway, where he opened another door. Behind that door was a small room with a beautiful, shiny Steinway piano in the center that had Rocky in awe. Why had she never heard about this room before?

"Whoa," Rocky said.

"I come in here to write my music during lunch sometimes," Renaldo said while taking a seat at the piano. He began playing some riffs and humming along to the melody.

Rocky knew Renaldo had a great voice, but she'd never heard him sing alone. He sounded *amazing!*

"Wow, that was awesome," Rocky said after he finished playing. "That sounded so beautiful."

"Thank you," Renaldo said with a shy smile. He closed the piano. "This room has phenomenal acoustics, let me tell you."

Things were starting to make sense. Now that Rocky thought about it, she'd never seen Aiden play the piano or write any of his — or Renaldo's — songs.

"I have more songs in my backpack if you're interested in hearing any of them," he said.

"I would love to," Rocky said. "So, you were seriously ghostwriting all of Aiden's songs?"

Renaldo nodded his head. "That's the only reason I'm still in the group."

Rocky couldn't believe it. How could Aiden not give Renaldo the credit he deserved for working on all the songs? It was worse that Aiden treated Renaldo horribly and made him sing backup. For his own songs!

Rocky shook her head. "Wow. I'm sorry I didn't believe you."

"That's okay," he said.

Rocky sat down next to Renaldo at the piano. "Don't you think you deserve some credit?" she asked him. "He should acknowledge you as the group's songwriter, or you should at least get to sing a verse. They are your songs, after all."

"You know how Aiden is. Everything is always about him. We're only here to make him look and sound better."

Rocky sighed and shook her head again. Then she decided to lighten the mood a bit. "Can I hear another one of your songs?" she asked.

"Sure." Renaldo opened the piano again and began playing a slower, ballad-like melody on the keys. Rocky figured it was more of a personal piece for Renaldo based on the lyrics and the song's Latin-like chord progressions. Everything about Renaldo's music sounded beautiful: the melody, the sincerity of the lyrics, and how he managed to transition from lower to higher register so flawlessly left Rocky speechless. She had to admit Renaldo had a God-given talent and had no business being a backup singer. He finished the song with a few Latin riffs.

"Amazing," was all Rocky could say.

Renaldo chuckled and shrugged his shoulders. "Eh, it's alright, I guess."

"No, that was more than just alright. Renaldo, that was incredible. The way you played, the way you sang, and the whole song were all phenomenal."

Renaldo started blushing. "Thank you, Rocky," he said. "I appreciate your kindness. I was younger when I wrote this song; it means a lot to me. It's basically about my first years' experience moving to this country."

"I think you told it well. The song is amazing. And I know I keep telling you that, but it's the truth!"

Rocky and Renaldo both laughed.

"You're too sweet," Renaldo said. "I call it '*Dulces Sueños*,' which means 'sweet dreams.' It's one of the few songs I wrote that Aiden didn't get a hold of, thankfully."

"I still can't believe he only uses you. Don't you want to do something about it?"

Renaldo rolled his eyes. "There's no point. I never win with him."

Things got silent for a moment. Rocky was beginning to see Aiden in a completely different way. How could he take credit for something that wasn't his? She also felt awful for Renaldo and couldn't begin to imagine his feelings about not being acknowledged for his hard work.

"Do you write?" Renaldo asked.

"Me? No, not really. Adam's the songwriter of the group. I've only written one song in my life."

"Can I hear it?"

Rocky laughed nervously. "It's stupid. I was little when I wrote it."

"Oh, come on."

"No, it's terrible."

"I sang for you."

Rocky laughed again. "Okay, fine."

Rocky hadn't played the piano in a few years, so she was a little rusty with the melody. She began singing her childhood composition, which was only about a minute long and a transition of two basic chords. When she finished, Renaldo did his best to contain his laughter but failed.

Rocky started laughing too. "I told you it wasn't that good," she said.

"No, it was cute," Renaldo told her. "What made you want to write that?"

"I was nine and wanted to know what it was like to write a song. As you can see, it's not my thing."

"Oh, it wasn't that bad, especially for composing it as a nine-year-old. You could tweak it a little bit and make a fun song if you wanted to."

"It'll need more than just a little bit of tweaking," Rocky joked. She checked her cell phone for the time and gasped when she saw three text messages from Hayley. "Oh my gosh!" she exclaimed.

"What's wrong?"

"I was supposed to meet Hayley for lunch. I completely forgot, and now lunch is almost over."

"Oh, I'm so sorry about that. I didn't know."

"No, you're fine. We should probably get back, though. She's going to kill me!"

As they both stood up, Renaldo closed the piano and then grabbed his backpack from the floor. "I can tell her I held you hostage, so she'll kill me instead," he joked.

Rocky laughed as she picked up her backpack. "No need for that," she said.

Rocky admired the grand piano one last time before going out the door. "I've never seen such a perfect piano in my life," she mused.

"Yeah," Renaldo agreed. "I think it's because no one knows about it or uses it, so it stays in good condition."

They both continued chatting as they headed back to the courtyard. Learning a little more about Renaldo made him a lot easier to talk to. Rocky had a feeling Hayley and Adam would get along with him well since they were alike in multiple ways.

Later that day, after practice, Rocky stayed behind to talk to Aiden. She wanted to have some alone time with him, and since her mom would be getting off work a little later, she had to take advantage of that. Rocky and Aiden were having a casual conversation, laughing, and getting to know each other better. It was the most at ease Rocky had seen Aiden in a while.

"Have you ever had an embarrassing moment while you were on stage?" Rocky asked him.

"Yeah, I've had a few," Aiden said.

"What was your most embarrassing moment?"

Aiden laughed. "If I tell you, you have to promise not to laugh."

"I won't laugh."

"I mean *really* promise."

"I promise. Tell me."

"Okay, this was back in middle school during a talent show. I was onstage, all hyped up, and singing my heart out. But I guess I got a little *too* hyped and didn't notice the microphone cords on the floor. While I was up there, I tripped on one of the cords and fell off the stage."

Rocky couldn't stop the giggle that escaped her, but Aiden also laughed.

"Hey, you promised!" he teased.

"I'm sorry," Rocky laughed. "Were you okay?"

"Yeah, I was fine. Some big fat teacher broke my fall. I was so embarrassed that I almost decided to stop performing on stage completely."

"Well, thank goodness you didn't stop."

"Yeah, I know. I can't imagine what else I'd be doing. Singing is my life."

Rocky was glad she and Aiden shared similar passions. It made talking to him much easier and being around him more fun. Slowly, she became more comfortable with and attracted to Aiden.

"Have you had any onstage embarrassments?" Aiden asked.

"Not necessarily," she said.

"Oh, so you're perfect then?" he joked.

Rocky laughed. "Of course, I'm not perfect. I just try to avoid the stage in any way possible."

"I don't understand why. Your voice is amazing."

Rocky smiled and looked down at her lap. "I don't handle embarrassment as well as you, so I try to avoid it."

"You can't avoid it forever. If it happens, it happens. You'll grow from it. I'm living proof." He smiled and put his arm around Rocky. "If I can overcome it, I know you can too. I believe in you."

Rocky snuggled up to Aiden and couldn't stop grinning. She honestly didn't believe she would overcome her fear of embarrassing herself on stage as smoothly as Aiden did, but she didn't want to ruin the mood with her pessimistic ways. It finally felt as though she and Aiden were a real couple. Rocky wanted to enjoy their moment together, but a burning question prevented her from doing that. She took a deep breath and dared herself to ask.

"Aiden, I have a question," Rocky said.

"I have an answer."

"Do you think the group should change things up a bit?"

"What do you mean?"

"The guys and I can still do backup, but don't you think it's about time one of us gets a solo?"

Aiden furrowed his eyebrows, clearly stunned Rocky would ask such a question. "You want a solo?" he asked.

"Well, I don't want to sing backup all my life. Also, I've heard the other guys sing alone, and they sound great. Each of us could sing a different verse and harmonize the chorus. Don't you think it would sound cool?"

"I'm not sure if you and the guys are ready for a solo yet."

"What makes us not ready?"

"Well, you just told me about how you avoid the spotlight because you're afraid of embarrassing yourself."

"But you just told me I could overcome it."

"Yeah, I know, but I want to make sure you're comfortable being on stage before letting you sing a solo."

It seemed to Rocky that Aiden contradicted himself, and his response puzzled her. Why would he not let her sing a solo if he told her before she could overcome her stage fright?

"Okay," Rocky said. "But what about the guys?"

"Well, they each have their voice parts, so who's going to fill in when one of them gets a solo? Angel, for example. Remember when he wasn't at rehearsal that one time, and we sounded off?"

Rocky nodded.

"The harmony will be incomplete without each of the guys singing their voice part, you know? Besides, Marcus sounds way better as a backup singer. Now Renaldo?" Aiden laughed. "Dude can barely even speak English. Why would I ever give him a solo?"

"Because he has an outstanding voice." Since they were on the subject, Rocky thought she should confront Aiden about Renaldo's ghostwriting. "He writes all the songs anyway, so why not give him a solo?"

Aiden tensed up and inhaled sharply. Rocky could feel his heart beating faster as she was lying on his chest. When she noticed Aiden's sudden change in behavior, Rocky sat up and looked at him.

"What are you talking about?" Aiden asked.

"You don't have any reason to lie now. I know Renaldo writes the songs for us to sing, and you take the credit for it."

Aiden rolled his eyes. And just like that, the sweet Aiden with whom Rocky was having a casual conversation vanished. It was back to the regular Aiden.

"What did he tell you?" he asked.

"He told me that he was writing all the songs you said you wrote. He showed me everything. Why would you lie about that?"

"Hey, I'm doing him a favor. I give his songs life when I sing them, while he makes them sound boring. I change up some of the lyrics and increase the tempo to sound more fun. They're basically my songs if you think about it."

Huh? "I don't think that's how it works," Rocky said, confused.

"Why are you sticking up for him so much?" Aiden asked.

"Wait, what?"

"You seem to care a lot about Renaldo's feelings."

"Well, I..."

"Are you interested in him or something? Is there more to your friendship with him that I don't know about?"

"No, of course not!" Rocky thought Aiden might have been overreacting. Rocky never thought of Renaldo as anything more than a good friend. She wouldn't be with Aiden if she had feelings for Renaldo. She was not that kind of girl. "You know I only like you."

"Well, it doesn't seem that way," Aiden fired back. "Are you only hooking up with Renaldo, or do you want Angel and Marcus, too?"

"I don't like any of the guys like that," Rocky explained. She felt a lump in her throat, and her eyes began to water. Why would Aiden accuse her of hooking up with the other guys? Rocky was a terrible flirt, and she was extremely awkward around boys. Also, she would never ruin her relationship with Aiden by sneaking around with another guy. It's a miracle that a guy like Aiden wanted Rocky to be his girlfriend anyway!

Rocky thought about what to say next without making Aiden even more upset than he already was. "Aiden, please," was the only thing that could come out. She tried to touch his hand, but he jerked it away. The tears became too powerful to hold back then.

"No, don't start with the tears," Aiden snapped. "Why don't you go cry to Renaldo or something?"

"I don't like him like that," Rocky told him again. "Why don't you believe me?"

Aiden got up from the couch and went to the other side of the room, keeping his back toward Rocky and his arms folded across his chest. "Why should I believe you?" he asked harshly.

Rocky couldn't stop crying. It always seemed like when things were going perfectly for her, something awful had to happen and ruin it. For some reason, Rocky couldn't get Aiden to believe she wasn't romantically interested in Renaldo and thought she would lose him. She just couldn't lose him.

"What do you want me to do?" Rocky desperately asked. "I'll do anything to prove I'm only interested in you."

Aiden remained silent.

"I would never do anything like that to you, Aiden," Rocky continued. "You mean everything to me. You have to believe me. Please."

His silence began to intensify Rocky's anxiety, and she felt herself hyperventilating. *Not now! I know this will fade away.*

"Aiden," she begged.

Aiden sighed and finally responded. "You swear you have no feelings for him?"

"I promise."

"I can't stand the thought of you being with another guy," he admitted. "It's making me sick just thinking about it. I guess I got a little jealous."

"You don't have to worry about me being with another guy. I only want you." Rocky walked up behind Aiden and reached to caress his back. "If it makes you feel better, I won't hang out with the guys as much. I'll do whatever it takes to prove I'm committed to only you."

Aiden turned around to face Rocky and took her hands into his. His touch gave her chills, and she stared into his eyes pleadingly.

"You're mine," he whispered to her. "You'll always be mine. Don't forget that."

"Of course," Rocky whispered back.

Aiden gently wiped the tears from Rocky's face and hugged her tightly. She felt a lot better knowing he was okay, but she had to make sure never to make that mistake again. Rocky couldn't lose Aiden, and she wouldn't be able to forgive herself if she ever made him feel that bad again.

Noticing the time, Rocky decided it was time to return home before it got too dark outside. Aiden walked Rocky out, and they continued their ritual of lingering on the porch for a few moments before one of them spoke.

"Let's do something this weekend," Aiden said. "Just the two of us."

"Like what?" Rocky asked.

"We could go see a movie if you want. Like on a Saturday evening."

"Sure, that would be great."

Rocky couldn't stop smiling. She was relaxed on the outside but was jumping for joy on the inside. It was their first time going out as boyfriend and girlfriend. Finally, an actual date!

"Sounds perfect."

Rocky sighed and fantasized about what her movie date with Aiden would be like. They'd share a large bucket of popcorn and occasionally touch hands when they both tried to reach for some. During a frightening scene, Aiden would put his arm around her, making her feel safe and secure. It all sounded perfect...until Rocky had a sudden realization.

"Wait, don't we have a concert on Saturday evening? When will we have time to see a movie?" Rocky regretted asking such a dumb question. There was a perfect moment between her and Aiden. Why was she bringing up work?

"We can go before or after the concert, depending on how things go that day," Aiden responded.

"But..."

Aiden lightly put his finger on Rocky's lips. "Shh. Don't ask any more questions," he said playfully. "All I need you to worry about is what to wear on our date."

Rocky smiled again. It sounded so real hearing Aiden say it. Before she knew it, he leaned down and lightly kissed Rocky on her lips. The kiss lasted for about a second, which was the most beautiful second of her life. She finally had her first kiss!

"I'll see you later, my love," he whispered in her ear.

Chills ran up her spine, and words couldn't begin to describe the euphoria she was feeling. It felt like Rocky was floating, and she and Aiden were the only ones in the world. Is this what it was like to fall in love?

"Okay," Rocky gasped. She had to collect herself and walk home. When she made it to her house, her cheeks were hurting from smiling so much.

14

Since Rocky and Aiden had their official first date, she spent much more time with him and less time with Hayley and Adam. It was never her intention to ditch her best friends for her boyfriend. It just sort of happened. Rocky tried making time to see Hayley and Adam more, but Aiden always wanted to be with Rocky. She was thrilled Aiden was giving Rocky more attention and wanted to prevent another conflict between them, so she did everything she could to make him happy. He was now a priority.

On a weekend when she didn't have to perform and Aiden was out of town, Rocky decided it would be the perfect time to meet up with Hayley and Adam at The Studio. It had been too long, and Rocky was ready to tell them everything that'd been going on.

"Hey, guys," Rocky cheered when she arrived.

Hayley placed her hand over her chest and gasped overdramatically. "Rocky, is that you?" she joked. "It's been so long; I almost didn't recognize you!"

Rocky rolled her eyes and laughed. "You're such a drama queen," Rocky joked.

"I'm a theater student for a reason, dahling," Hayley giggled. "But seriously, it feels like ages since we last saw each other. I miss you, girl."

"I miss you guys so much," Rocky replied. "I'm sorry about not being able to spend as much time with you. It's just Aiden." Rocky couldn't stop herself from smiling when she said his name.

"We completely understand," Adam said. "You get a boyfriend, and we get pushed aside."

Rocky didn't expect such a hurtful comment from Adam. Rocky hung her head, feeling even more awful about not having enough time for her friends.

"Adam!" Hayley hissed, smacking his arm. "Seriously, dude?"

"It was a joke," Adam said, though he and Rocky both knew there was some seriousness behind it.

"It wasn't funny!" Hayley snapped.

"No, it's fine, Hayley," Rocky said. "He's right. I'm not pushing you guys to the side on purpose. You know that, right?"

"Of course, we know that," Adam reassured her.

"Aiden and I are finally starting to do more stuff as a couple. We went on our first date last weekend."

"Aww," Hayley cooed. "It's about time! How was it?"

Rocky reminisced about their movie date and couldn't help but smile. They saw a romantic comedy at a high-end movie theater with reclining chairs, a gigantic screen, insane surround sound, and workers who delivered food to you in the auditoriums! Rocky had only ever been at her smaller neighborhood theater, so it was incredible to experience something more upscale. Although they couldn't hold a conversation during the film, Aiden did hold her hand the entire time and gave her a short goodnight kiss after he dropped her home. It was a night she would never forget.

"It was perfect," Rocky sighed. Thinking about her first date with Aiden gave her butterflies all over again.

"Quick question," Adam said. "Why did it take him four months to take you out on a first date?"

Hayley rolled her eyes. "Here we go," she said.

"I just want to know," he said with a shrug.

"We can finish talking about it when it's only the two of us," Hayley said to Rocky. "Because clearly, there's a hater amongst us."

"Clearly, you've got me all wrong," Adam retorted. "The day I hate on Aiden is the day that pigs fly."

"Hmm, I thought I saw a pig fly the other day," Hayley said.

Adam shook his head and rolled his eyes.

"I'm just happy, you guys," Rocky told them. "Things are finally going well with me and Aiden."

"If you're happy, then we're happy," Hayley said.

"There was a talent agent at our most recent concert, and he loved us," Rocky gushed. "He worked with other famous singers and said he would consider signing us!"

"That's amazing, Rocky!" Adam exclaimed.

"I know! It's almost like a dream come true. The only thing missing from it is you guys."

"You know we'll always be there," Hayley said. "Every step of the way."

"I wish you guys could live the dream with me. I don't want to do this alone."

Hayley and Adam didn't respond right away.

"You have Aiden," Hayley said. "And as for Adam and me, it's not our time yet. Until then, we're content with being your number one fans."

Adam nodded in agreement. Their support meant everything to Rocky. She couldn't imagine becoming successful in her singing career without Hayley and Adam. She genuinely didn't think she would survive without having her two best friends by her side.

*＊＊

A few days later, Aiden, Rocky, and the guys arrived at the amphitheater for their performance. Rocky went straight to the restroom to relieve herself as soon as they got backstage. Her mouth would always get dry before a concert because of her nerves, so she drank tons of water. All the water she was drinking made her use the bathroom more often. Once Rocky finished, she found Angel and Marcus backstage.

"Hey, guys. Where's Aiden?" Rocky asked them.

"I have no idea," Marcus said.

"Haven't seen him," Angel told her.

"Aren't we going to be performing in a little bit?" Rocky asked. "Where could he be?"

The guys shrugged their shoulders, seemingly uninterested in Aiden not being present. Rocky sighed and went looking for him. As she passed by a cracked open door, she heard a familiar voice and stopped to listen.

"Why would you tell her?" shouted a male voice. That sounded like Aiden, but who was he yelling at?

"I didn't have to. She just found out," replied another voice. Rocky noticed the Spanish accent and knew it was Renaldo.

What's going on in there? Rocky thought. She cracked the door open a little bit more to see the guys. Renaldo was standing in a corner with wide eyes and tightly clasped hands in front of him. Aiden stood over Renaldo with his fists clenched.

"What do you mean she just found out?" Aiden asked. "She said you told her and showed her everything! If she knows, then soon everyone will know, and I'm going to end up looking bad. I ask you to do one simple thing, and you can't even do it! What's wrong with you, man?"

Rocky wondered what on earth they could be talking about or even if she should be listening to their argument.

"Look, I said I was sorry," Renaldo said. "I didn't mean for it to happen like that."

"Well, it happened. What are you going to do about it?"

Renaldo didn't answer right away. Every time Aiden made the slightest move, he would flinch. He was terrified, and Rocky felt awful. She'd never seen Aiden so upset before.

"I'll tell you what you're going to do," Aiden said. "You're going to tell Rocky you're just a desperate loser who tried to get away with being the ghostwriter of my songs. And you better not let her know about it."

"She already knows."

"She's gullible enough already. Make up some believable excuse, and she'll fall for it."

"So, you want *me* to seem like a bad guy and a liar?"

"You wouldn't have to do this if you didn't get caught or made up one little excuse. Seriously, how dumb can you get?"

"Come on, Aiden..."

"Do it already! And if you try to pull something, I swear I'll make your life a living hell."

"Like you don't already," Renaldo snapped back.

"Excuse me?"

Renaldo stood up a little straighter. "You don't understand how hard it is. You always put so much pressure on me and treat me like I'm worthless. How do you expect me to do my best when you treat me like this?"

"You better suck it up and do it, or else no one will ever hear your precious songs."

"Then I guess we'll both suffer if you get rid of me. You can't even make your own music, so how do you think you'll survive without me?"

Aiden punched Renaldo in the face, causing his head to fly backward. Rocky gasped and then quickly covered her mouth, praying she wasn't loud enough for them to notice her. She couldn't believe what had just happened! Renaldo dropped to his knees and held his nose while groaning. Aiden forcefully picked Renaldo back up to his feet, slammed him against the wall, and got in his face.

"Listen to me, you stupid immigrant." Aiden's nostrils flared, and he was talking through clenched teeth. "Don't you ever think you can get away with talking to me like that."

Rocky was frozen in fear and couldn't do anything but watch helplessly. She wished she was bold enough to walk in and stop Aiden from hurting Renaldo, but her feet seemed to weigh a ton.

"You better check yourself, fool," Aiden continued. "You need me way more than I need you. I'm doing *you* a favor by keeping you here. I run things, and you stand there and do as I say. Okay?"

Renaldo didn't say anything. He kept his hand over his nose and glared at Aiden with hatred.

"Okay then," Aiden said. He pushed Renaldo by the face into the wall, causing his hand to slip and reveal his bruised and bloody nose. Renaldo covered it back up and winced in pain.

"Get yourself cleaned up," Aiden told him. "We've got a show to do."

When Aiden started heading for the door, Rocky ran to another room before he could spot her. Her eyes filled with tears as she recalled what had just happened. Rocky knew Aiden had a bit of a temper, but she never thought he'd hit any of the guys. Her heart pounded so hard in her chest that she thought she would throw up.

Rocky peeked to see if anyone was in the hallway. She saw Renaldo with tissues in his nose and a few drops of blood on his shirt. He was uttering some words in Spanish. Even though Rocky couldn't understand what Renaldo was saying, she knew he was furious by hearing his harsh tone. Even though the coast was clear, Rocky still couldn't bring herself to leave the room. She felt like she witnessed a crime she could've and should've prevented.

Her thoughts wouldn't stop racing, and her mind replayed that incident repeatedly, causing Rocky to start hyperventilating and feeling faint. Tears were streaming down her face as she sat on the floor and tried to clear her mind and control her breathing. *I know this will fade away. I know this will fade away.*

It took Rocky a few minutes to get her anxiety attack under control. She closed her eyes and started thinking about being in The Studio with Hayley and Adam to calm herself down. She heard Aiden's voice in the middle of her fantasy, which threw her back into reality.

"Rocky, where are you?" he called out. "We're about to perform now."

Again, Rocky felt helpless and glued to the floor as Aiden's voice appeared to come nearer to her. So much for her happy place.

"Where is that little...?" Aiden turned the corner and spotted Rocky sitting on the floor. "There you are. Come on," he said impatiently. "They're about to announce us."

Aiden took Rocky by the arm and led her back to the rest of the guys. She wondered if he even noticed she was recovering from a panic attack.

"I don't think Renaldo's going to be able to sing like this," Angel said. He and Marcus were standing over Renaldo, who was sitting in a chair with a cloth over his nose. "His nose won't stop bleeding."

"What happened?" Aiden asked.

"He said he fell," Marcus said. "He must've hit his nose on something pretty hard for it to keep bleeding like that."

Yeah, Aiden's fist, Rocky thought to herself. She stood quietly next to Aiden, forcing the incident out of her mind so it wouldn't consume her thoughts again.

When Renaldo removed the cloth from his nose, blood continued to drip from it. He covered it back up and sighed.

Aiden shook his head. "He obviously can't sing with a bloody nose," he said. "I guess we just have to go without him and change things up a bit."

"But how?" Marcus asked.

"And now, without further ado, please give it up for Aiden and Company!" the announcer on stage called out. The sound of the audience cheering followed right after.

"Figure it out," Aiden said, walking on stage shortly after.

Marcus and Angel exchanged glances before following behind Aiden. Rocky looked back at Renaldo, who sat with his head down while holding the bloody cloth over his nose. She then joined the rest of the boys on stage.

"How's everyone doing tonight?" Aiden said enthusiastically into his microphone. The audience responded with a round of applause. "Obviously, one of my backup singers isn't here. He had an unfortunate accident and can't perform today, but the show must go on. We'd appreciate it if you could bear with us through this performance, and let's hope he feels better soon. Thank you."

The group sounded and felt different without Renaldo. Since he usually sang the melody, they couldn't create a harmony, and the song didn't sound the same. They had to make it work, so they did, and the audience didn't seem to complain.

Fortunately, Rochelle was at the concert and brought Hayley and Adam along. Rocky was elated her mom would take her home, considering the ordeal between Aiden and Renaldo still had her shaken.

"What happened to the other backup singer?" Rochelle asked on the way home. "Is he okay?"

"Um, he'll be okay," Rocky said. At least she hoped he would be okay. By the time they finished their song, Renaldo was gone. The people backstage said his parents picked him up and took him to the hospital to get his nose checked out. "He...he fell and hurt himself."

"How did he fall?" Hayley asked from the backseat.

Rocky had flashbacks of the incident and couldn't sit still in her seat. She felt terrible for Renaldo and hoped he would recover soon.

"Um, I'm not sure," Rocky said. "He just approached us with a bloody nose and said he fell."

"Oh no, that's awful," Rochelle said. "He might've broken or fractured it. He should take it easy for a while."

"I hope he feels better soon," Hayley said. "Poor guy."

"I know," Adam replied. "That has to suck."

Rocky adjusted herself in her seat again, and Rochelle noticed her uneasiness.

"You okay, Rocky?" she asked.

"I'm fine," Rocky lied. "Just worried about him."

"I'm sure he'll be okay," Adam reassured her.

"Yeah, I hope so," Rocky said.

The rest of the ride home was quiet. Rocky didn't feel like talking, and she couldn't stop that horrific scene from replaying in her head throughout the ride home. She had never felt so terrified in her life. When they got to Rocky's house, Hayley and Adam started noticing how unsettled Rocky was.

"Rocky, don't worry about it," Hayley told her. "Everything will be okay with him."

"What about it is bothering you so much?" Adam asked.

Rocky took a few deep breaths to try and calm herself down. She couldn't keep it to herself anymore. She had to tell someone, or she was going to lose it.

"You guys, he didn't fall," Rocky admitted.

Hayley and Adam exchanged looks.

"So, what happened then?" Adam asked.

"Aiden punched him in the face."

"No way!" Hayley exclaimed.

"Are you serious?" Adam asked.

Rocky nodded. "I saw what happened, but he doesn't know. It was so scary, you guys. I've never seen Aiden that upset before."

"Now do you see how horrible he is?" Adam said in exasperation. "Rocky, you need to leave him and his group for good. He's dangerous."

"I don't know," Rocky said.

"You don't know?" Hayley repeated, almost as exasperated as Adam. "Rocky, Adam is right. From what you've told me about his erratic behavior, I started losing trust in him. He doesn't seem like such a good guy after all."

"I don't know," Rocky said again. "I'm just so scared right now. I can't even think."

"Please don't do anything stupid," Adam warned her. "You saw him punch that guy in the face. You don't think he'll do the same to you?"

"Adam, please don't go there," Hayley said.

"But it could happen. Aiden is corrupt. He's evil. He's — he's all the bad words you could think of! And now you can see it, Rocky. You need to run before it's too late."

Rocky didn't want to believe Aiden was corrupt. She wanted the sweet Aiden back who supported her and told her nice things. What would make him go off on poor Renaldo like that? None of this made sense to Rocky.

"Haylcy, can you spend the night here?" Rocky asked. "I could use the company."

"Of course," Hayley told her. "I'm here for you."

Hayley, Rocky, and Adam sat quietly in the living room until Adam's parents came to pick him up. Shortly after Adam left, Hayley and Rocky were lying side by side in Rocky's bed.

"I don't want to believe Aiden is corrupt," Rocky told Hayley.

"Well, someone who isn't corrupt doesn't go around giving other people bloody noses," Hayley said. "Did you hear anything they said before Aiden punched him? Maybe there was a reason Aiden blew up on him, not that I'm justifying his actions."

"Aiden was upset about something Renaldo did. I don't remember much of what they were arguing about. I think Aiden wanted Renaldo to lie about something?"

"Why would Aiden need to lie about something, though?"

"Their argument was a blur," Rocky admitted. "When Renaldo stood up for himself, Aiden got mad and punched him. It didn't even feel real."

"You're not giving me any good reasons to prove Aiden isn't corrupt," Hayley joked.

"I don't know," Rocky sighed. "He has a bit of a temper and gets stressed out easily, but this isn't like him."

"It sounds like he has anger management problems and control issues. I'm not sure I trust him anymore."

"But you don't understand, Hayley. He's usually nicer when he isn't stressed out. What happened tonight was a first."

"But it might not be the last."

Rocky started crying. This couldn't be the Aiden she fell for. There was no way he was a jerk. He just had a bad moment, and with a few stress-relief practices, nothing like that would ever happen again. She knew Aiden could be better.

"I understand you care about him a lot, but I don't want you to get hurt," Hayley said. "I'd be super careful around him if I were you, Rocky."

Rocky had to shift her focus to something else, or she would be up all night thinking about what had happened before the concert.

"Could we talk about something else now?" Rocky asked.

She and Hayley spent some time watching a compilation of funny and viral videos on YouTube before Hayley started dozing off. It was 1 a.m., and Rocky was still lying awake in bed, trying to clear her mind. No matter how hard she tried to forget about what happened, she couldn't get it out of her head. It took a while for Rocky to finally fall asleep, and she had trouble staying asleep.

15

Rocky was feeling a little better on Monday. She had schoolwork, assignments, and friends to keep her distracted, so she didn't have to focus on what happened between Renaldo and Aiden. When Rocky got to rehearsal and saw Renaldo for the first time since the incident, she began feeling uneasy again. His nose was black and blue and swollen. She ran up to him.

"Are you okay, Renaldo?" Rocky asked, worry in her voice. "Are you feeling any better since your, um, accident?"

Renaldo gave Rocky a friendly smile. "I'm okay," he said. "My nose is still a little sore, but it gets better every day. I appreciate you asking."

"Is it broken? Will there be any long-term damage or anything?"

"Nothing's broken. I just badly bruised it." Renaldo must've noticed Rocky's worried expression because he chucked and said, "Seriously, I'm fine. I'll try to be less clumsy next time."

Rocky sighed. She couldn't believe Renaldo wasn't honest about what really happened to his nose. She had to do something about it.

"I saw what happened," Rocky admitted.

Renaldo tensed up, and he couldn't meet Rocky's eyes. "What do you mean?"

"I know you didn't hurt your nose by falling. I saw Aiden hit you."

Angel and Marcus stopped what they were doing and turned their heads toward Rocky and Renaldo.

"Wait, what?" Marcus asked in shock.

"He hit you?" Angel asked.

"Shh!" Renaldo hissed. His eyes darted to the garage door, looking for Aiden.

"Dude, Aiden seriously hit you?" Angel asked again. "What happened? Why didn't you tell us?"

Renaldo's eyes widened in terror. He looked almost as terrified as he did during that altercation with Aiden. "Can we talk about this later?" Renaldo whispered. "He might be coming in soon. Please."

Seeing how scared Renaldo was of Aiden nearly broke Rocky's heart. Rocky didn't blame him, though — she would be scared, too.

"Can you at least tell us what happened?" Marcus asked quietly. "Why would he do that to you?"

Renaldo looked over at the door again without saying anything.

"Give him a minute," Rocky told Marcus. "It was a traumatizing situation. He'll talk about it when he's ready."

"Unbelievable," Angel said while shaking his head. "Aiden is such a..."

Angel stopped mid-sentence when the garage door opened, and Aiden walked in. Renaldo kept his eyes on the floor while Angel and Marcus glared at Aiden. Rocky hoped they wouldn't say or do anything to upset him. She did not want to see Aiden that angry again.

"Ready to start, guys?" Aiden said once he got to the center of the room.

Silence. Angel and Marcus stood with their arms folded across their chests and glared disapprovingly at Aiden. Renaldo's wide eyes begged the boys not to say a word about what happened the other day.

"What's wrong with you guys?" Aiden asked.

More silence. It was intimidating how quiet it was because Rocky had no idea what would happen next.

"Somebody talk," Aiden urged, getting impatient.

Marcus was the brave one to bring up the situation. "What is wrong with you, man?" he asked.

"Excuse me?" Aiden asked in shock.

"The other night at the concert," Marcus continued. "Renaldo's nosebleed. Ringing any bells?"

"I told you guys I fell," Renaldo spoke up.

"Cut the crap, Renaldo," Marcus said. "We all know what happened. There's no way you could've fallen and hit your nose on something hard enough to make it bleed the way it did."

"Marcus, please," Renaldo said quietly. "I'm fine now. Let it go."

"No," Marcus said. "I want to know what gives Aiden the right to go around punching people in the face. You didn't deserve that."

Aiden didn't seem to be angry. He had a blank expression on his face, so Rocky couldn't tell what could be going through his mind at that moment.

"I know Aiden can be a jerk sometimes," Marcus continued. "But hitting you in the face and giving you a nosebleed crosses the line. And because of that, Aiden, I lost a lot of respect for you. Why would you do that to Renaldo?"

Aiden didn't say anything for a while, still wearing his poker face. Everyone waited to see if he would admit to what he did or deny everything. Finally, Aiden sighed.

"Okay," he said. "You're right, Marcus. I did punch Renaldo and gave him that nosebleed at the concert."

"Why?"

"I don't know. Nothing was going as planned. I got mad and had to let off some steam. Renaldo just happened to have been there right when I blew up."

Renaldo kept his head down.

"You guys know I have a hot temper," Aiden continued. "And maybe I do have trouble controlling my anger."

"You're not wrong," Angel muttered under his breath.

"But it's hard," Aiden said. "Whenever I feel like I have no control over a situation, I get so angry." He looked at Renaldo. "I'm sorry about what happened at the concert, Renaldo. What I did to you was awful, and you didn't deserve that."

With his head still down, Renaldo exhaled sharply. His face was slightly reddening, and he kept his fists balled.

"I understand if you're still mad," Aiden told him. "Honestly, I would be too. Sometimes, I feel helpless. I've tried so many ways to manage my anger, but nothing works."

Aiden sighed and bowed his head. Rocky felt terrible that Aiden had such a hard time controlling his anger because she knew how sweet of a guy he was. She sat next to Aiden and gently placed a hand on his back.

"Maybe we all can try and help you better manage your anger," Rocky told him. "Right, guys?"

The guys didn't have anything to say; their faces were masked with bewilderment.

"I've already tried anger management classes," Aiden said. "If professionals couldn't help me, what makes you think you guys can?"

"When my mom used to be stressed out and angry from work, she started doing yoga and meditation," Rocky said. "That always helps her relax, especially after a stressful day. Maybe you should give it a try."

"Yeah, right," Aiden said, rolling his eyes. "I don't believe in any of that."

"You have to try it first before you start doubting. It works, and I want to help you get through this."

Rocky looked at the guys again for extra support, but they kept quiet. She wondered why nobody could see the good in Aiden the way she could. Rocky thought that if he only learned to control his anger, everyone would see the genuine sweetheart she knew Aiden was.

"I know you can get through this," Rocky told him.

Renaldo stood up from his seat. "There's an emergency at my house," he uttered. "My family needs me now. I have to go." As Renaldo rushed out of the room, he stuffed his hands in his pockets and made no eye contact with anybody.

"I should probably go, too," Angel said. "Maybe see if he could use some extra help or something."

Marcus looked at Aiden and Rocky, then followed Angel out the door.

"I bet they don't believe me," Aiden said once he and Rocky were alone. "I bet they think I'm making all this up and that I'm a terrible person." He looked at Rocky with sad puppy dog eyes. "I'm not a terrible person, Rocky."

"I believe you," Rocky reassured him.

"Why don't they believe me?"

Rocky shrugged. "I don't know. I guess you'll have to prove you're not a bad guy to them."

"How?"

"By learning how to manage your stress and anger. There are better ways to cope with stressful situations than using your friend's face as a punching bag. You have to learn to control your temper."

"But it's so hard. I don't think I can do this."

"Yes, you can. I'm here to help you, Aiden. Please let me help you."

Aiden took Rocky's hands into his own and looked at her. She could see in his eyes that he wanted to change for the better.

"You're the best thing to ever happen to me," he told her.

Rocky laughed nervously. "You think so?"

"I know so. Even at my worst, you still see the good in me. Nobody else does that."

"I always try to see the best in people."

"When everything in the world has me feeling down, you somehow manage to bring me higher. How do you do it, Rocky?"

"I know what it's like to be at a low point. I'd hate to see the people I care about feeling that way, so I try everything possible to make them feel better."

"Sometimes, I feel like I don't deserve you."

Rocky watched Aiden caress her fingers with his, which made her stomach get intense butterflies.

"Rocky," he called her name.

"Aiden," she answered.

"I love you."

Rocky felt a surge of joy run throughout her entire body and was in disbelief at what she had just heard. Her eyes felt warm, her heart fluttered in her chest, and she couldn't stop smiling. Aiden loved her! She tried telling him she loved him back but was too in the moment for the words to come out.

"You — you love me?" Rocky stammered.

"I do. I feel so lucky to have you in my life. You complete me." Aiden squeezed her hand and smiled. "I love you so much, Rocky."

Once Aiden said it for the second time, Rocky knew it had to be real. Her hands were shaking in Aiden's as she processed this magical moment.

"I love you, too," Rocky finally said.

Meeting Aiden was the best thing that ever happened to Rocky. He'd given her the support and confidence she desperately needed over the past few months, and she was now a better version of herself because of him. Aiden helped Rocky change for the better, so she knew she'd always support him when he needed it.

***

Rocky had been doing everything she could to help Aiden with his anger issues for the last few weeks. She showed him the breathing exercises she learned from her mom and gave him words of encouragement when he felt overwhelmed. Rocky even helped him come up with his own calming mantra when he was ready to explode in rage. Aiden always told Rocky that being next to her made him feel calmer, so she never left his side.

As a result, Rocky barely saw Adam and Hayley, even at school. She started having lunch with Aiden to keep him in a better mood for the day. She didn't have the time or sometimes the energy to call, text, or respond to their messages. Rocky was sure they would understand that it was only to help Aiden.

Unfortunately, it also seemed like some of Aiden's negativity began to rub off on Rocky. After spending so much time helping him manage his anger, Rocky had been grouchier than usual. She felt so drained at the end of the day that she went straight to her room to lie down when she got home. It seemed like everybody was even more demanding of Rocky's time. Her teachers, mom, and friends were all constantly asking for something. Rocky felt like she was drowning in extra responsibility.

In the middle of the week, Hayley asked Rocky to come to her house after school to help her replace a broken string on one of her guitars. Rocky couldn't understand why Hayley would ask for her help when she had an army of people at her house who could do it. Plus, she knew Rocky had to rehearse after school! Rocky agreed to help, thinking it would be a quick process and that she could go straight to Aiden's house when she finished.

Rocky left school late because her last-period teacher wanted to talk to her about her performance in class. Of all the days, why did it have to be today? That took about five minutes, and then Rocky rushed to Hayley's house. She was focused on not showing up too late to rehearsal, so she didn't look at or speak much to Hayley during the entire process. It took Rocky about 20 minutes to restring and tune the guitar, which was much longer than she had hoped it would take. She knew Aiden would freak out on her for being this late.

After strumming the guitar one last time to make sure it was properly tuned, Rocky handed it back to Hayley.

"Good as new," Rocky said. "I have to head out now."

"Wait, Rocky," Hayley called out.

"I'm already late, Hayley," Rocky huffed. "What do you need now?"

Hayley stared at Rocky in disbelief. "You've changed so much," she said quietly.

"What do you mean?"

"I don't remember the last time we had a real conversation. Adam and I reach out to you, but we're always getting ghosted. And don't even get me started with your sassiness."

Rocky rolled her eyes. "You know I've been busy. It's been nonstop concerts every weekend, and I'm always tired after them. I have to deal with school, homework, and now I'm practically Aiden's therapist. Juggling all of this isn't easy."

"That's always your excuse."

Rocky didn't understand what Hayley's problem was. She already told her she wasn't ghosting her and Adam on purpose. Rocky was doing everything she could to please everybody, but it wasn't working anymore.

"I don't think you realize what he's doing to you," Hayley continued.

"What are you talking about?"

"Aiden is taking advantage of you."

Rocky's face was getting hot. "No, he's not! What would make you think that?"

"He knows how vulnerable you are and uses that to his advantage. I think he's holding on to you because you're making him more noticeable."

"Aiden loves me. He would never take advantage of me!"

"Adam was right about him the whole time. He's selfish and would do anything to get praise, even if it means stabbing his own group in the back."

"You don't know him, Hayley! He comes off as mean, but he's a caring guy. All these concerts stress him out, and he just has a problem controlling his temper. I'm helping him get better with that."

Hayley rolled her eyes. "Seriously, Rocky? He punched his backup singer in the face and gave him a nosebleed, for crying out loud. If Aiden's capable of doing that to him, I don't even want to begin to imagine what he would do to you."

"He would never hurt me, Hayley. He cares about me."

"He only cares about himself. I think you should quit his group and break up with him."

"Weren't you the one who convinced me to join his group?"

"Yeah, but I was wrong to do that. I don't like how Aiden is making you change like this."

Rocky put her hands on her head. "Oh, my goodness," she said. "It all makes sense now. I know exactly what's going on."

Hayley sighed with relief. "You do?"

"Of course. You're jealous of me."

Rocky should've known all along. Hayley wanted herself and Rocky to become more noticeable at Lennox by singing together. They had their moment of fame until Rocky joined forces with Aiden. Now Rocky was singing at concerts. She was the hot topic at school while Hayley was on the outside looking in.

"What?" Hayley asked in disbelief. "You seriously think I'm jealous of you?"

"I know you're jealous of me and everything I've become. You're mad because, for once, I'm popular, and you're not."

Hayley crossed her arms, scoffed, and glared at Rocky. "Okay, Rocky. I'm totally jealous of the girl who's a backup singer for a selfish, hotheaded jerk who emotionally manipulates her and never lets her sing. That sounds about right."

"At least I still get to perform at concerts, and at least I have a boyfriend."

"Oh, I'm sure singing backup is every aspiring singer's dream. And your 'boyfriend' doesn't even care about you or anyone else who isn't benefiting him."

"Envy isn't pretty, honey."

"Get off your high horse."

"You've always been the popular one, the pretty one, the fun one, the social one. You're freakin' flawless, Hayley! Why can't I have the spotlight for once? You know how much being popular means to me."

"I know how much it means to you, but you can't gain attention by losing respect. It's like you've become this slave to Aiden, and you can't even think for yourself anymore. Can you not see he's taking advantage of you?"

"He cares about me."

"No, he doesn't, Rocky."

"Apparently, neither do you."

"Could you just listen to me, Rocky?"

"No, you listen to *me*. If you really cared about me, you wouldn't try so hard to ruin everything I worked for. You don't support me because you can't accept that we come from the same place, I'm evolving, and you're still in the same place. I'm getting noticed by talent agents, and you're still trying to get noticed by the student body. Since you can't get on my level, you try to knock me off my game. You're no friend of mine. You're just a hater."

Things were quiet as Hayley and Rocky stared at each other. They've had many arguments before, but never one this heated.

"Wow," Hayley finally said. "Anything else you want to get off your chest?"

Rocky looked up at the clock on the wall in front of her. If she didn't leave for rehearsal now, Aiden would lose it.

"I need to go," Rocky sighed, walking out the door.

"Fine, go run to him like you always do. When he turns his back on you, I'll be right here waiting for an apology."

"Yeah, that won't be happening," Rocky retorted.

Hayley slammed the door shut as Rocky left. Hayley's parents and younger brother were out in the dining room, and Rocky had to pass them to get to the front door to leave. She was embarrassed they might've heard everything. Maybe if Rocky walked quickly and with her head down, they wouldn't ask any questions.

"Is everything okay with you girls?" Hayley's father asked as Rocky was heading down the stairs.

"Nope," she said so softly that it was almost inaudible. Rocky rushed out of the house before Hayley's parents could ask more questions. She didn't feel like talking to anyone right now.

16

When Rocky got to Aiden's house and rang his doorbell, she expected him to answer and scold her for being late. Kaylah answered the door, and Rocky's heart dropped to her stomach when she saw her. She hadn't seen or spoken to Kaylah since what happened to her hair and was terrified Kaylah would say something about it.

"The guys are waiting for you in the studio," Kaylah said without even saying hello.

Rocky faked a smile and made her way to Aiden's studio. *Guess she still feels some type of way.* She could hear the guys singing as she got closer to the garage door. Once she opened it, they all stopped and looked at her.

"Ooh, someone's late," Marcus teased.

"I'm sorry," Rocky said.

"You're thirty-five minutes late," Aiden told her. "Where could you possibly have been for you to show up this late?"

"I had to deal with some things and lost track of time." Rocky put her backpack on the table and plopped on the couch. She was emotionally and physically exhausted and had much rather been at home sleeping than hearing Aiden's mouth.

"What if this was a concert you showed up late for because you 'lost track of time'? You can't keep an audience waiting that long, Rocky. Timing is important."

"It won't happen again," Rocky promised.

"You're damn right it won't happen again. Having us wait thirty-five minutes is unacceptable. Do better."

Rocky was still on edge about her fight with Hayley, and how Aiden spoke to her about being late didn't improve her mood. She also knew Aiden was right. Showing up to practice over half an hour late without a reasonable excuse was unacceptable. At the same time, it wasn't like she arrived late every day. Rocky was always on time and sometimes even showed up early.

Rocky sighed, tried to clear her head, and joined the guys for the last 20 minutes or so of rehearsal.

***

Rocky and Hayley had been avoiding each other at school, leaving Adam to choose which of the girls he would hang out with for the day. Rocky knew it wasn't fair to him, but she was still mad at Hayley and wasn't planning on speaking to her anytime soon. Plus, Hayley always got to Adam first and hung out with him more than Rocky could. It had gotten to the point where when Rocky saw Adam by himself, she'd rush to approach him before Hayley could and pull him away.

"You and Hayley need to make up already," Adam told Rocky in between classes. "I'm tired of getting pulled around and forced to choose sides."

"Nobody's making you choose sides," Rocky said.

"You're practically trying to hide me from Hayley."

"Because she's acting extremely petty! She always gets what she wants, and I'm not letting her take my other best friend away from me."

Adam sighed. "Can you at least try to work things out? You're both putting me in an awkward position, and I don't like it."

"I don't want to talk to her right now. Besides, you'd probably just agree with her anyway and tell me to drop Aiden."

"I've been telling you to drop him since the beginning. I can't believe you still don't see how evil he is."

Rocky rolled her eyes. "He's not evil. He just has a hard time controlling his temper. Everything you said about him was wrong."

Adam sighed again and shook his head.

"Can we please not do this right now?" Rocky asked irritably. "I'm dealing with enough already."

"I don't want you to get hurt," Adam said. "He's not a nice person."

"You don't know anything about him!"

"Rocky, I've known him longer than you have. Trust me. I know more about him than you do."

"Okay, so there was that one time he acted out when he was twelve. He's matured since then."

"He's still the same selfish jerk he was back then. You don't see it because you're so hung up on him."

Rocky rolled her eyes again. "If you're going to keep saying all these lies about my boyfriend, then go hang out with Hayley. I don't feel like having this conversation again."

"Please just listen to me," he called out before Rocky could walk away.

"What?"

"He only cares about himself and thinks he's better than everyone else. I don't want you to get hurt, Rocky. Please just talk to Hayley and leave him for good."

Adam gently took Rocky by the arm, but she forcefully pushed him away. "Why are you always trying to tell me what to do, Aiden?"

Adam's brows furrowed in confusion. "Huh?"

Rocky then realized what had happened and felt embarrassed. How could she mix up Adam's and Aiden's names like that?

"Um, Adam," Rocky corrected herself. "You're always trying to make decisions for me like a child. Newsflash. I'm fourteen years old and perfectly capable of making my own choices."

"All I'm trying to do is help you."

"Well, don't!" Rocky shouted. "I know what I'm doing, I know what I want, and I don't need you telling me what to do. You're not my father."

"Rocky..."

"You're just jealous because of my popularity."

Adam's eyes widened. He had the same reaction as Hayley when she told her the same thing.

"Excuse me?" he asked in shock.

"You and Hayley are jealous of what I've become. I've broken out of my shell, I'm close to being famous, and you can't seem to accept that I don't need you guys anymore."

"Rocky," Adam tried to explain.

"I made the best decision of my life to join Aiden's group because if I had stuck around with you guys, I wouldn't be who I am right now. You guys were holding me back from doing everything I'm doing now."

"Wait a minute," Adam said. "Are you forgetting we were the ones encouraging you to break out of your shell in the first place? Unlike that punk you call a boyfriend, Hayley and I want to see you improve for your own benefit."

"He does, too."

"Yeah, right. He's only using you to benefit himself and doesn't realize how much talent you have. You don't deserve to be singing backup all your life, especially not for him. I'm sure it was a good experience for you, but now it's time for you to move on."

"Stop trying to control my life. I already told you I know what I'm doing, Aiden."

"What?" Adam asked.

Not again! Rocky was so upset that she couldn't even think straight. She put her hands on her temples.

"You know what your name is," she said.

"Listen," Adam said seriously. "I'm not trying to control you, and I understand you can make your own decisions. I only want what's best for you, Rocky. You have so much talent, and it'll go to waste if you keep singing with Aiden. You need to..."

"Yeah, are you done yet?" Rocky cut him off. She was starting to get a headache and had enough of people trying to control her.

Adam's jaw dropped as he stared at Rocky in complete shock. Rocky was even surprised by how rude she was toward him. They rarely ever fought.

"I guess I am," Adam said after a while. "You win. If Aiden makes you so happy and you know what you're doing, who am I to hold you back? Good luck to you."

Adam walked away without looking back as Rocky stood alone with her arms folded across her chest. She'd officially lost Hayley *and* Adam.

I guess they weren't my best friends after all. Whatever. I don't need them anyway. I have Aiden, I have the guys, and I'm popular now. I have everything I need.

When school was over, Rocky made it a priority to get to Aiden's house on time. Since she wasn't speaking to Adam or Hayley, she had no distractions after school. She was going to make Aiden proud of her again.

About thirty minutes in, they took a quick break from rehearsing. As usual, the guys went out in the living room while Rocky stayed in the garage to be alone with Aiden. She figured she was mostly over her stage fright. Her anxiety wasn't nearly as intense since she was getting more used to being on stage. Now, Rocky was ready for a challenge. After considering it, Rocky decided that Adam had made a valid point earlier. She didn't want to be a backup singer all her life. Since it was only her and Aiden, she took a deep breath and dared herself to bring up the idea.

"Aiden, can I say something?" she asked.

"What's up?" Aiden said.

They both sat on the couch next to each other. "Um, don't you think it's time for one of us to have a solo? You know, just once?"

"Rocky, we've talked about this already."

"I think we're ready. Or at least *I'm* ready. Being on stage doesn't give me that much anxiety anymore, and I want to challenge myself."

"I don't want you rushing into anything. You think you can do these things, but you can't. Not yet."

"Well, how long am I supposed to wait?"

"Until I say you're ready."

Once again, Rocky felt like she was being controlled. Why doesn't anyone believe she can make the right decisions for herself? Rocky sighed. "But Aiden," she tried to explain.

"I said no, Rocky," Aiden snapped. "You're not getting a solo yet, so stop asking."

The guys came back inside shortly after. Rocky's face started getting warm, hoping the guys didn't hear their conversation.

"Okay, let's continue," Aiden said as if nothing had happened.

After a while, Rocky and the guys became restless. Marcus kept looking at his phone the entire time. Angel kept getting distracted, and Renaldo was sitting in the corner with his head down. Rocky wasn't in the mood for rehearsing anymore and missed singing when it was just a hobby. She missed the joy of having fun with her music. Now, she was always pressured to be perfect and live up to Aiden's high expectations.

"Okay, what's up with you guys?" Aiden finally asked, noticing everyone's lack of enthusiasm.

Nobody answered. Everyone was still in their own worlds.

"Let's not do this again," Aiden said with frustration. "What is it this time? What did I do this time? Whose feelings did I hurt? It's always something with you guys."

"Aiden, relax," Rocky told him gently. "You're getting frustrated again."

"Well, what's going on?" he asked. "It's like you guys aren't even trying anymore. Don't you want this?"

"I don't know," Marcus said. "I'm not feeling it for some reason."

"Well, what can you do to make things better?" Aiden asked him.

"Huh?"

"What do you think you're doing wrong, and how will you fix it?"

Marcus glared at Aiden. "I'm not the problem," he told him.

"Well, *I'm* not the problem," Aiden said with a shrug. "I'm doing fine. If something seems off, it must be because of one of you."

"Oh, brother," Angel muttered under his breath.

"Is there something you need to say, Angel?" Aiden asked.

"I have nothing to say, Aiden," Angel retorted.

"It just feels like...I don't know how to say it," Marcus said. "Can we do something different?"

"Different how?" Aiden asked.

"We do the same thing all the time, and it's starting to get old," Marcus said. "Why don't we change things up a bit or something?"

"I tried with the dancing," Aiden said. "None of you liked it, so we got backup dancers."

"I'm not talking about dancing."

"Well, what else do you want to be done differently? You're not suggesting we alternate who sings lead, are you?"

"What?" Marcus furrowed his brows in confusion.

Aiden looked at Rocky with hard eyes. "You told them about the whole solo thing, didn't you?"

"No," Rocky said.

"What makes you guys think you'll be singing front and center stage?" Aiden asked. "That's my position. You guys stay in your lane as my backup singers."

"Do you not get tired of singing lead all the time?" Angel asked.

"Of course not," Aiden answered. "I'm proudly using the gift God gave me."

"We have that gift too, you know," Angel said.

"But none of you guys are as good as me, which is why you're backup singers."

Was Aiden serious right now? Why was he saying these things?

"Don't you think that's kind of messed up?" Renaldo asked.

"Nope, not at all," Aiden said with a shrug.

"We all want to be successful in this industry," Renaldo continued. "It's not fair that you get all the attention while we're in the background. We all want the same thing, so we should help and support one another instead of bringing each other down."

"Renaldo, this is America," Aiden said. He was talking to Renaldo as if he were a child. "I know you're not used to our customs since you're not from here, but I'll be happy to teach you."

Renaldo narrowed his eyes at Aiden. The way he talked down to Renaldo didn't sit well with Rocky.

"Here, nobody cares about your feelings. People will do whatever it takes to get to the top. Nobody tries to help each other. They'll do anything to knock you off your guard so they can be more successful than you."

"So, you're basically admitting you would sabotage us for your own gain," Renaldo told him.

"I didn't say that. You took it that way."

"So, why can't one of us sing lead for once?"

Aiden laughed at Renaldo. "I see you're hard of hearing, too."

"Knock it off, Aiden," Angel told him. "Stop being so horrible to him. We all helped you get to where you are, so we should at least get to sing once. It's not fair."

"That's where you're wrong," Aiden said. "You guys are successful because of me. You couldn't have done all this on your own. You should be thanking me instead of acting ungrateful and greedy. You're already living like stars. Don't push it."

Rocky decided it was time for her to speak up. "We're just asking for a chance to let our voices be heard," she said timidly.

"You're pushing it again," he said.

The conversation wasn't going anywhere. Rocky thought Aiden was being unusually stubborn and cocky. They would be there all night if they tried to continue convincing Aiden to let someone else sing a solo.

Rocky and the guys left rehearsal together for the first time in a while. Rocky usually liked staying later to get alone time with Aiden, but she couldn't deal with him now. She made up an excuse about needing to help her mom with something so she could leave. As soon as they left Aiden's house, Rocky stopped and faced the guys.

"Don't you think our voices deserve to be heard, too?" she asked them.

"Nothing is going to change his mind," Angel said. "It's his band; we're just his backup singers."

"You don't want to be backup singers forever, do you?"

"Of course not."

Rocky had a risky idea. "We should change the song around at the next concert and add a solo for each of us."

"Are you out of your mind?" Marcus laughed. "Aiden would kill us if we did that."

"He might want to at first. Once he hears how good we sound, then maybe he might consider letting us have more solos."

Marcus continued laughing, which made Rocky roll her eyes and smile.

"Come on, Marcus," Rocky said. "It's not that funny. Angel? Renaldo? What do you guys think?"

"I think you're getting a little *too* bold," Renaldo said with a slight chuckle.

Rocky thought about how ironic this situation was. Usually, Hayley and Adam were the ones convincing Rocky to take risks and let her voice be heard, and she was always reluctant about it. Now, she was trying to convince the boys to take this huge risk and let their voices be heard. Rocky was really breaking out of her shell!

"Well, I think it'll be fun," Rocky said.

"What happened to the Rocky who always did what Aiden said?" Angel asked jokingly.

Rocky laughed. "She got tired of being controlled and wants to do her own thing now."

"The shy exterior has been broken!" Marcus cried out. "But sadly, underneath that exterior is a lunatic. There's no way we'll pull this off, Rocky."

"Yes, we *will* pull this off."

"How?"

"We'll have our own rehearsals in the room where you write your songs, Renaldo," Rocky explained. "We can practice during lunch."

"You seriously want to do this?" Angel asked.

"Sure. We'll probably get yelled at, but at least people will hear us. We don't deserve to sing backup all the time, guys. Your voices are a special gift. Don't let Aiden keep you from sharing your gift."

"Wow," Marcus said in awe. "That means a lot, Rocky. Thank you."

"It's the truth," Rocky said with a smile. "How about we meet tomorrow during lunch to figure out what we'll add to the song?"

Angel, Renaldo, and Marcus all exchanged looks.

"We can meet at the auditorium entrance," Renaldo said.

"Perfect!" Rocky said. "This is going to be so exciting. I can't wait!"

As they parted to go home, Rocky couldn't stop thinking about how the concert would turn out. Who knew taking risks and being bold would be so exciting? She just hoped it wouldn't come back to bite her.

17

All week, Rocky and the guys practiced their revised version of the song during their lunch period. Renaldo came up with a short outro, giving each of them a part to sing when Aiden thought the performance was over. Rocky was impressed at how Renaldo made it flow so easily with the rest of the song — it was almost as if that should've been its true ending. If Aiden didn't consider giving one of them a solo after this performance, then Rocky wouldn't know what to do.

Rocky thought they sounded perfect during Friday's lunch rehearsal after only two takes. They had everything down pat! Rocky knew this was a bold move for her, and she couldn't believe she was still going through with it. Who knew doing something bad could feel so good?

Rocky had such an intense adrenaline rush on the night of the concert that she couldn't keep still. She thought it was exhilarating to know she and the guys added an alternate ending to the song, and Aiden didn't even know about it. Although she was a little anxious about being onstage and about Aiden's reaction, she couldn't wait to perform.

Aiden noticed Rocky's restlessness and chuckled.

"Are you okay over there, Rocky?" he asked.

"Yup," Rocky said. "Just ready to get this show on the road."

"That's the spirit!" Aiden turned to the rest of the guys. "Do not mess this up, guys. There are important people out there watching, and it could be something major if they like us."

Marcus rolled his eyes.

"We have to make sure this is a performance no one will ever forget," Aiden continued.

"It will be," Angel said.

"Let's give it up for Aiden and Company!" the announcer called.

"Alright, let's do this!" Aiden said. "And don't embarrass me."

"Would you relax already?" Marcus said. "We've got this."

Rocky and the guys exchanged looks before following Aiden on stage. *Tonight was definitely going to be a performance to remember*, Rocky thought.

"How's everybody doing tonight?" Aiden greeted the crowd enthusiastically.

The audience responded with cheering and a round of applause.

"This song is called 'The Good Feeling,'" Aiden continued. "It's something I've been working extra hard on, so I hope you all enjoy it."

From the corner of her eye, Rocky saw Renaldo roll his eyes and shake his head. He then turned to look at Rocky and smiled at her. She returned the smile, already knowing what he was thinking. *This is going to be so great!*

"Come on, everyone. Get on your feet and clap along. It's going to be a good one tonight!"

Aiden started singing while Rocky and the guys provided backup vocals. The audience seemed to enjoy the song, but Rocky knew they would love the ending even more.

Aiden put a lot of effort into this performance, Rocky noticed. He was running around on stage more and encouraging the audience throughout the show. Once the song was over, Rocky and the guys exchanged looks. It was time.

"Thank you so much, everyone!" Aiden called out. "I loved the energy out there. Thank you!"

As Aiden was heading off the stage, Angel started singing. Aiden stopped in his tracks and looked at him with dagger eyes. After Angel finished his part, Rocky sang hers, then Renaldo, and finally Marcus. They completed their alternate ending with the four singing together with perfect harmonization.

The crowd cheered just as loudly, if not louder, for them. Aiden's face was a mixture of shock and exasperation. As they all left the stage, Aiden had his fists tightly clenched while trying to keep a smile on his face.

"Wow, that was unexpected," he said as soon as they were backstage.

"Yeah, that's what we were going for," Angel said.

"We wanted to surprise you," Renaldo said.

"You sure did," Aiden said with a big, fake smile.

"You said you wanted this to be a performance no one would forget," Marcus said. "So, you're welcome."

"Well, you're right about that," Aiden told him. "I don't think anyone will forget this show tonight. I know I won't."

"We were pretty good, don't you think?" Rocky asked. "Didn't you like how we sounded?"

"Oh, yeah. You all sounded wonderful. You know, I have a little something for you guys, too. I wanted it to be a surprise for another day, but I think it's best to show you tonight. Meet back at my place for a few?"

Renaldo tensed up, and Rocky began to worry her plan might backfire way worse than she thought. Maybe she should've left the whole thing alone instead of trying to change things.

Aiden's parents dropped the guys and Rocky back at his house. Rocky reached for her phone to let her mom know she'd be home a little later, but it was dead. Hopefully, her mom would understand and let it slide this once. Rocky and the guys waited in the garage for Aiden to return.

"What do you think he's doing?" Renaldo asked, his voice slightly shaking.

"Planning on how he's going to murder us and hide the evidence," Marcus said.

"Marcus, seriously," Angel snapped.

"I mean, I wouldn't put anything past that psycho," Marcus explained. "He was so pissed about what happened tonight. I told my parents to call the cops if they don't see me by 10."

"Okay, you need to stop," Angel said.

Rocky's heart began to race as her thoughts went straight to the rumors of the kid losing his voice because of Aiden.

"Do you think he'll get us expelled from Lennox?" Rocky asked. "Will he seriously hurt us? Will we be able to sing the same again?"

"We're not getting expelled, and he's not going do anything to hurt us," Angel said.

"I don't think I've seen him so mad before," Rocky asked. "Will he kick us out of the group?"

"Aiden can't get rid of all of us," Angel said. "He'll never admit this, but he needs us way more than we need him. We're the ones doing him a favor by singing for him."

"You think so?" Rocky asked.

"I know so. Aiden has something on each of us he holds over our heads anytime one of us wants to quit. That's why we're all still here."

"Really?"

"If that weren't the case, I would've left a long time ago," Marcus told her.

"Same here," Renaldo agreed. "The guy is crazy."

The garage door swung open, startling everyone. Aiden stormed inside and slammed the door shut. "What the hell was that?" he asked angrily.

Nobody answered — this was the maddest Rocky had ever seen Aiden. It was quiet until Marcus was brave enough to speak up.

"You mean our surprise ending to the song?" he asked casually.

"Yes, your 'surprise ending.' You guys completely embarrassed me."

"But I thought you liked it," Rocky said meekly.

"Of course, I didn't like it! You idiots never do anything right and wonder why I'm always so harsh. You wanted a solo so badly that you made yourselves look stupid and desperate. *And* there were some powerful talent agents out there!"

"Well, maybe if you had given us the solo like we asked..." Marcus started, but Aiden cut him off.

"Shut up," Aiden said. "I don't want to hear anything you have to say."

When Aiden usually interrupted Marcus, he would stop talking and move on. However, Marcus wasn't having any of it today.

"We've been asking to sing for months," he continued. "We do so much for you and deserve something because of it."

"So, I should do more for you guys after the stunt you pulled tonight?" Aiden asked. "You can't possibly expect something good to happen when you do stupid stuff like that."

"I mean, we wouldn't do stuff like that if you treated us with the same respect you would want from us."

As Marcus was getting visibly upset, Rocky started feeling guilty. She should've known something like this would happen. Why did she ever think her dumb plan would work anyway?

"The way I treat you is based on your behavior," Aiden said. "When you guys goof around during rehearsals, show up late, and act like everything is a big joke, how do you expect me to react? I'm trying to make something of ourselves, and you guys are ruining it!"

"You don't care about us!" Marcus snapped. "None of this is about us. It's always about you!"

"It's my singing group."

"Which you wouldn't have if it weren't for us. We all make this group."

"I'm the voice of this group. It's your job to sing backup and make me look great. That's all you're good for anyway."

"Okay, you know what?" Marcus sighed. "If you want things done so perfectly and all we do is tear you down, then do all of this yourself. I'm done with you."

Marcus tried to leave, but Aiden stood in his way.

"Since when did you get a backbone?" Aiden said threateningly.

"Move out of my way," Marcus warned him.

"Move me."

Rocky was scared Marcus would hit Aiden and start a fight. Aiden was making Marcus even angrier by taunting him. Angel sprang up and held his arm in front of Marcus, holding him back.

"It's not worth it, man," Angel said.

"No, let him go, Angel," Aiden said, clearly enjoying Marcus's anger toward him. "I dare him to hit me. He knows what happens when he picks a fight he can't win."

As Aiden walked up to Marcus, his expression went from angry to slightly embarrassed. His face turned bright red, either from shame or rage.

"Come on, Marcus," Aiden provoked him. He pointed to his jaw. "Hit me right here."

Rocky held her breath as she waited to see what Marcus would do. Aiden seemed to be getting a kick out of making Marcus feel the way he did. He was practically ready to strangle Aiden a minute ago. What made him back down?

"Do it!" Aiden shouted.

Rocky, Angel, and Renaldo all watched in fear. Marcus wouldn't budge. Aiden laughed in his face.

"That's what I thought," Aiden said. "Sit down, punk."

Marcus sat back down and didn't say anything else. Seeing such a carefree and easygoing guy like him get this angry was hard. Rocky wanted to kick herself now for convincing the guys to add an alternate ending to the song.

"Now listen to me," Aiden said to everyone. "You guys are backup singers, so you sing backup. This is the Aiden Show, and you idiots are here to make me look good. Got a problem with it? Build a bridge and get over it. I don't care how you feel. You need me way more than I need you."

Angel quietly scoffed.

"There's rehearsal on Monday after school," Aiden continued. "Be there on time." He glared at Rocky as he said that. "And be serious. If you guys ever do something like this again, you'll regret it. Now get out of here."

Marcus was the first to get up and leave, while Rocky, Renaldo, and Angel followed shortly after. Rocky didn't even think about staying behind to calm Aiden down. He was too upset, and she was scared of what Aiden might do to her in his moment of rage.

When they got outside, it was dark and windy. It would pour rain any minute. Marcus was standing in Aiden's driveway with his hands stuffed in his pockets.

"You okay, Marcus?" Renaldo asked.

"No, I'm not," Marcus muttered, shaking his head. "I should've hit him."

"You know what happened the last time you tried to fight Aiden," Angel told him. "Be glad you didn't."

"Did you see what he did in there?" Marcus asked. "I can't take this anymore. I don't need this kind of stress in my life."

If Rocky hadn't come up with that ridiculous idea, then none of this would have happened. She and the guys would be content, and Marcus would still be his easygoing self. Rocky was so upset with herself for thinking of the stupid idea and convincing the guys to go through with it. Tears started rolling down her cheeks.

"I'm so sorry, guys," Rocky said. "This is all my fault."

"It's not your fault, Rocky," Renaldo reassured her.

"Yes, it is. I shouldn't have told you guys to change the song around. You said Aiden would be mad about it, but I didn't listen. The idea was so stupid anyway."

The night sky lit up with lightning, and a deafening thunder rolled right after. It started raining hard.

"Let's go to my house until it lightens up," Angel said.

Angel lived two houses down from Aiden, so the four ran over there to shelter from the rain. Angel opened the garage for everyone to get inside. As they stood there soaked, Rocky thought about how the weather outside perfectly matched her feelings now.

Angel brought everyone towels to dry off.

"Marcus, if you're going to be mad at anyone, it should be me," Rocky said.

"No way," Marcus told her. "I don't have any reason to be mad at you. Your idea was great. I don't like singing backup anymore."

"What does Aiden have on you guys that's making you stay with him?"

As the boys sat quietly, Rocky felt embarrassed for asking.

"Never mind. I'm sorry I asked," she said.

"I don't mind explaining," Angel said. "My story, at least. It's kind of similar to yours."

Everyone turned to face Angel as he spoke.

"I wasn't always the coolest guy in school," he continued. "I was the nerdy, socially awkward kid who just wanted to fit in."

"You're still nerdy," Marcus mumbled jokingly.

Renaldo and Rocky chuckled as Angel glared at Marcus.

"But you're a cool nerd," Marcus added with a smile.

Angel rolled his eyes but laughed too. "As I was saying," he said. "I do musical theater, but I consider myself more of an actor than a singer. I knew I could carry a tune, but I never thought I'd end up singing at concerts since that wasn't a priority. One day, Aiden overheard me singing a song that was stuck in my head. He told me how great I sounded and asked why I was wasting my true talent on theater.

Marcus and Renaldo were already part of the group at the time. Aiden practically begged me for weeks to join because he needed a tenor. He also kept telling me he could get me noticed quicker than the theater program ever could. He said his uncle was a big-time television producer and would give me a good word if I sang with him. So, I decided to join. Obviously, singing with him did get me noticed, but not in the way I wanted. I was always 'the guy who sings with Aiden' when I wanted to be just me.

"Aiden told me if I quit his singing group, then I'd go back to being the geek at school, and he'd tell his uncle never to consider me for a film or TV show. He was going to sabotage my dreams of being an actor. I kind of enjoyed the bit of attention I was getting, and the singing was okay. So, I felt like I had no choice but to stay."

Angel sighed, and Rocky held her head down.

"You already know why he has me," Renaldo said softly. "He knew I was a songwriter and wanted some of my music to get noticed. He told me he knew some record producers who could get my songs out there. But only if I joined forces with him."

Aiden sure knows how to manipulate people, Rocky thought.

"After I agreed to sing with him, he asked to see a few of my songs so he could show his record producer friend," Renaldo continued. "I let him hold some of my favorites. You know, the ones I wanted to record and release first. After some time, I asked Aiden about it because he never got back to me. When he gave me my songs back, a lot of the lyrics were changed.

"Naturally, I got angry with him for changing my songs without my permission. He told me the only way his producer friend would consider the song was if he revised it. I was ready to tell Aiden to forget about it, but he kept reminding me that he pretty much held the key to my success in music. This producer friend was big in the music industry, and Aiden threatened to give me a bad rep if I left.

"He ultimately got me to write all the songs for the group. After I write one, he makes a bunch of changes, and all my hard work gets ruined and credited by Aiden."

Renaldo held his head down in shame.

"I'm so sorry, Renaldo," Rocky told him. "That's awful."

"Yeah," he sighed. "At one point, he threatened to deport my family and me back to Mexico if I stopped singing with him. He was *that* ruthless."

Angel rolled his eyes, and Marcus shook his head.

"Music is my life," Renaldo continued. "I love what I do and want to make my family proud. I can't be happy if I keep letting Aiden take credit for my hard work. I can't..." Renaldo was too overwhelmed with emotion to continue. He put his head down in his lap, and Angel gave him a gentle pat on the back for support.

It continued to pour outside, and there were no signs of it lightening up.

"My reason is kind of embarrassing," Marcus said softly. His arms were folded over his chest as if he were protecting himself. "Last year, there was a casting call for a play at school. It was a remake of *Aladdin*, and the audition was open for students of all majors. As a certified Disney fan, I decided to try out for the Aladdin role just for the heck of it. I didn't think I would get the part anyway, and I thought it would be fun to test my acting skills. As it turned out, our boy Aiden was also there to audition for the role of Aladdin."

Rocky rolled her eyes. "Of course, he tries to go for the lead," she said under her breath.

"I went, I auditioned, and the judges loved me. Not to toot my own horn or anything, but they said they loved my enthusiasm, and I brought the character such life," Marcus chuckled. "Fast forward to a few weeks later. They posted the cast list in the courtyard, and I got the part of Aladdin! Guess who got the understudy? That's right — Aiden. He wasn't too pleased about it."

Rocky thought about how Marcus's story with Aiden was similar to what happened with Adam when they were in the church choir together.

"Long story short, Aiden did everything he could to get me to drop out so he could be the star. He tried bribing me and making threats. The dude even tried to get me to hurt myself. Soon, he found out something personal and embarrassing about me. I have no idea how, but he did.

"We had a literature class together that year. Aiden kept volunteering for me to read the passages we were discussing out loud in front of the class, but I couldn't. I was too embarrassed because I have dyslexia. It makes my music classes harder since all the letters on the sheet music get jumbled up, so I have a private tutor to help me. When I tried to confront him about it, he threatened to tell everyone in the school unless I dropped out of the play and let him have the lead role. So, I did."

Rocky wouldn't have guessed that Marcus had dyslexia. He seemed to play it off so well and didn't seem to have any difficulty in their chorus class. It saddened Rocky that Marcus was fighting this battle all on his own.

Marcus turned his back to Rocky and the guys and was quiet for a while. "I watched that jerk perform my role."

Rocky shook her head. "That's awful," she whispered.

"Afterward, he asked if we could start a singing group. Or rather, he forced me to sing with him, or else he would expose my secret. He uses my dyslexia against me whenever I try to leave or fight him." Marcus sighed again and turned to face Rocky and the guys. His eyes were glossy. "And that's how I ended up in this mess."

"I'm sorry to hear that," Rocky said sincerely.

Marcus nodded his head and kept quiet.

"He's using all our vulnerabilities against us to keep us from leaving," Angel said. "Marcus's secret, Renaldo's desire to get noticed..."

"And he's keeping me because he knows how much I want to be popular," Rocky gasped. She put her hands to her head. "I can't believe this."

"It's like what we've been trying to tell you, Rocky," Angel said. "Aiden isn't a nice guy. He's nice at first, but his true colors start to show once he gets what he wants."

This realization was like a slap in the face for Rocky. The guy she fell in love with — the guy who was supposed to love her — was only using her. It killed Rocky on the inside because she thought Aiden genuinely liked her.

"I don't want to believe it," Rocky said tearfully. "I would do anything for him. I dropped my two best friends for him. I thought he really cared about me." Tears began rolling down Rocky's cheeks. "Was any of it real?"

Marcus hugged Rocky when she started sobbing. She couldn't stand the fact that she cared so much about Aiden, and he used her. Everything was a lie. Rocky felt foolish for defending him when her friends told her he was no good. She was crossing oceans for someone who wouldn't even jump a puddle for her.

While Rocky and the guys were waiting for the rain to stop, she knew it was way past her 10:00 curfew. She didn't want to begin to think what her mother would say about her coming home so late without calling.

"I don't think the rain is going to lighten up soon," Angel said. "Do you want me to drive you guys home?"

"Why didn't you do that when we first got here?" Marcus asked.

"We were all bonding," Angel shrugged. "I didn't want to ruin the moment."

Rocky, Renaldo, and Marcus burst into laughter. Angel then took an umbrella from the corner and walked them to his car in the driveway. Since Rocky's house was the closest, Angel dropped her off first.

"Do you have the time?" Rocky asked once he pulled into her driveway.

"It's 11:40," Marcus said.

"It's that late already?" Rocky asked in disbelief. "Hopefully, my mom is asleep now. Thanks so much for the ride home, Angel."

"Of course," he said. "You want me to walk you to your door with my umbrella?"

"I'll just run. Thanks again."

Rocky got out of the back seat of Angel's car, ran to her front door, and waved goodbye before going inside.

18

When Rocky got inside her home, she quietly closed the door and proceeded to tiptoe to her room. About halfway to the staircase, she gasped once she noticed a figure on the couch next to her. After realizing it was her mom, Rocky relaxed, but Rochelle wasn't too happy.

"Where were you?" Rochelle asked.

"I told you I had to sing at a concert this evening," Rocky explained.

"It's almost midnight. You never come home this late, and you know you have a 10:00 curfew."

"The concert ended a little late, and Aiden had a group meeting that lasted a while. Then it started pouring, so we stayed at one of the other guys' houses for a while. I promise I wasn't anywhere you wouldn't want me to be."

"You couldn't have called me to let me know you were coming home late?"

"My phone battery was dead." Rocky had had enough scolding for the night. She was tired and wanted to get out of her wet clothes and sleep. "I'm sorry for missing curfew, and I'm sorry I couldn't call you. At least I'm home now, Mom. Can I please just go to bed?"

"You better watch your attitude, young lady."

"I don't have an attitude. I'm just cold and exhausted, and you keep asking all these questions. Can I get whatever punishment you're going to give me tomorrow?"

"I don't know how much I trust that boy anymore," Rochelle said, shaking her head.

Rocky sighed. She knew she wouldn't get into her warm bed anytime soon.

"Ever since you got with him, you haven't been yourself. You're coming home after curfew; you have a bad attitude..."

Rocky tried to go upstairs. She couldn't deal with this. Not now. "Goodnight, Mom," she said.

Rochelle stood in front of the stairway, preventing Rocky from going any farther. "Excuse me, Rocky. Don't walk away while I'm talking to you."

Rocky rolled her eyes. "Mom, please. I had a long day today."

"That doesn't excuse your rude behavior toward me, young lady. I have long days at work, too."

"I don't mean to be rude, but you don't understand how I'm feeling right now."

"What I do understand is that you're acting like you're grown when you're not."

"I already apologized for coming home past curfew and said it wouldn't happen again. Leave me alone!"

Rocky didn't know what had come over her. She had never raised her voice at her mother before, but she was just annoyed. Before Rocky could see it coming, Rochelle slapped her across the face. She touched her stinging cheek and had tears in her eyes as she stared at her mom in disbelief.

"That's enough out of you, Raquel!" Rochelle yelled. "The last time I had to smack you for being disrespectful, you were seven years old. I don't know what this boy is doing to make you change like this, but it has to stop now. Don't you ever think it's okay to talk to me like that. I'm your mother, and you need to show me some respect."

Rocky was shocked but knew her behavior was wrong. She had never realized how bold she had become until this moment.

"Go upstairs to your room now," Rochelle said. "We'll finish talking about this in the morning."

Without hesitation, Rocky did what she was told. She went into her room, changed out of her wet clothes, and climbed into bed. Rocky couldn't even sleep due to her racing thoughts — and her cheek was still stinging.

***

Not talking to Hayley or Adam was beginning to make Rocky feel lost. She had no idea what to do with herself on Monday morning in the school courtyard since she was used to always hanging out with them. Embarrassed to be sitting alone, Rocky spent that morning and her lunch period hiding in the bathroom.

The extra time she spent there gave her a chance to think about what she wanted to say to Aiden about his behavior on Saturday night. She thought he overreacted, especially with how he embarrassed Marcus. Rocky started to lose some respect for Aiden when she found out how manipulative he'd been with the boys. She didn't like his nasty attitude and thought having a serious conversation with him might change things. Maybe she could convince him that what he's doing is wrong and needs to stop.

After the dismissal bell rang and everyone scrambled to go home, Rocky went to Aiden's locker, hoping he would be there so they could talk. He was there alone, transferring textbooks from his backpack into his locker.

The hallways were gradually clearing as everybody was heading home for the day. Rocky took a deep breath before walking over to Aiden. Hopefully, he wasn't in a bad mood and didn't lash out at her. *You can do this, Rocky.*

"Hey, Aiden," Rocky said as she approached him.

Aiden turned around and smiled slightly. This one was different than the ones he used to give Rocky when they first started talking. His face used to light up when he smiled at her in the beginning. This slight grin seemed forced and patronizing.

"Hey, what's up?" Aiden said.

Rocky looked down at her feet. "Um, we need to talk," she said softly.

"About what?"

"A lot."

"Rocky..."

"You're not treating me like you did when we first met. You've been kind of rude — actually, you've been *very* rude. And I deserve better than what you're giving me now."

Aiden opened his mouth to speak, then closed it. He furrowed his eyebrows as he thought of what to say next. "You're right," he finally said. "I have been harsher on you lately, but you know I'm not that kind of person. It's just..."

"The stress from all the concerts," Rocky finished for him. "But even when you aren't worrying about concerts, you've still been rude. I think you're using that as an excuse now."

"No, I'm not, Rocky. How could you even say that? You try booking concerts and shows with a group of guys who don't seem to care and tell me that doesn't stress you out."

"Maybe they'd show more appreciation if you showed them more respect. You're always putting the guys down, and you talk to them like they're worthless. Your actions are going to dictate your consequences, you know."

"What are you, a life coach or something?"

"I thought I was supposed to be your girlfriend and a singer in your group."

"What point are you trying to make, Rocky?"

"I know you're only using me, Aiden."

"What gave you that idea?"

"You always tell me how great of a singer I am, but you never let me sing."

Aiden sighed and grabbed his temples. "You know I don't let you sing because of your stage fright."

"Do you know how long ago I got over that? I don't even remember the last time I had a major panic attack before singing on stage. It's more than that, Aiden. You don't want the spotlight on anyone except you."

"Listen, I'm so tired of having this conversation with you. I asked you to join my group as a *backup singer*. Do you know what backup singers do, Rocky? They sing backup. Get used to being the underdog because, like I said the other day, this is the Aiden Show. I'm the star, not you."

Rocky took a deep breath and tried her hardest to keep a neutral face. She didn't want to show Aiden how hurtful his comment was to her. "If you think I'm exceptionally talented, why would you have me sing backup?"

Aiden rolled his eyes. "Okay, I'm done talking to you." He turned around to leave, but Rocky was going to make it clear *she* wasn't done talking to *him*.

"Answer me!" she shouted. Rocky had never been bold enough to stand up to Aiden because she was afraid of what he would do to her. She had to admit it felt good to stand up for herself for once.

Aiden turned around and glared at her. "Who do you think you're getting loud with?"

"Answer my question, Aiden," Rocky demanded. "Were you only using me to make yourself sound better? Did you even want me in your group?"

Aiden took a step toward Rocky, and she took a step back. He clenched his fists and had the same threatening look in his eye the day he punched Renaldo in the face. Surely Aiden wouldn't hit Rocky, though. Would he? If Aiden ever put his hands on Rocky, that would be a deal-breaker. He stared down at her.

"Okay, you want the truth?" Aiden asked. "You suck. Your voice is so squeaky, and it sounds horrible. You sopranos think the world revolves around you. I had to put you in your place, which is singing backup for a real singer."

At that moment, it felt like the first day of Lennox all over again for Rocky. She was insecure, helpless, and wishing every minute she was back in the comfort and protection of her bed. No matter how much Aiden's comments cut her like a knife, Rocky kept her poker face. She took another deep breath.

"Don't talk about me like that," Rocky said.

"You wanted the truth, didn't you?"

Rocky didn't want to believe the Aiden in front of her was the same Aiden she fell so hard for. She defended him, stuck up for him, and chose him over her best friends. But here he was, talking down to Rocky as if she didn't mean anything to him. It was as if everything she ever did for him didn't matter. Rocky wondered if any of it was real. She shook her head.

"You're crazy," Rocky told him. "I don't know what I ever saw in you." As Rocky turned around to leave, Aiden grabbed her wrist and squeezed it. Rocky yelped in astonishment and pain.

"Where do you think you're going?" he asked.

Rocky pulled her wrist free from Aiden's firm grip. "Let me go!" she shouted.

"You think you can leave that easily?"

"You never wanted me in the first place. Not as your backup singer or your girlfriend."

Aiden took Rocky by the face with one hand, squeezing her jaw like a misbehaving toddler getting scolded by their parent. Rocky couldn't move her head. The harder she fought to get away, the tighter Aiden would squeeze her face. Her heart began racing, and she wanted nothing more than to get out of there before Aiden could hurt her.

"You wouldn't be who you are right now if it weren't for me," Aiden told her. "If you hadn't joined forces with me, you'd still be that awkward little nobody with stage fright. I gave you the chance to sing on national television and at real concerts and record actual songs. I made you into someone, and this is the thanks I get?"

Rocky finally managed to get free from Aiden's grip, and her jaw was aching.

"You're nothing without me," Aiden continued. "If you choose to leave, you'd be making the biggest mistake of your life."

"My biggest mistake was trusting you."

"You were a loser before you met me."

"Stop talking to me like that!"

"Stop talking to me like that!" Aiden mimicked her.

Rocky felt her eyes begin to water as Aiden laughed at her. *Get it together, girl!* She squeezed her eyes shut and took another deep breath. "You don't faze me anymore," Rocky said with a shaky voice. She was hoping to sound more assertive.

"You're lying," Aiden said. "Look, I made the poor baby cry."

Rocky quickly wiped her tears away with trembling hands. She didn't know how much longer she could keep up her tough-girl persona.

"That's all you do — just cry." Aiden stepped up to Rocky again, but she didn't move this time. "Just cry like the little bitch you are." He laughed at her again.

Rocky still didn't say anything. She kept her head down.

"You know what?" Aiden said. "You don't even have to worry about trying to leave the group anymore because I'm kicking you out. I don't know why I let a girl into the group, especially one like you. You're so weak and timid. You never stand up for yourself. I thought you would toughen up after all this time with me, but I see you're a slow learner. You're untalented, you're stupid, you're worthless, and you'll never amount to anything in life."

Rocky had had enough of Aiden's belittlement. How can a person make such harsh comments about someone? She felt her chest tightening from holding back her tears.

"Why don't you go and kill yourself already? You're so..."

With all her might, Rocky pushed Aiden from in front of her. He stumbled a bit but regained his balance. Even angrier than before, Aiden walked back up to Rocky and slapped her so hard, she went flying backward. He then grabbed her by the throat and started to squeeze.

"You want to go there with me?" he asked angrily. "Bring it."

Aiden now had both hands firmly grasped on Rocky's neck, and she was struggling to breathe as he held her against the wall. She scratched Aiden's hands as hard as she could as tears streamed down her face.

"Let me go," Rocky gasped. "Please!"

Aiden only choked Rocky harder. Everybody had already left for the day. She and Aiden were the only ones in the hallway, so calling for help wouldn't do anything. Rocky's vision was starting to blur, and she thought she heard a slight humming in her ears. As her body was becoming limp, she noticed Aiden loosen his grip. It sounded like there was another person in the hallway yelling.

"Let her go now!" she heard a male voice shouting.

Rocky was able to turn her head slightly and thought she was hallucinating. She saw Adam standing across the hallway. Before Rocky could collect her thoughts, Aiden groaned and threw Rocky against the wall. Rocky fell to the floor and was still groggy as the oxygen returned to her brain. *Wait, is that really Adam?*

"I'm so sick of you," Aiden said to Adam.

"Do something about it then," Adam challenged.

As Rocky was slowly becoming more aware of what was happening, she couldn't help but watch in horror as Aiden approached Adam. What was Adam getting himself into? Aiden was nearly twice his size. Surely, he wouldn't try to fight him.

"Do you know what I could do to you?" Aiden asked.

"Do you think I'm scared of you?"

"You should be, little man. I'll destroy you."

"Do it, then."

Rocky respected Adam for sticking up for her — but at the same time, she thought he was out of his mind. Rocky had never even seen him fight anyone before. Her heart started racing as she thought of all the terrible things that could happen to Adam — and it would be all because of her.

Aiden laughed at Adam. "Why are you even wasting your time?" he asked. "You know you can't stand a chance against me."

Adam threw a punch directly to Aiden's chest when he least expected it. Aiden grunted and doubled over, now leveled with Adam. Taking advantage of the opportunity, Adam sucker-punched Aiden in the face. He hit the floor and was stone still.

Rocky's jaw dropped. She didn't know if it was the lack of oxygen in her brain, but it took her a while to process what had happened. Did Adam just knock Aiden out?

"Don't you ever underestimate the little man again," Adam told the unconscious Aiden.

"Adam," Rocky whispered.

Adam rushed over to Rocky's side and hugged her as she cried. The tighter he held her, the harder Rocky sobbed. Adam just saved her. She felt protected while he held her close.

"You're okay," he reassured her. "You're okay." He kept repeating those words as he caressed her back.

19

The school principal *conveniently* showed up shortly after Adam calmed Rocky down. Noticing Aiden lying unconscious on the floor, the principal used his walkie-talkie to contact the school nurse. Mr. Anderson told Rocky and Adam to wait outside his office until he returned. Rocky had never been sent to the principal's office, and the one time she did, it was because she was the victim of an attack. How crazy was that?

Rocky didn't leave school until about 5:30 that evening. After getting everyone's stories straight, the principal called her mom to inform her about what had happened. Even though Rocky couldn't see her mom's reaction, she could hear her yelling through the phone. She couldn't recall ever hearing her mother sound that angry. Rochelle was on her way to pick her up from school.

While Rocky was in Mr. Anderson's office, she explained how Aiden was physically violent with her and how Adam was trying to help. Luckily, they were in an area with a security camera, so Mr. Anderson could see what happened for himself. Rocky was off the hook, but unfortunately, Adam got suspended. Aiden woke up to find out he'd been expelled from Lennox.

When Adam and Rocky got to the student pickup area, Adam's mom was already waiting for him.

"Rocky, are you okay, sweetheart?" Adam's mom asked. "I'm more than happy to take you home if you need a ride."

"No, thank you, Mrs. Marin," Rocky said. "My mom is almost here."

"Would you like us to wait with you until she comes?"

Rocky's first instinct was to decline the offer, but she was still shaken about what had happened and didn't want to be left alone.

"I'd appreciate that," Rocky said, holding back her tears.

Adam put his hand on Rocky's shoulder as his mom gave her a warm smile. Less than five minutes later, Rochelle was pulling into the school. She thanked Adam and his mom for waiting with her, and Yolanda said she'd check in later today.

When Rocky opened the passenger door to her mom's car, Rochelle had tears in her eyes.

"Rocky, baby, are you okay?" she asked frantically.

"I'm okay, Mom," Rocky said. As she got in the car, Rochelle gave her a big hug and started sobbing, which made Rocky tear up as well.

"Rocky, I swear if I weren't a saint, I would take the sharpest machete I own and chop that boy up," Rochelle said.

Rocky giggled at her mother's silly threat.

"Don't laugh. I'm crazy, and you know I'd do it." Rochelle held Rocky's face and looked at her. "No boy will ever get away with hurting my daughter, do you hear me?" she said.

"I'm sorry about everything, Mom," Rocky said. "I was just so happy about being popular and finally having a boyfriend."

Rochelle wiped the tear rolling down Rocky's face. "Sweetie, I'm just happy you're okay," she said. "I hope you learned something from this."

"Oh, for sure. I'll never be that naïve again. And I hope Aiden gets everything his karma owes him."

"Karma takes too long. I'd rather punch him now."

Rocky chuckled a bit, not too sure if her mother was being serious or not.

"You think this is a game? He'd better pray I don't run into him out there. I don't play about my child."

"Thanks for caring so much, Mom. He's going to regret treating me like this."

"Yes, he will. He'll learn not to mess with Caribbean folks ever again." Rochelle gave Rocky another hug. "I love you so much," she whispered.

"I love you, too," Rocky whispered back.

***

The next morning at school was strange for Rocky. Random students she'd never seen or spoken to approached her and asked questions like, "Are you okay?" and "Did Aiden really hurt you?" The whole thing happened less than 24 hours ago, and most of Lennox already knew about it. How was that even possible?

Rocky politely answered all the questions and tried to leave before she got too overwhelmed. Hayley ran up to Rocky and hugged her tightly, nearly sending them both tumbling to the floor. It sounded like Hayley was crying.

"Rocky, please tell me you're okay," she said frantically. "Please tell me he didn't hurt you too bad."

"I'm fine, Hayley," Rocky said breathlessly. Hayley was hugging her a little too tight. "But *you're* hurting me right now."

Hayley let go, and Rocky exhaled. Hayley stared at Rocky with wide, concerned eyes.

"He didn't hurt me too bad," Rocky told her once she could breathe normally.

Rocky and Hayley hadn't spoken since their fight a few weeks ago, and she felt awful about what happened between them. She didn't realize how much she missed her best friend until her eyes started welling up. "Hayley, I'm so sorry about how I acted toward you. You and Adam were right about Aiden, but I couldn't see it because I was so in love with him. Please forgive me."

"Of course, I forgive you, Rocky. The only thing that matters right now is you're okay, and Aiden is out of your life."

"Oh, I never want to see that jerk again," Rocky said. "He convinced me that you were holding me back from making it big as a singer. He told me all I needed was him, but he was wrong. I don't know what I would do without my best friend."

Hayley smiled. "Aw, Rocky. I missed having you around."

Rocky and Hayley hugged again, and things were finally starting to feel right.

"Can I ask you something?" Hayley said, wiping the tears from her eyes.

"Anything," Rocky answered.

"Did Adam really knock Aiden unconscious?"

Rocky laughed. "He did, and it was so cool. While Aiden was talking about how Adam wouldn't stand a chance against him, he winded him and knocked him out cold."

Hayley and Rocky couldn't stop laughing about it.

"That's what he gets for underestimating Adam," Hayley said.

"I still need to thank him for what he did for me. I tried calling him yesterday, but his dad took his phone. He's on punishment for getting suspended."

"Ooh, harsh. But fair, I guess. I totally respect him for helping you the way he did."

"I know. That was brave of him." Rocky thought about how horrible she was to Adam and felt guilty. Even after how horribly she spoke to and treated him, he still went out of his way to protect her. "Man, I need to apologize to him."

People kept asking Rocky about what happened with Aiden throughout the day, sending her anxiety through the roof. She wanted to forget that yesterday happened, but everyone brought it up. During lunch, she had to hide in the bathroom because she felt an anxiety attack coming on as she had flashbacks.

As she sat on the toilet thinking back on what happened, it made her feel foolish. There were so many red flags, and it baffled her how she flat-out ignored them. She was angry at herself for wanting a boyfriend and popularity so badly that she put up with Aiden's gaslighting.

After she left the bathroom, she walked with Hayley, who was waiting outside for her. The two returned to the courtyard, and Rocky noticed Angel, Renaldo, and Marcus. It was odd seeing them without Aiden.

"There are the guys," Rocky said to Hayley. "I'm going to go talk to them. Want to come with?"

"Sure, I'll come," Hayley said hesitantly. "But can you give me a minute?" She dug through her backpack, took out a compact mirror, and started fixing her hair.

Rocky laughed and rolled her eyes. "You look fine, Hayley."

Hayley blushed as she started checking for food in her teeth. She mentioned to Rocky that she had finally started talking to Angel, but they hadn't officially started dating.

"Should I put on a little lip gloss first?" Hayley asked. "Do you think he'll notice the zit on my forehead? Should I...?"

"Hayley," Rocky laughed again. "You look beautiful. You always do, and Angel will always think so, too."

Hayley took a deep breath. Rocky had never seen Hayley stress herself out over a boy before. She must like Angel a lot!

"Come on, let's go," Rocky said.

As Rocky and Hayley approached the guys, they had that look of concern everyone gave Rocky all day.

"Rocky," Marcus said. "I heard about what happened yesterday. Please tell me it was all a lie."

"I wish it were all a lie," Rocky admitted. "But I'm fine now, I promise."

"I knew Aiden was a jerk," Renaldo said. "But for him to hit you like that is unacceptable. If I ever see him again, I'd tell him *métetelo por el culo*."

"Not too sure what that means, but you know Renaldo is upset when he starts speaking Spanish," Marcus joked.

"Have you guys talked to him yet?" Rocky asked them.

"No way," Angel said. "We're done with him and his stupid group."

Hayley and Rocky exchanged looks.

"Really?" Rocky asked.

"Do you think we'd continue singing for that fool after what he did to you?" Marcus asked.

Rocky smiled at the guys. She's glad Aiden was out of the picture for good. She could see how much he was affecting each of the guys, and they all deserved way better than what Aiden was giving them.

"From one survivor to another," Marcus joked, holding out his fist. "We conquered Hurricane Aiden."

Rocky laughed at him as they bumped fists.

"Did Aiden physically hurt all of you?" Hayley asked out of curiosity.

The guys hesitantly nodded, and Hayley looked down at the ground. "I'm sorry to hear that," she added. "But at least he won't be a problem anymore."

"Yeah, and even though we all had a negative experience with him, some good came from it," Rocky mentioned. "I finally got over my stage fright."

"I guess some of my songs are finally out there," Renaldo added. "Even though Aiden has all the credit for them."

"I finally learned how to dance well," Angel said, busting out one of the old moves from their dance routine.

Everyone laughed at his failed attempt.

"You still could use some practice, my guy," Marcus joked.

"Hey, I'm getting there!"

"Best of all, I made three amazing new friends," Rocky added.

"Aww," Marcus cooed. "That's so sweet. Group hug, everybody!"

"Yeah, let's not," Angel said.

Marcus still held his arms open. "Don't be lame, Angel. You can't fight the feeling. You know you want to."

Rocky giggled and hugged Marcus, and soon Angel and Renaldo shrugged and joined in.

"Come on," Marcus told Hayley, who was standing off to the side, watching and holding back her laughs. "You're family, too. Join the hug-fest."

Hayley smiled and shook her head but joined in. Sure, the whole group hug thing was corny, and they all probably looked ridiculous. Rocky didn't care. These people meant a lot to her and didn't make her feel like a loser.

After they finished hugging, Rocky noticed Hayley and Angel standing awkwardly beside each other and grinned.

"You know," Rocky said. "I think Marcus, Renaldo, and I should go over there for a moment."

When Rocky turned to look at Hayley, her eyes widened, and Angel's face turned bright red.

Marcus and Renaldo soon got the hint.

"Oh, okay," Marcus said.

"We'll be over there then," Renaldo said.

"And you two can stay here," Rocky said.

The three of them ran away while Angel and Hayley stayed behind. Rocky knew Hayley would probably kill her later for pulling that stunt. She also knew Hayley would be thanking her after she got comfortable being alone with Angel.

After school, Rocky walked straight to Adam's house. She had to thank him for what he did and apologize for how she treated him. She wouldn't feel right with herself if she let another day go by without seeing him.

When Rocky got to his house and knocked on the front door, Adam's father, Reverend Trenton Marin, opened the door and smiled at her. He was the pastor at the church they attended.

"Sister Rocky," he greeted her. "How are you?"

Rocky smiled back. "I'm great, Reverend."

"I'm so sorry to hear about what happened to you yesterday."

"Thanks, but I'm okay now. It was scary, and I'm hoping to just forget about that day."

"It's a good thing he got kicked out of school, and you'll never have to deal with him again. Now, what brings you here?"

"Would it be okay if I talked to Adam for a bit?"

"Oh, Sister Rocky, he's on punishment for the next two weeks. I thought I told your mother about this."

"You did, but this is important. I don't think it can wait until Adam is off punishment."

"If you need me to give him a message for you, I'd be more than happy to do so."

"I'd feel better telling him myself, Reverend," Rocky said timidly. "I haven't been the greatest friend to him lately, and I need to apologize and tell him how much I appreciated his help yesterday."

Reverend Marin stared at Rocky for a moment.

"Please?" Rocky pleaded. "I promise it'll only take a few minutes, and it'll feel more sincere if he hears it from me."

Reverend Marin smiled at her again and chuckled. "Oh, all right," he said. "But five minutes, okay?"

"Perfect. That's all I need. Thank you so much."

Reverend Marin let her into the house, and Rocky went straight to Adam's bedroom door, which was halfway open. She knocked anyway.

"Hey, Adam," Rocky called out. "Can I come in?"

"Yeah, sure," Adam called back.

Rocky let herself in and saw Adam lying comfortably in his bed with a bible in front of him. He sat up when Rocky came in.

"Catching up on the Word?" Rocky joked.

Adam laughed. "I don't have a choice. My dad took everything from me — my phone, my TV, my music. All I have left is my bible."

Rocky laughed too. She stood next to his door with her back against the wall. "Adam, I want to thank you for saving me from Aiden yesterday."

Adam shrugged. "It was nothing. I was only looking out for you."

"I appreciate that a lot." Rocky smiled at him. "I can't believe I've known you all this time and had no idea you were such a fighter."

Adam laughed again. "I'm not that great of a fighter," he admitted. "Once I saw him messing with you, I knew I had to do something, so I acted quickly."

"Again, I appreciate it," Rocky said.

"It's no big deal."

"I'm also sorry for how I treated. I should've believed you when you told me Aiden was no good. You're probably waiting to say, 'I told you so.'"

"No, I'm not," Adam joked. "But yeah, I told you so."

Rocky laughed again. "I should've listened to you. I was just so happy to be popular and convinced myself you were trying to keep me from being happy."

"You know I would never try to keep you from being happy. All I want is for you to be happy."

Rocky sighed. "I'm such a horrible person."

Adam got out of bed and stood next to Rocky. "Rocky, you're not a horrible person," he told her.

"Yes, I am. Listening to Aiden was the stupidest thing I could've ever done. I can't believe he turned me against my own best friends."

"Rocky," Adam said, but she wouldn't stop talking.

"I was so horrible to you. You didn't have to protect me from Aiden yesterday, but you did. I don't know how I can ever repay you."

"Rocky," Adam tried again. Still, Rocky didn't listen and continued to talk.

"I just want you to know how sorry I am about everything, and I'm so thankful..."

Adam stopped Rocky from talking by gently turning her face toward his and kissing her lips, much to her surprise. After he broke the kiss, Rocky looked at him in disbelief.

"Can I speak now?" he asked.

"Okay," she answered.

"First, you don't need to apologize so many times," Adam joked. "And I'm not mad at you anymore. I was looking out for you because I care about you. Even when we're not on the best terms, I'll always care about you. You're special to me."

Rocky and Adam timidly smiled at each other. For as long as she'd known him, she never got those intense butterflies when she looked at him until now. Rocky never saw him as more than her best friend and began wondering how long Adam had felt this way about her. Also, why didn't he tell her about how he felt sooner?

Adam's door opened, and the two quickly separated before Adam's mom walked in. Did she see them kissing? Did she think something else was going to happen? Rocky held her head down in embarrassment, and Adam was just as embarrassed.

"Hey, Rocky," she said. "Adam's dad wanted me to let you know it's about time for you to head out."

Time seemed to fly by! Even though Rocky wished she could stay and learn more about what just happened, she did promise to only be there for a few minutes to apologize and thank Adam. She didn't want to get on the Reverend's bad side, so she obliged.

"Okay, Mrs. Marin," Rocky said. "Thanks again for letting me talk to Adam for a bit."

"No worries! We always love having you over, sweetie. Please come back whenever you want once Adam's off punishment."

Rocky turned around and waved at Adam. "I'll talk to you later," she said. "You know, once you're off punishment."

Adam chuckled. "See you in two weeks," he said before Rocky left.

ONE MONTH LATER

The end of the school year was only a few weeks away, and Rocky was glad to get freshman year out of the way. Her first year of high school was nothing like how she expected it to be, and she has come a long way since the beginning of the year. Her time and experience at Lennox made her more confident in herself and her singing. Rocky also had the chance to learn more about herself.

Since Aiden was expelled from Lennox, more people were willing to show off their talents without worrying about being "too good." Nobody feared what Aiden would do if he thought they were better than him. In other words, the atmosphere was a lot lighter since he left.

Rocky hadn't spoken to or heard about Aiden since he attacked her. In a way, he had a lot to do with how she was today. Rocky wondered —wherever Aiden was — if he would ever take advantage of other vulnerable singers again.

Rocky still hung out with the guys often. A music executive reached out to Renaldo after he posted a video of himself singing an original song. Rocky was thrilled for him because all he ever wanted was acknowledgment for his work. The other day, Renaldo eagerly told her how he had the opportunity to professionally record the song he posted online. It was available on all major music streaming services, and he was getting a lot of listens. The music executive planned on working with Renaldo to get more songs recorded and released. Rocky was excited that he got to do what he had dreamed of for so long.

Marcus always mentioned the only thing he loved more than music was sports. Since he wasn't as busy with singing, he had plenty of time to train with Lennox's football team. He was stoked to join the team next year. Marcus made Rocky promise she would be at every one of his games and playfully threatened to never speak to her again if she missed even one game. Rocky was sure Marcus would be a valuable player for the team next year. Marcus also switched his major from vocals to instrumental with a concentration in percussion. He mentioned enjoying playing instruments more than singing.

Angel always talked about how excited he was about being a senior next year. He'd been busy looking at different colleges, narrowing his top choices, and applying for scholarships. Since Angel didn't have to worry about singing, he could maintain good grades to get into the best schools. Angel told Rocky that he and Hayley were still talking every day and went out on a few dates. Anytime she asked for more details, he would only smile and not say anything. Hayley did the same thing when Rocky tried to ask her about their relationship. To Rocky, they were already a couple.

Rocky and Hayley started singing together again. They performed every so often during the lunchtime concerts and did a couple of impromptu performances in the courtyard. Rocky still wasn't too keen on randomly singing in the middle of the day, but they always received positive feedback. Rocky was relieved to be singing with her best friend again and even more relieved about not worrying about Aiden's antics. She felt free and fully comfortable singing in front of her peers for the first time.

Adam and Rocky were going strong as a couple, and she'd never been happier. He was the main one encouraging her to start singing more at the lunchtime concerts and had been nothing but supportive of her. Rocky did what she could to support him as well. Adam was basically everything Aiden wasn't. He even tried looking up venues for amateur singers to get her more practice singing in front of different crowds. Adam still wrote songs and sometimes joined in with Rocky and Hayley's harmonization. The three of them recently sang one of Adam's songs during a lunch concert, and everyone at school had been talking about it for weeks. Rocky introduced Adam to Renaldo, and they hit it off instantly. They even agreed to work on writing some songs together.

***

Rocky had been home from school for the day and was in the living room watching television. In the middle of her favorite show, Rochelle came home from work. She was visibly exhausted and seemed to have a lot on her mind.

"Hey, Mom," Rocky said. "Long day at work?"

Rochelle sat next to Rocky and sighed. "Don't get me started," she said. "Hey, what was that jerk's name again? The one you were singing with a while ago?"

"Aiden?"

"Is his last name Benjamin?"

"Yes. Why? What happened?"

"He got admitted into the hospital today."

Rocky's jaw dropped. "Oh, my God. What happened?" She looked at her mother. "Mom, did you do something to him?"

Rochelle laughed. "I didn't do anything to him, Rocky. It had something to do with his throat; I think he needed surgery."

Rocky was sure that had to be Aiden's karma. At the same time, she couldn't help but feel bad for him. Throat surgery isn't anything a singer would want.

"Can I visit him?" Rocky asked.

Rochelle looked at Rocky with one eyebrow raised. "You really want to visit him?" she asked.

"Sure. You know, just to check on him."

It was wild how a month ago, Rocky never even wanted to see Aiden again. Now here she was, asking to visit and check on him. No matter how petty she wanted to be, she had to make sure Aiden was doing okay. Throat surgery couldn't have been easy for him.

"I think he's in too much of a vulnerable state to try and hurt me if that's what you're worried about," Rocky said. "And as a singer, I know this must be hard for him. I want to make sure he's okay."

"I'm coming in there with you," Rochelle said seriously. "And if he or his family try any funny business..."

"Mom," Rocky laughed. "It'll be fine."

"Rocky, I'm not too sure about this."

"Please, just trust me."

Rochelle sighed. "Give me five minutes, and we can go," she said. "I guess nine hours at the hospital just wasn't enough."

Rocky laughed and hugged her mom.

Rocky never enjoyed being in hospitals. Something about them always creeped her out. Maybe it was the fact that people die in hospitals every day. After Rocky and Rochelle got their visitors' passes at the front desk, they made their way to Aiden's room. It was odd seeing him in the state he was in. The last time Rocky saw him, he physically abused her. Now a month later, he was lying in a hospital bed.

Aiden's demeanor changed when he saw Rocky and her mom standing at the door. It was like she was the last person he expected to see.

"What are you doing here?" Aiden asked. His voice was hoarse.

"I heard you were in the hospital, so I wanted to check on you," Rocky said shyly. She noticed Aiden's mother sitting in a corner, minding her own business. She didn't even say anything to Rocky or Rochelle.

"Why?" Aiden asked.

Rocky shrugged. "Just because."

Aiden rolled his eyes. "Yeah, right. You're probably here to watch me suffer. You didn't visit 'just because.'"

Same old Aiden, Rocky thought to herself. Luckily, Rochelle jumped in on this one.

"Young man," she said. "Rocky asked to see you after you've put her through a lot. The least you can do is show her some appreciation."

"What if I don't believe her intentions are true?"

Kaycee finally stood up. "The doctor said you shouldn't be talking!" she told him. She still hadn't said anything to Rocky or her mom.

"Who cares what the doctor says?" Aiden snapped.

"This is the same reason why you had to have the surgery in the first place. You never listen, Aiden. All people want to do is help you, and you completely disregard them. I don't understand why you're so hardheaded."

Aiden rolled his eyes again. "Whatever."

"I think I might know why he's so mean," Rochelle whispered to Rocky.

"Keep playing, then," Kaycee said. "You're going to end up not being able to sing at all. And once your career is over, you'll wish you had listened."

"That's not going to happen."

"Believe what you want."

"Mrs. Benjamin," Rochelle interjected. "It's nice to see you again after all this time, but I wish it weren't under these circumstances."

"My son is never going to be a successful singer because of this stupid surgery," Kaycee said with her hand on her forehead.

"Okay, let's be reasonable," Rochelle said. "Why don't you step outside with me, and we can talk. Mom to mom."

Rochelle guided Aiden's mom out of the room. Rocky couldn't get over how Aiden's mom didn't even acknowledge her presence. Not once did she look at or speak to her, but she was so friendly the first time they met. Adam might have been right. Maybe Aiden's whole family is corrupt and two-faced. It would make sense why Aiden was the way he was.

"She seems a little stressed," Rocky joked. Aiden wasn't laughing. "So, what did you have surgery for?"

"Do you honestly care?" Aiden asked with attitude.

"If I didn't care, do you think I would be here right now?" Rocky shot back. "I'm not trying to get even with you or get revenge for everything you did to me. I'm over that. Being in the hospital after surgery is serious, and I was genuinely concerned. I figured you've known me long enough to realize I'm not a bad person."

Aiden kept his head down and didn't say anything.

"I can guarantee if it were anyone else, they wouldn't have bothered to visit or even cared about what happened to you. They probably would've thought you deserved to suffer. And here I am. When I could be doing so many other things, I took the time to visit the guy who took advantage of me and physically hurt me."

Aiden was still silent.

"I didn't have to come, but I chose to."

Rocky hoped what she was saying would at least talk some sense into Aiden. Maybe it could teach him that what he'd been doing was wrong and that he should treat people with the same respect he would want from others. What goes around does come back around.

"But if you don't want me here, I'll leave."

"Please don't," Aiden said before she could walk away.

Did Rocky finally get to him?

"I had vocal nodules," he admitted.

Rocky winced just thinking about it. She'd never had vocal nodules before, but her mother did, and she mentioned how painful they were.

"They were so severe that surgery was the only way to get rid of them," he continued.

"Why didn't you get them checked out sooner?"

"I never knew I had them. I just thought I was hoarse from all the performances."

"Will you be able to sing again?"

Aiden sighed. "Yeah," he said. "But I lost my vocal range. I'll never be able to hit those notes I used to."

Poor Aiden, Rocky thought sympathetically. Aiden had a wide vocal range, and being unable to sing the same had to be rough. Wasn't it ironic how the rumors around the school were about Aiden getting a student expelled and ruining his singing voice? And now the exact thing was happening to him.

"I'm really sorry to hear that," Rocky told him. "Even though you won't sound the same, you'll still be able to sing. That's a good thing."

Aiden finally looked at Rocky, and she noticed he had an expression of guilt and sadness on his face. It looked like he was holding back tears.

"Thank you for listening, Rocky," he said. "You know, you're the only one who actually cares."

"Seriously?" Rocky asked. "That can't be true. What about your parents?"

"They only care if I'll ever have a successful singing career again. When the doctor said my vocal range wouldn't be the same, my parents had nothing positive to say."

"I'm sure it was just because they were stressed about you being in the hospital?"

"They told me to start learning a new talent since my singing career was in the toilet. They didn't show any kind of concern for me as a person."

Aren't parents supposed to support and encourage their children with positivity? Rocky finally understood — Aiden grew up dealing with a lot of negativity from his parents, who treated him more like a client than a son. He had to be the best singer in the school, or he wouldn't get support from his parents. That explained a lot about how he acted, and it broke Rocky's heart. At least she knew deep down that Aiden wasn't mean because he wanted to be.

"You saw how my mom reacted when you first walked in," Aiden continued. "My dad still hasn't come to visit me, and who even knows where Kaylah is? None of them asked about how I was feeling after the surgery."

"Aiden, I'm so sorry," Rocky said quietly. She didn't know what else to say.

"But after everything I put you through, why would you still come to visit me? Why would you even care to see me?"

"I told you, I'm not a bad person. You need someone to be here for you, and it seems your family isn't the best support system. Nobody deserves to be alone after having major surgery."

"Thank you so much," Aiden said, putting his hand on top of Rocky's. She quickly but gently pulled away. She was here for Aiden, but only as a friend and nothing more. Rocky wasn't going down that road again. She nervously laughed and put her hands in her pockets.

Aiden cleared his throat and looked slightly embarrassed. "How are the guys?" he asked.

"They're great," Rocky said. "They're doing their own things now. Renaldo has a new single available on music streaming platforms."

Aiden looked down again. "That's good for him," he said quietly. "He writes incredible songs. I have no idea how he does it."

"Yeah, he's great at what he does. He's passionate about it, too."

"I'm happy for him. He deserves it all." Aiden paused for a moment. "I owe him an apology. I owe all of you an apology. I shouldn't have used you guys." He looked at Rocky again. "And I shouldn't have played with your emotions."

Rocky looked down. She always knew Aiden had a heart deep, deep, *deep* under his crusty shell. It took a lot of digging and this unfortunate circumstance, but Rocky was happy to see Aiden show some vulnerability — for real, this time. Nobody is ever cruel to other people without having a reason behind it. Not that being mean is ever okay.

"Yeah, you shouldn't have," Rocky said quietly.

"You have no idea how sorry I am for treating you like I did, and I'm not just saying that. I mean it from the bottom of my heart. You're an amazing person, Rocky, and you didn't deserve any of that."

"I accept your apology. I'm glad you realize how wrong it is to use other people."

"Yeah, I know."

There was a knock at the door, and a nurse walked in, along with Rocky's mom.

"Oh, I didn't know you had a visitor with you, Aiden," the nurse said. "Remember, you should be resting your voice so your throat can heal."

"That's my daughter," Rochelle said. "She asked to visit him."

"Aww, that's so sweet. Are you two dating?"

"No," Rocky and Rochelle blurted at the same time.

The nurse chuckled as she went to check Aiden's vitals.

"I guess we should head out, then?" Rocky said to her mom. "Let Aiden rest his voice."

"Sounds good to me," Rocky's mom said.

Aiden looked down, seeming disappointed about Rocky leaving. She wished this could've been the Aiden she had gotten to know, not the arrogant jerk who enjoyed manipulating people. Rocky could only hope he would stay this way and not be cruel anymore. This might be a lesson for him.

"Okay," Aiden said. "Thank you for visiting, Rocky. I really appreciate it."

"No problem," Rocky said. "I hope you have a quick recovery."

"Goodbye, Mrs. Coleman," Aiden said.

"Bye, Aiden," Rochelle said. "Feel better soon."

Rocky and her mom left and sat in the hospital parking lot for a moment.

"He seemed pretty depressed in there," Rocky's mom said. "And that mother of his is something else!"

"Yeah, she never even looked my way."

"He must go through a lot with that family. I almost feel bad for wanting to kill him a month ago." She chuckled.

Rocky laughed, too. "You know, he really opened up to me in there. He even apologized for everything."

"That was nice of him. He'd better not do anything like that to you or anyone else again."

"I don't think he will. I'm sure this was a wake-up call for him."

Before going home, Rocky and her mom stopped at a restaurant to order takeout for dinner.

The following morning at school, Rocky met Hayley and Adam in the courtyard. Rocky hugged Hayley before holding Adam's hand. Hayley giggled.

"I still can't get over the fact that you two are together now," she said. "You guys look so cute."

Rocky and Adam looked at each other and smiled. Rocky honestly couldn't get over the fact that she and Adam were together, either! She'd never been happier. As the three of them waited for the first bell to ring, Angel, Marcus, and Renaldo joined them. Rocky smiled as Hayley gave Angel a long hug.

"Are we on for a double date anytime soon?" Rocky asked.

"Of course," Hayley told her.

Marcus chuckled. "Angel and Rocky found love, but what about Marcus? What does he get?"

Renaldo gave him a friendly nudge. "Hey, you have me," he said.

"So, they get dates, and I'm stuck with you?"

They all burst into laughter.

"Hey, you'll never guess what happened," Rocky said.

"What is it?" Hayley asked.

"Aiden's in the hospital."

Everyone's eyes widened at the shocking news.

"What happened?" Renaldo asked.

"Vocal nodules. They were so bad that he needed surgery. He lost his vocal range because of it, too."

Nobody said anything for a moment. They all kept their heads down as if they were deciding whether to feel bad.

"I went to visit him yesterday," Rocky said, breaking the silence.

"How is he?" Adam asked.

"Pretty bummed. He was super vulnerable with me and told me how he feels like more of a client than a son to his parents."

"I guess that explains a lot," Adam said quietly.

"Yeah, he actually has a heart underneath that tough shell." Rocky looked at Marcus, Renaldo, and Angel. "He asked about you guys."

"He asked about us?" Angel repeated in shock.

"What did he say?" Marcus asked.

"He wanted to know how you guys were. I told him you were doing great, and he said he owes you guys an apology."

"He's not wrong about that," Renaldo said quietly.

"I think you guys should visit him when you get the chance," Rocky said. "He might appreciate it."

The guys must've thought Rocky was out of her mind to even think they'd want to see Aiden after everything he put them through. Nobody said anything.

"I know he treated you all horribly," Rocky continued. "But he's sorry about it."

"Are you sure he's not messing with your head again, Rocky?" Angel asked.

"Something about it seemed genuine this time," Rocky said. "He was at his lowest point in there, and you just can't fake feeling that way. Maybe you'd understand what I mean if you saw it with your own eyes."

There was another pause.

"All he wants is someone who cares," Rocky said. "He doesn't get much of that from his parents or anyone, really."

More silence.

"I guess I could visit him today after school," Angel said.

"I'll tag along," Marcus said.

"Me too," Renaldo added.

"Wow, you guys are good people," Adam said.

"He might enjoy seeing you too, Adam," Hayley teased.

"We'll talk about it later," he said.

Rocky truly surprised herself this year by breaking out of her shell. She also realized she never cared too much about being popular. All she wanted were true friends who she could be comfortable around and who brought out the best in her, and that's what she found. Even when Rocky felt scared about being on stage or talking to new people, she had a good support group to get her through it. She wouldn't trade what she had for all the popularity in the world.

Featured Songs

- If I Ever Fall in Love Again – Shai
- Pump it Up – Joe Budden
- We're All in This Together – *High School Musical* cast
- Listen to the Music – The Doobie Brothers
- Titanium – David Guetta & Sia
- On Bended Knee – Boyz II Men
- Stand by Me – Ben E. King
- More Than Words – Extreme
- Oceans – Hillsung UNITED
- Mary Did You Know – Various artists
- I'm Your Baby Tonight – Whitney Houston
- I Wanna Dance with Somebody – Whitney Houston
- Bleeding Love – Leona Lewis
- Suddenly – Billy Ocean
- (I've Had) The Time of My Life – Bill Medley and Jennifer Warned
- Time After Time – Cyndi Lauper
- Soul Man – Sam & Dave
- Unbreak my Heart – Toni Braxton
- Do You Hear What I Hear – Various artists
- Emotions – Mariah Carey

Acknowledgements

I'm incredibly grateful for the many people who helped make this book possible. Thank you to my developmental editor, CaTyra, for your guidance and expertise. You helped me shape my story into the best that it could be. Thank you to Adrienne, my copyeditor and proofreader, for your meticulous attention to detail. You've helped polish my book and make it shine. Thank you for also creating an absolutely stunning book cover. Thank you, Karina, Kayla, Makkedah, and Biannett, for being my beta readers. I appreciate all the honest feedback you gave me to help make the improvements I needed to make this book rock. I'd also like to thank my aunt, Laura Jones, for providing mentorship and support throughout the process. You've helped me learn a lot about what it takes to get a book published, and I'm excited for there to be another published author in the family now! My immediate family and partner have also been incredibly supportive during this journey. They've always believed in me and pushed me to keep going, even when I doubted myself and didn't think it would be possible to finally get published. I wouldn't be where I am without you. I also want to thank the one and only Sharon M. Draper for igniting my love for reading and writing. This book actually began as a short story I wrote for a writing contest in high school. The winners had the chance to meet Sharon Draper for a writer's workshop, where she gave valuable writing tips and resources that I use whenever I write my stories. I knew I wanted to write incredible stories for young readers after reading *The Battle of Jericho*. *Rocky Crescendo* was over ten years in the making, starting as a short story written when I was only 16. What began as a dream has finally become a reality, and I couldn't have done it alone.